"Everything I love about Lara Vapnyar's vision and voice—her blazing intelligence, skewering wit, and exuberant prose—is contained in this wild and witty novel. I don't know how her work manages to feel absolutely timely and perfectly timeless all at once. *Divide Me by Zero* is an inventive page-turner that explores familial and romantic love, passion, the inevitability of grief, and the ways we manage all of those things in compassionate and wonderfully surprising ways. I was so sorry when I finished and I'll think about this book and its characters for a very long time."

—CYNTHIA SWEENEY, author of *The Nest*

"Lara Vapnyar is one of my very favorite writers: funny and true and with the rare talent to assemble one ideally telling scene after another. She is also one of the few writers I would recommend to all my friends, with all their varying tastes, because the charisma of her storytelling is unmissable."

—RIVKA GALCHEN, author of *Little Labors*

DIVIDE ME BY ZERO

Published by Tin House Books, Portland, Oregon

Distributed by W. W. Norton & Company

Library of Congress Cataloging-in-Publication Data

Names: Vapnyar, Lara, 1971- author.
Title: Divide me by zero / by Lara Vapnyar.
Description: First U.S. edition. | Portland, Oregon : Tin House Books, 2019.
Identifiers: LCCN 2019013808 | ISBN 9781947793422 (hardcover)
Subjects: | GSAFD: Love stories.
Classification: LCC PS3622.A68 D58 2019 | DDC 813/.6--dc23
LC record available at https://lccn.loc.gov/2019013808

Photo credits: p 43: 1. Anonymous / AP / Shutterstock, 2. Andrey Oleynik / Shutterstock; p 75: Oxy_gen / Shutterstock; p 98: n7atal7i / Shutterstock

First US Edition 2019
Printed in the USA
Interior design by Diane Chonette
www.tinhouse.com

DIVIDE ME BY ZERO

LARA VAPNYAR

TIN HOUSE BOOKS / Portland, Oregon

DIVIDE ME BY ZERO

ONE

One week before my mother died, I went to a Russian food store on Staten Island to buy caviar. I was brought up in the Soviet Union, where caviar was considered a special food reserved for children and dying parents. I never thought of it as extravagant or a romantic delicacy. My mother would offer me some before important tests in school, because it was chock-full of phosphorus that supposedly stimulated brain cells. I remember eating caviar before school, at 7:00 AM, still in my pajamas, shivering from the morning cold, seated in the untidy kitchen of our Moscow apartment, yawning and dangling my legs, bumping my knees against the boards of our folding table, holding that piece of bread spread with a thin layer of butter and thinner layer of caviar.

I did eat caviar in a romantic setting once. With a very rich Russian man who I agreed to marry even though I was still married to Len and still in love with B.

"Caviar," I said to the sullen Russian woman behind the fish counter, and pointed to the smallest plastic container. She had blonde bangs pushing from under her white cap, uneven skin, thin lips with the remains of the morning's lipstick in the creases. Most probably she was a recent immigrant who had had to leave her family in Ukraine or Moldova and come work here so she could send them money. I imagined how much she must hate her well-to-do customers, wearing leather and gold, choosing their gleaming cuts of smoked salmon, pointing to the sushi rolls, ordering caviar.

She regarded me with wary puzzlement. I was dressed in sweatpants and a T-shirt I hadn't changed in days, and didn't look well-to-do or well.

She squinted at me, spooned the caviar into the container, and put it on the scale.

"It's for my mother," I said.

I don't understand what compelled me to share this. I'm a private person. I don't chat with strangers. I don't share things. Except, of course, in my fiction.

But I said that to the woman behind the fish counter. I wasn't sure if she heard me. There was loud music playing through the speakers, alternating with advertisements. "Buy your kitchen sink from Alex's Stainless."

The muscles around my mouth started to twitch, and I wanted them to stop, but I didn't have any control over them.

The woman behind the counter did hear me. And she understood what I meant right away. She stood there as if frozen, holding that container with caviar in her hands.

I think she was the one who started to cry first. Then I started to cry. Or it could've been that I was crying the whole time.

The woman behind the counter seemed to be as shocked by her tears as I was. I was ashamed. I didn't have the right to pull her into my grief. I used her. The silent anguish was getting impossible to take—I needed an explosive release, and I used that woman to help me explode. Or perhaps, I needed a tiny bit of kindness, of connection, right there, right at that moment, in front of the fish counter with those gleaming cuts of smoked salmon, and colorful sushi rolls, and caviar.

Then I saw she wasn't crying for me, or for my mother, but that something about my experience momentarily clicked with hers. I became exposed to her, and she became exposed to me. And perhaps she needed it as much as I did.

I think about that woman often.

My mother didn't want the caviar. I waited until she woke up, and then I made her a sandwich that looked exactly like the ones she had made for me before school. She studied it and raised her eyes to me. She still recognized me as a caretaker or as some sort of parental figure, but I don't think she knew who I was anymore. She looked at me with that pleading expression she had had for the last week or two, as if she knew that I wanted something from her, and she would've been happy to oblige, but could I please, please, please leave her alone?

I fixed her pillow and stroked her on the side of her head above her right temple. She closed her eyes and turned away from me.

I went upstairs to look for my kids. I found both of them in their rooms. Nathalie, thirteen, was curled up on her bed, asleep, her tear-streaked face pressed into the open paperback of Curtis Sittenfeld's *Prep*—the book that she kept rereading over that summer.

Dan, sixteen, greasy hair, unwashed clothes, was hunched over his laptop playing *Minecraft*, building a virtual castle with a virtual tower that led right into the virtual sky. I walked up to him and touched him on the shoulder.

"What? Grandma's calling?" he asked, ready to rush downstairs.

I shook my head and walked out of his room. Both kids seemed to be a picture of neglect but also a picture of normalcy. Neither of them wanted me at the moment.

There was no excuse not to do the work that I urgently needed to do. I went into my bedroom and opened my laptop. A long queue of emails filled me with panic. Some were from my students, who wanted me to look at their stories, others from the college admins, urging me to order books or confirm my schedule. A few were from various editors offering me one or another freelance assignment. My book editor was politely inquiring when I was going to deliver the novel I hadn't started. I had been earning my living as a writer for about twelve years now, a fact that made me immensely proud, especially since I had been earning my living as an American writer, working in my second language. But the thing about making your living as a writer is that you need to be writing in order to make a living. You need to be writing a lot, and writing well, and I wasn't writing at all. Then there was an urgent email from my agent asking me to describe my future novel in a hundred words or less.

"I'd love to write the novel about Love and Death," I typed. "How both of those words lost their majestic old meanings. People don't really 'love' each other anymore, they either 'worked on a relationship' or 'succumbed to sexual desire.' People don't 'die' either, they 'lost their battles' with various diseases or they simply 'expired' like old products on a shelf. Neither love nor death is considered the most important passage in the life of a person anymore. In my new novel, I would try to restore their proper meanings."

My agent shot back an answer almost right away.

"Is it going to be a comedy?"

I was shocked and even a little insulted. Comedy? Why comedy?

But then I thought that comedy, a very dark comedy, a comedy so dark that it made you cry, was the only form that would allow me to write with all honesty. If I were to truly open up in this novel, and there wasn't any point in writing it unless I did, I would need comedy, a lot of comedy, to create a protective layer shielding me from being too exposed, guarding me from sounding too bitter. And then wasn't life itself a perfect dark comedy too, with its journey to an inevitable tragic ending interspersed with absurd events providing comic relief?

I was about to put that in writing when I heard a strange sound coming from my mother's room. I shut my laptop and rushed to her.

It was all quiet. My mother was still asleep, in the same position, breathing hard. Perhaps I had simply invented the strange sound so I wouldn't have to deal with my emails.

I sat down at my mother's table, which also served as her desk, littered with pill bottles, grocery receipts, hospice papers, random medical equipment, various food items, and yellow flash cards with my mother's notes for her new book.

In Russia, she had been a famous author of math textbooks for children. She had published her last right before we emigrated, so this was going to be her first book in twenty years, and her first book written in English. She said that she had this sudden and stunning insight on how to make a math textbook that would guide you through life.

My mother kept working on that book for as long as her mind was still functioning and for a time after it stopped.

There were about twenty of these cards dispersed around the room. Some perfectly coherent, even brilliant, others showing both the inevitable deterioration of my mother's mind and her desperate attempts to stave it off.

One of the cards had fallen to the floor. I picked it up and put it back on the table.

It said: "Divide me by zero." Nothing else. No date. I wasn't sure if my mother had written it in a state of confusion or if she had had some deeper meaning in mind. As a child I was fascinated by this concept. I kept asking my mother what would happen if you divided something by zero. She would say: "Nothing!" But I didn't believe her. I thought of division as a physical action. You could take a piece of bread and divide it by two, and you would have two pieces. "Nothing" happened when you divided something by one, the piece would stay intact then. Dividing by zero must have a different outcome! I kept pushing buttons on my mother's huge calculator, forcing it to divide something by zero again and again. It would beep and the screen would scream "ERROR," as if guarding the answer from me, refusing to let me into this mystery. What was that mystery? I'd pester my mother. "Not all mysteries can be solved," she told me once. "Certain things are simply beyond our grasp or understanding."

Could the "Divide me by zero" card mean that she had finally been let in on that mystery? As she was about to die?

It's tempting to say that my mother started working on her last book right after she received her terminal diagnosis, but this wouldn't be true. It was good news that inspired her to start writing. The first flash card for my mother's book is dated December 10, the day her GE told her that she definitely didn't have cancer. He had scheduled the colonoscopy because the symptoms pointed to colorectal cancer. Turned out that she did have metastatic cancer at the time. Just not colorectal. Her cancer was someplace else, so the colonoscopy didn't show it. He couldn't see it.

My mother had told me about her symptoms too, but I didn't really believe her, because her symptoms appeared when I decided to leave Len. She was vehemently against the divorce, and I felt that she developed her symptoms to stop me or, if she failed to stop me, to punish me. We've had a history of doing that to each other—you'll see.

I wouldn't let her health worry me. I needed to focus on my divorce, which was a long time overdue. Sixteen years overdue to be precise.

On the day of my mother's colonoscopy I was hiding out in Victor's Manhattan apartment, fending off angry phone calls from Len. At one point Len called to tell me that he was going to take my kids away. I ran out on the roof terrace so I could listen to Len scream at me in private. The terrace was covered with snow. I was barefoot. The sun reflecting off the snow was blinding me, but my feet were freezing. I had to run across the terrace from one snowless spot to the next, hunched over as if it could shield me from the cold or Len's hatred. I was a monster, Len said. I had ruined his life and the kids would be better off if I died. The kids were at my uncle's place in the Poconos—I had sent them there so they could absorb and store as much normalcy as they could along with fresh mountain air. I had a quick scary thought that Len might drive there and kidnap them, but I managed to recognize this thought as crazy right away. As much as Len wanted to destroy me, he would've never done anything to hurt the kids. I imagined Len pacing across the living room of the New Jersey home of his skiing buddy. Pale, balding, scared, confused, holding on to the idea of me as a monster, because this was the only thing that dulled his pain. Fighting a devious monster must feel so much better than accepting the banal situation of his wife leaving him for another man. I hadn't loved Len for a long, long time, and I feared and hated him at the moment, but I also couldn't help but feel perverse affection for him. We'd been married for seventeen years, we were used to taking care of each other. I felt like it was my duty to protect him from this pain, even though I was the one causing it. But then I knew that any gesture of kindness would only make his pain worse.

Len finally hung up, and I cleared snow off the edge of a lawn chair and sat down, savoring the moment of peace before I had to go down and face Victor. He was angry at me for not being more resolute about the divorce. He suspected that I wasn't fully committed to him. He was right.

Even if I didn't love Len anymore, I still had feelings for B., no matter how hard I tried to kill them. In fact, there was nothing

I wanted more at that moment than to see B., right then and there, on that snowed-in, blinding roof. To see him walk up the stairs and to rush into his arms, to feel his warmth, his smell—he smelled like cigarettes and hay—to move a wisp of his graying hair off his forehead and look into his eyes.

I had to stop! I really had to stop thinking about B.!

This was precisely why I had started seeing Victor in the first place, in a crazy, or perhaps crooked attempt to get over B. I've discovered that Victor wasn't perfect, far from it, but he was strong, extremely intelligent, and somewhat kind. A romantic self-made man, a Russian Great Gatsby. He was also very rich, have I mentioned that? I'm sure I have and I'm probably going to mention that again and again. Not because I'm proud of the fact of dating a rich man but because I still find it disturbing and even a little disgusting.

Victor promised to help me with the divorce, to come up with a fair solution for Len, to make sure that the kids stayed with me and that they were well provided for, that my mother had a decent home. All of that in exchange for a sincere assurance that I was going to be his loyal partner. I couldn't possibly deceive Victor. I could accept his help only if I felt that I could be that for him. He knew that I didn't love him yet—he didn't love me either—but he believed that love would develop with time, from our mutual affection and respect. My problem was that I doubted that. But maybe love wasn't necessary at all? I had married Len for love. I'd later experienced the most intense love for B. and look where it got me.

I was sitting on that roof, literally freezing my ass, while trying to persuade myself that I didn't need love and will myself into wanting to be with Victor, so I could go back and face him.

This was when my mother called to tell me about her colonoscopy results. "It's all good," she said. "No cancer!"

I said: "Okay."

"I thought you'd be relieved." She sighed.

At that moment, I didn't have any patience for hypochondria.

"I am not relieved, because I never thought you had cancer in the first place!" I said.

"But what about my symptoms?" she asked.

"Your symptoms are not real!" I screamed.

I said that. The words were out and gone, I immediately forgot about them, as if they had gone to some sort of memory landfill, but apparently that landfill wasn't very far or very deep, because when my mother got the correct diagnosis just a few months later, my words came right back to stay with me forever.

On the card dated December 10, my mother wrote that her new book would have so-called "notes or asides to readers" that would try to engage them directly with the text. There were no examples in the following cards, but I imagine the notes were supposed to look something like this.

Note to a reader about to scream at her mother that her symptoms are not real. Don't do it! You will never be able to forgive yourself. You hear me? Never!

I ate the caviar at that desk, right out of the container, trying to justify eating it by telling myself that I couldn't afford to waste money, or that I simply needed it for nourishment, with my mother and my kids all depending on my strength at a time like this. It didn't work. I felt as if I were robbing a grave.

Writing this book often feels like that too.

MENTAL MATH:

Since the invention of calculators, people became lazy to do math in their heads.

Mental math, however is crucial to the development of memory, attention, creativity, and situational problem solving.

TWO

The first few months of my affair with B. were the simplest and the happiest. By a silly twist of fate, it so happened that we both worked at the same Enormous University in New York. I taught creative writing, and B. taught film studies. We had classes in different departments and different buildings, but on the same day. We would usually steal an hour or so, right after our classes ended and before we had to rush back to our respective families, and spend it in the sprawling park by the river.

One of my students posed this question once: "Why is it so much easier to describe bad sex than great sex?" After a heated discussion, the class came to the following conclusion. Writers usually base complex sex scenes on their own experience, and while they remember bad or ordinary or even good sex in great detail, they fail to evoke the specifics of great sex because they weren't lucid enough while it was happening to make observations. "You're too much in the moment!" one of my students complained.

LARA VAPNYAR

The same goes for happiness.

I can't possibly describe what B. and I did in that park in detail, because the happiness was so extreme and all-consuming that it completely erased my ability for observation.

The thing I remember the best was the crazy urge to touch each other, as we walked along the water edge or sat on one or another bench. We were apprehensive about a stray student or a colleague who might see us, so we tried our best to resist that urge, but we didn't always succeed. I can't help but think what a strange sight we must have presented to an onlooker. B., with his graying long hair, neat Russian beard, wearing his frayed leather jacket, I, wobbly in my ridiculously high heels, my dark hair drawing crazy shapes in the wind. Kissing like mad. This phrase comes from "What Is Remembered," my favorite story by Alice Munro, and for the life of me I can't think of a better expression. Kissing like mad, but also talking like mad, talking about anything at all with the intense focus that came to signify love for me.

There was another strange thing that I noticed. Since this was the very beginning of the affair, we both tried to impress each other, claiming obscure films and books as our favorite, dropping names of especially dense philosophers, spouting nonstop intellectual insights, but at the same time the process of falling in love made us too vulnerable and overwhelmed to maintain cerebral cool.

One time B. was in the middle of a complex argument about Bergman's lack of sentimentality when his eyes suddenly filled with tears.

"Do you remember that shot at the end of *Wild Strawberries,* where the elderly professor is sitting next to his ancient mother?"

I didn't remember it.

"He is an old man. But he's also a child at that moment. A lonely child. Nobody can understand true loneliness, except for children and people approaching death."

B. choked on his words and couldn't speak for several minutes.

I think it was the "talking like mad" rather than the "kissing like mad" that made it so hard for us to face our respective spouses afterward. I hadn't loved Len for a long time before starting an affair with B., but I still cared about him, and what filled me with unbearable guilt was that I couldn't force myself to listen to Len with genuine attention, no matter how hard I tried.

Ever since I was a young child, love was something that I badly wanted. This was what my parents had. I knew that that was what they had, before I even knew the word "love."

Here is how the story goes.

My mother and father met at a party in somebody's crowded apartment. Within an hour, they sneaked out and spent the rest of the night walking along the streets of Moscow. It was summer, my mother was wearing a stiff sleeveless dress and a pair of too-tight sandals. She mentioned those sandals every time she told me the story. They made it to the Moscow River embankment and walked along the river until my mother's feet were chafed raw. Then they sat down on the bench facing the Kremlin. They wanted to see the sunrise, but it was too cloudy that night, and by the morning a warm drizzle started, so they couldn't really see anything. My father pulled the *Pravda* newspaper out of his briefcase, checked the sunrise time for the previous day, subtracted one minute, and proposed to my mother exactly then. She thought it was a joke and started to laugh. She wouldn't stop laughing. He said he was completely serious. She still wouldn't stop laughing. She said, "Fine, I'll marry you." He said he needed this in writing. She asked: "What do you want, an official document?" He nodded. My father had a pen on him, but no paper, so he had to tear off the corner of *Pravda's* front page.

"I, citizen Nina Kopeleva, promise to marry citizen Daniil Geller. Signed and registered." There are also the words "Workers of the world, unite!" printed in huge letters in the background.

My father lived in Sevastopol, a town on the Black Sea, famous for its bloody military history, vast pebble beach, and the ruins of an ancient Greek town called Chersonesus. He was an oceanographer, employed by a lab that specialized in studies of the ocean. Because of his job, my father couldn't live anyplace else, so it was my mother who had to leave everything behind, including her job at the Ministry of Education, and move to Sevastopol to be with him. She told me that she didn't mind. She had just published a very successful math textbook for children, and she hoped she would be able to work from home and earn her living by writing more textbooks.

This was the peak of the so-called stagnation period in the Soviet Union, when people were allowed to live and work in peace, unless of course they tried to stir things up. Those ended up fired or exiled (if they were very lucky) or locked in psychiatric asylums (if they weren't). I wonder if this was why both my parents found fields that were timeless and infinite, to exist beyond politics, like the Ocean and Math, so they wouldn't be tempted to stir things up.

In Sevastopol, my father had to spend a lot of time away, crossing the oceans and seas on specially equipped ships, gathering data, making up formulas for the activity of the currents, but also watching those currents live, how they shifted and breathed, making the whole mass of the ocean move and rise and fall. The ocean was his curved space, magical in its enormity and disregard for human concerns.

My mother stayed home, where she worked on her books and took care of me. We would go to the beach every day, even when it was chilly, and do math with pebbles. One of my first memories of my mother is our doing math with pebbles. I was only three, I think. The pebbles were all cold and rounded, but of different sizes and colors, so you could do all kinds of mathematical operations with them. You could count them up, you could arrange them from smallest to largest, you could build various geometrical shapes out of them.

"See?" my mother would say. "This is a square. Now let's make a triangle."

Her black curly hair flew in all directions in the wind, falling over her eyes, which were brown and gleaming like the eyes of a horse. Everybody said that I had the same eyes.

The cold often made my nose run, and my mother would wipe my face with a sandy handkerchief that felt scratchy against my skin. All of our things were sandy, because we spent so much time on the beach.

Every time my father came home from a trip, we would go to the port to meet him. My mother would hold me by the hand, and her hand would be sweaty and throbbing because she squeezed mine hard when we had to push through the crowd.

She kept craning her neck and rising on her toes to see above other people's heads. Her lips were painted bright pink, and she wore so much perfume that every time a gust of wind blew in my direction, it felt like being slapped across the face by a bouquet of flowers. One time, when I was about four, my mother left me in the crowd. She couldn't spot my father for a long time, and when she finally did, she dropped my hand and ran toward my father to jump into his arms. I was scared, but I wasn't mad at my mother, or at least I don't remember being mad.

When my father was home, we would take long walks on the beach. I remember one of our walks well. I was five, still small enough to be hoisted up onto my father's shoulders. He taught me how to spot ships that were far away, tiny shimmering spots on the horizon, indistinguishable from seabirds. I remember thinking that if the ships on the horizon were that tiny, that meant my father had to turn into the tiniest speck to fit in there. The ships would reach an invisible line and then disappear beyond the horizon. "Look, another one vanished!" I would point to the empty space where we had just seen the ship. "They don't vanish!" my father would say, chuckling. "They go beyond your line of vision. If you can't see something, it doesn't mean it's not there."

He died two months after that.

His sister Rosa had immigrated to Israel, and my father's Communist Party membership had been revoked. Then my father had been summoned by a KGB officer assigned to oversee the lab. My father was told that he wouldn't be allowed on overseas research trips, because he wasn't trustworthy anymore. "But this work is my whole life!" my father pleaded. "You should've explained this to your sister," the officer said.

My father had a heart attack and died within twenty-four hours. He was only forty. I was only six. My mother was only thirty-six.

Her hair turned gray overnight. There is proof of this in the photos. Here she is at the funeral, leaning against a brick wall, sparse gray tufts sticking out from under her black scarf. And here is a photo taken just a few days before, where my mother is posing on the beach with a full head of black curly hair.

There was a box with their letters and photographs. My mother gave it to me when I was eighteen, during a time of true and intense friendship. I was recovering from my first heartbreak and I was reading everything I could find about love (novels, memoirs, essays, poems). I thought that if I could study love the way I used to study math, the knowledge would arm me with some power against the colossal incomprehension and fear I was experiencing.

Most of my mother's photos from our time in Sevastopol turned out to be of her striking silly poses on the beach. There were two or three photographs of my mother and father together. They don't really look glowing with passion in any of them, but rather at ease with each other. Each perfectly comfortable in the other's space, each absolutely sure that he/she is with the right person, each wearing the sly, smug expression of somebody who is sure of being deeply loved.

There were also letters. Tons of letters that my parents wrote to each other while my father was away.

I was disappointed at first. Neither of my parents was a good writer, and neither of them employed the grand words of love. But then I saw something else, something more important and powerful than grand words: genuine hunger for each other's presence.

My dear and dear and dear and dear Danka!

You asked me to tell you about my day minute by minute. Unfortunately, I had to spend many minutes standing in line to buy underpants. It was worth it though. They are made in Poland and have these little blue flowers all over them. I think you're going to love them!

I'm worried about what you eat on that ship! Every time I cook something delicious for Katya and me, I feel sad that you can't eat it. Things with the new book are still tough. The artist failed to submit the illustrations by the deadline, and now everything has to be postponed. It's not like he's a good artist either. He mostly draws little pigs. I can't have every problem be about little pigs. There are other animals, you know!

I'm still having trouble falling asleep without you. The empty space on your side feels wrong. Luckily I know math, so I just stretch diagonally to minimize the empty space.

Love you, miss you, kiss you!
Your Nina

Nina, Ninochka, Nochka!

I don't sleep very well either, I keep dreaming of you and reaching for you and wake up on the very edge of the bed about to fall down. Food is actually pretty good here. The cook makes borscht with ham and sausage, it's really good, nothing like yours though. I agree that math problems should employ different animals. Kids should be able to count sheep and cows and goats. Counting pigs alone won't make them ready for the real world. Speaking of animals, I think I saw a whale yesterday. I wanted to take a picture for you, but it

*was gone before I got the camera. I have to go to a meeting
in a minute.*

You can't imagine how much I want you right now.

Your D.

Note to a squeamish reader. No, I didn't find the sexual in-
nuendos in my parents' letters embarrassing. I found them
heartbreaking.

There was one more item in that box. The note scribbled on
the yellowed corner of the *Pravda* front page: "I, citizen Nina
Kopeleva, promise to marry citizen Daniil Geller. Signed and
registered."

A love letter in the language of Soviet bureaucracy written on
the corner of a Soviet newspaper.

I came to think of that note as my talisman and my written
oath. What my parents had was real love, and I promised myself
not to settle for anything less.

In 1994, my mother and I immigrated to the US. Most of our
letters and photographs were lost in the process, but that note sur-
vived, because I had it tucked between the pages of my passport and
never touched it, except one time, in 2010, when I'd started seeing
B. By then the note was forty years old. Forty years old, can you
imagine that! Completely yellowed and so thin that I was afraid it
would crumble in my fingers. I stroked it, choking with a mix of
emotion and being embarrassed by emotion, and put it back.

Encourage kids to
do math in their
heads ALWAYS, no
matter what.

THREE

Our apartment in Sevastopol belonged to the lab, and they wouldn't let us stay there after my father's death. My mother and I had to move back to the Moscow apartment she used to share with her parents. My uncle Grisha, my mother's younger brother, came to help us pack and take us back to Moscow.

The train wasn't full, so we got the entire compartment for the three of us. Grisha slept on the upper berth, and my mother and I slept on the lower ones.

My mother spent most of our journey in the compartment, lying on her berth with her back to us, howling into the pillow. She would sit up only to drink tea from a thick glass in a massive metal holder. And she would stand up only to wobble down the corridor to the bathroom.

I spent most of the time crying too, but my grief wasn't absolute like my mother's. It was possible to distract me. I had never been on a train before, and there were many exciting things that managed to steal my attention. It was exciting to lie on the narrow berth with my ear pressed to the pillow, listening to the rumble of the wheels, or to sit balancing that huge glass holder in both hands. It was thrilling to get off the train when it stopped at the little stations—to jump off the stoop into my uncle's arms. He was very handsome—he had the same eyes and the same thick black eyebrows as my mother, but on him they looked better somehow, and I loved it how people turned to follow us with their eyes.

The most fun though was to watch the changing scenery and occasional animals through the window. Once I saw a fawn chasing another fawn across a field, and started to clap and laugh. I stopped myself right away, but it was too late, everybody heard me. My mother heard me. I touched her on the back and I said that I was sorry, then I started to cry from embarrassment.

"It's okay, dear," Grisha said. "It's really okay, to laugh, and to play, and to have fun." I wasn't sure if I could trust him. Especially since my mother didn't laugh or play or have fun.

My first impression of Moscow was that it was humid and smoky, with crowds of people hurrying, pushing, shoving each other, while eating ice cream. It seemed like every single person was eating ice cream. Licking chocolate squares on sticks, nibbling on waffle cups, biting into whole bricks of ice cream, staining their chins and their hands. I wanted ice cream, but I didn't ask for it, because I thought it would be awful of me to ask.

The neighborhood where my grandparents lived was on the outskirts of Moscow. It had been a village two decades before, then all the little houses were demolished to make space for highrises, but the gardens stayed. My grandparents lived in a long nine-story, ten-entrance building (buildings like that were nicknamed "supine skyscrapers," and they did resemble skyscrapers lying on their sides) that along with other identical buildings formed a half circle around a school and a kindergarten. There were fruit trees in front of the buildings, behind the buildings, and between the buildings. Apple trees, peach trees, plum trees, and cherry trees. They would bloom every spring and bear fruit every summer. The fruit from the neglected trees wasn't good enough for eating, but people would go and pick it for jams and compotes. Late August was the time for apples. The year my father died was a crazy year for apples. Everybody said they had never seen so many.

The first thing I noticed upon entering my grandparents' place was that it was very hot and reeked of rotten fruit.

The apartment was a small one-bedroom. My grandparents gave the bedroom to my mother and me, claiming that they would be perfectly fine on the sofa in the living room. My mother's bed was moved to the wall, and a narrow foldout bed was bought (from the neighbors) and placed at a ninety-degree angle to my mother's bed, right next to the bookcase. I was six when we arrived in Moscow, and I slept on that foldout bed for sixteen years, until I married Len and left for Saint Petersburg.

As soon as we entered, my mother marched into the bedroom, got into bed, and stayed there for what seemed like months.

I was left in the care of my grandparents, whom I hardly knew and didn't love.

What the three of us did every day was pick apples and make jam out of them.

I would sit at the Formica folding table across from my grandfather, and my grandmother would stand at the stove. I was a child of six, so I wore nothing except for my little underpants.

My grandmother dressed in her sleeveless housecoat. Her body was all jittery and lumpy, as if thick soup had been poured into her skin. My grandfather dressed in his old boxers and a wifebeater, and his limbs looked crumbly and dry like discarded firewood.

Sometimes they would even exchange insults in what I took for a funny made-up language (later identified as Yiddish).

My grandmother was "Nafka!"

And my grandfather was "Khazer!"

My job was to sort the apples—good ones were for jam, bad ones for compote. I would pick better apples and push them toward my grandfather, and he would take them from me and cut them up and pass them to my grandmother, who was stirring the bubbling sputtering matter in aluminum washing basins at the stove. The process was really boring. I tried to entertain myself by engaging my grandparents with math the way my mother did with me, but it didn't work out, even though I picked the easiest possible problems for them.

"Look, Grandpa, there are five apples in the bowl. If I take two, how many would be left?"

He wouldn't answer me at all or would give a deliberately wrong answer, like "a thousand fucking apples."

His disrespect for math was shocking, but it was better than my grandmother's indifference. She wouldn't even try to solve my problems, or she would say that I was "a poor little orphan" and start to sob.

When the fruit season finally ended, my grandparents took to spending their days either reading or going to the store.

They lay on their foldout sofa, side by side, two pairs of feet facing me. My grandfather's clad in carefully mended socks, my grandmother's bare, crooked, and yellow. There was hardly enough space for both of them so they would grunt and push each other off their assumed sides.

My grandfather liked to read Soviet newspapers—thin, rustling, and smelling strongly of fresh print, the smell that my grandmother hated more than any other smell.

My grandmother liked to read novels—with yellowed pages, worn-out spines, and occasional illustrations.

As for me, I refused to read. First of all, I didn't know how. I could do math on a fourth-grade level, but I couldn't put letters and sounds together. My grandmother tried to teach me, but I resisted her efforts. My mother had been a voracious reader in Sevastopol, but now she kept saying that stories about love or death were unbearable, and all the books that ignored these two subjects weren't worth reading. I didn't fully understand what she meant, but it seemed like an admirable sentiment. I could kill time playing with my toys, but eventually I would find myself curled up on the rug in the middle of the room, wanting my mother.

The only thing that made that time more or less tolerable were the days when somebody came to take me away for an hour or two. My mother's friend Rita would take me to play with her boys, Sasha, who was my age, and Misha, who was older. Rita's husband (formerly a heavily drinking artist, now a full-time alcoholic) was always sleeping on the couch, his head hanging off the edge, his mouth agape, his snores like a mad dog's gnarls. "God help you if you wake him up!" Rita said, and we took her words very seriously. Sasha and Misha kept kicking and punching and biting each other, grimacing in pain, but not making a sound.

And I sat on the floor cheering them on in a low whisper. "Good for you, Misha . . . Sasha, now bite him back!"

And there were rare weekends when Uncle Grisha came to take me for a walk. He would have to sit in our kitchen first, eating reheated soup, wincing at my grandmother's sticky hugs and frowning at my grandfather's nagging. "I already have a job, Dad. I'm a photographer. Yes, it's a real job! No, Dad, I don't want you to speak to your veteran buddies on my behalf. I don't care how high they are in the Communist Party!" I could see that Grisha was as eager to leave the apartment as I was.

He usually took me to Kuskovo Park. The park itself was leafy and sprawling and seemingly endless, with the woods, and the lake, and beautiful mansions, and even a small amusement park. Grisha explained to me that before the revolution, this entire territory used to belong to Count Sheremetev and nobody was allowed in except for his family and his servants.

"But now everybody is allowed in!" I said with the due eagerness of a Soviet child.

"Yes," Grisha said under his breath, "and everybody can shit all over the place."

He did say stuff like that often, and sometimes he even made jokes about communism, or Brezhnev or even Lenin, making it seem as if he didn't believe that the Soviet Union was the best country in the world. His attitude confused me, but I enjoyed our outings too much to think about it.

In October, a spot opened in the Ministry of Education, and Rita, who used to work with my mother and now held her former position, begged her bosses to give it to my mother. Every day my mother would put on a black dress and black shoes and leave for work. I once asked her what her work was, and she said: "To stare at some papers and shuffle them around."

It took her two years to start wearing gray and brown—I don't remember any other colors in her wardrobe—and about the same amount of time to resume working on her books.

My mother came home from work around seven, and at a quarter of six I would be waiting for her at the door. Every time, I was hoping that the woman who walked through the door would be my old mother from our Sevastopol time, dark-haired and smiling, and happy to see me. Seeing my mother the way she looked now, gray-haired and zombie-like, came as a shock. I would still rush to hug her, but those hugs brought me little joy, worse than that—they frightened me. She still felt like my mother, with her familiar smell and familiar texture—soft and pliable in the same places as before, bony and scratchy in others. But she didn't react to me the way my mother used to react, or the way any mother would. Not just her facial expression but even her hugs were devoid of warmth. This upset me so much that I felt like biting or punching her, but instead I ran away and cried.

There were pills to alleviate the sadness, and my grandmother and Uncle Grisha kept begging my mother to take them. She vehemently refused. She said that doing something to ease the pain would be the act of betrayal. She didn't want to betray Daniil! she screamed. She didn't want to feel nothing! She didn't want to numb down her love for him. Danya might have died, but her love for him hadn't!

Many years later, in fact just a few months before my mother died, she told me that the thing that tortured her the most back then was the intense sexual desire she still felt for my father. He was dead. Wanting him, dreaming about him, imagining all those things he would do to her, felt like the ultimate violation. I told her that I found it perfectly natural to want somebody who had died. If the death of a person doesn't make longing for him any less, why should it diminish sexual desire?

But still her confession made me cringe. I found it especially embarrassing that I couldn't help but compare her experience to mine, when B. had told me that we had to break it off. What I felt was a proverbial heartache—sharp pain in the left side of my chest—intensified by all these stubborn little urges: to say his name out loud, to touch his hand if even for a second, to feel him breathe down my neck, to have him inside me.

I didn't share this with my mother. First of all, this was her time, she was the one who was dying, she was the star of the show. I was a supporting character, a sidekick. Other reasons were that I found it embarrassing to compare the loss of a husband to the end of an affair, and humiliating to admit to wanting a man who had left me of his own volition.

Unlike my mother, I didn't have the strength to refuse the pills. I couldn't handle the pain, I didn't care if I betrayed our love or not. Perhaps this was precisely what I wanted, to betray our love, to make it die. Or perhaps I simply didn't believe that it was over with B. and hoped that one day some miracle would happen, the space would curve, the reality would bend, the impossible would become possible, and he would come back to me. Perhaps my goal was to preserve myself until that happened.

The first year in Moscow, I didn't miss my father at all. I was used to his absences, and his being dead didn't differ that much from his being away. When I thought of him at all, I imagined him being far away, a tiniest speck on one of those tiny ships that crossed the horizon line and disappeared from view, but not altogether. Even though I couldn't see them, they were still there, as my father had explained to me, out there, somewhere, or just There.

With my mother it was the opposite. She was right here, and yet she wasn't. My entire life up to this point had been filled with her presence, and I couldn't function without her. I would make up prayers to make her come back to me. It was my mother who had taught me how to pray. My father, like most Soviet scientists, was an atheist, but my mother said that she was agnostic. She explained that agnostics didn't believe in Anything Specific, but they believed in Something, because it was too scary not to. She said that by saying the prayer, we let Something know that we believed in it so that it wouldn't get mad at us. We would make up our own prayers that resembled nursery rhymes and included silly rituals like biting on our little fingers. "Water, air, metal, wood. [Bite.] We be happy, we be good."

Now I had to make up my own lonely prayers. My bed was pushed against the bookcase, and I made a habit of touching the book spines before I went to sleep, and naming the animals on the covers of the books that stood on the level of my bed. "Bunny, mouse, doggy, cat. Make my mommy love me back." I would end my prayer by pressing my face to the spine of the last book and licking it from top to bottom.

And guess what? My prayer worked.

Exactly nine months after we arrived in Moscow, I developed a cough accompanied by occasional fever that wouldn't go away. My grandmother tried to cure me with chicken soup and raspberry jam, but none of that was helping. One day my fever rose to 104, and my grandmother insisted that my mother stay home and call a doctor. I remember that doctor as a monstrously tall woman with huge hands as hard as wooden boards. She tapped and poked and squeezed various parts of my body with those hands, hurting me, making me cry. And then she spoke to my mother, making each sentence land like a hard slap.

"The child has pneumonia!" she said.

"And it's very far gone!" she said.

"What kind of a mother are you?" she asked.

They took me to a hospital, and my mother never left my side there. She kept begging my forgiveness and promising that she would never ever leave me again. I was too sick to understand her words, but I understood that she had returned to me from that strange place she had inhabited for months, and that she was with me now, possibly more with me than she ever was before.

you can't really
understand an
object unless you
look at it from
all sides.

FOUR

One evening about ten years into our marriage, I found myself screaming at Len that I had had a very happy childhood.

Like most of our screaming fights, this one started with a pretty innocent dinner conversation. The kids were outside with their friends, my mother was in her apartment downstairs, on the phone with Uncle Grisha. Len came home after work, and I rushed to greet him as he was changing his shoes in the hallway He smiled at me, and as I hugged him, enjoying his familiar warmth, I thought maybe my marriage wasn't that deficient after all. Maybe this was everything that marriage was supposed to be—longing for your husband to come home, feeling happy when he opened the door, feeding him, providing him with comfort after a busy day.

I put Len's dinner on the table and sat down across from him with a fresh issue of the *Magazine*, hoping to come up with a topic for conversation. I wasn't eating, myself, I had just had dinner with the kids—we rarely had dinner as a family, because Len never came home from work before eight. So here we were, I leafing through the magazine while throwing occasional glances at Len; Len silently working on his salmon with steamed broccoli, his long nose moving along with his mouth, his blue eyes trained on his plate, his large forehead shiny in the light of the overhead Ikea lamp. I stumbled on a cartoon I found funny. A young woman was complaining to her parents that they ruined her chance at becoming a writer by giving her a happy childhood. I showed the cartoon to Len and said: "I had a happy childhood too, but it didn't stop me from becoming a writer!" He looked at me as if I were insane, then made a visible effort to get his expression back to neutral.

"What?" I asked.

"Nothing," he said and went back to his food.

I could've gone back to my magazine too, that would've been the smart thing to do to ensure marital peace or at least the appearance of it, but I either caught or imagined sarcastic notes in his "nothing," which annoyed me so much that I continued to insist.

"Fine," Len finally said. "You couldn't seriously mean that you had a happy childhood, could you?"

I asked him why I couldn't. He said that I knew why. I said that I didn't. I insisted that despite losing my father I had had a very happy childhood.

He swallowed the last unappetizing bit of broccoli, put his fork down, and said in a straining-to-be-calm voice: "No, you didn't!"

"Why not?" I asked, my voice quivering with anger.

"Because your mother is a monster."

I threw my magazine at him and screamed that this wasn't true.

He stood up, pushing his chair away so hard that it fell, and screamed back: "Your mother is crazy. She's treated you like a guinea pig her whole life! She ruined you! Just look at you! She is a witch, a lunatic! And so are you!"

Note to a reader who knows what I'm talking about. Why is it that fighting partners so often attack each other's parents? Is this blind groping for the most painful spot? Or a focused attempt to destroy the person starting with her origins, with something that made her who she is? And don't you think that I was a blameless victim. I once called Len's parents "vile brainless pigs."

Usually, when your spouse tells you that your parent is a lunatic who fucked you up, it is hard to refute his point, because you don't have any concrete evidence to prove the opposite. But I had the evidence. I had the actual documents to prove that I had been a happy child. My school essays, the letters and photographs in the blue plastic box on the bottom of the linen drawer in our bedroom. I ran upstairs to fetch the box, but when I got back, Len was already heading out of the kitchen. "No, wait," I screamed, "You have to see these." Len wouldn't. I had to chase him up and down the three floors of our Staten Island house—tall and narrow like a pencil case, skipping and slipping, scraping my knees against the rough wood of the stairs. With the box pressed to my chest, screaming: "Just look at one letter, one!"

I kept chasing him, until he fled down to the garage and shut the door in my face.

Note to an astute reader thinking that my behavior actually confirmed Len's assessment of my mental state. Like you've never done anything crazy in the middle of a vicious fight!

I ended up going back to the bedroom and looking through the contents of the box on my own, hunched on top of our marital bed, trying to hold my tears so my face wouldn't look all blotchy and puffed-up by the time the kids came inside to get ready for bed.

On top of the pile were four green copybooks filled with my school essays, most of which happened to be about my mother. Every time the school would assign an essay on one or another aspect of Soviet people's heroism, I would naturally write about my mother, because she wasn't just my role model, she was my hero of heroes. Take this one, for example. "Heroism of Soviet Children during WWII."

"When the war started, my mother was five. My grandfather went to war, and my grandmother took my mother and her younger brother (my uncle Grisha) away from Moscow to a village in the mountains. On the way there, Nazis dropped bombs right on top of their train. My five-year-old mother covered her baby brother with her body and saved his life. Because of Soviet children like my mother we defeated Hitler."

Or this one, "Soviet Ideals in Everyday Life."

"One day, when my mother was twelve, my grandfather decided to punish my uncle Grisha. (He was eight and belligerent.) My grandfather pulled the leather belt out of his pants and started hitting Uncle Grisha on his back and butt. My mother ran into the room and screamed: 'Soviet people don't hit their children!' My grandfather stopped."

Note to a politically astute reader. This strikes you as a cult of personality, right? Well, what did you expect? I didn't grow up in a totalitarian society for nothing.

I realized that I had never really reread my school essays until now, and what struck me about them was how similar they were to the essays my kids were writing in their American public school. Even though the political system in the United States isn't totalitarian, the teachers seem to praise the same simple language, the same unwavering logic of the structure, the same tendency to hammer the main point, and the same ideological steadfastness.

"The US is the land of opportunities," they would go. "My grandmother is a great example. When she came to the US, she was a poor clueless immigrant. Then she saw an opportunity . . ."

Or, "Before feminism, women used to be powerless, but when my grandmother got a job at the Ministry of Education, she could make important decisions. This is an example of great progress for feminism."

But it wasn't the dogmatism that bothered me about my kids' essays; it was the fact that they'd always choose my mother as the example. My mother, and not me, their mother.

This wasn't fair! My mother had already had her share of essays written about her. I wrote them. My jealousy suggested that perhaps the essays weren't the greatest proof of the normalcy of my upbringing, so I hurried to tuck them away behind the photographs and other stuff.

But there were also letters. Letters and postcards to my grandmother filled with my hurried childish handwriting, bursting with happiness.

> *Dear Gran,*
>
> *You are probably wondering how our journey went. It was amazing!* [See Len, see?] *The train compartment was pretty clean—unlike the last time—haha! We shared it with two drunk men. They were very nice though. They gave us two peaches and they dropped two more on the floor, so we got those too.*
>
> *How are my dear hamsters?*
> *Love, K.*

I used to send letters to my grandmother from the trips my mother and I took every summer. We couldn't afford a real vacation, but my mother got invited to speak at teachers' seminars all over the country. They paid very well and covered all our travel expenses, except for my train ticket. One summer the seminar would be in Latvia, another summer in Belarus, or Georgia, or Ukraine, or Moldova.

I wrote to my grandmother not because I missed her—I didn't—and not because I thought she'd enjoy my letters—I knew she wouldn't care—but because I wanted to revive and relive all the wonderful moments of our trips through writing and because the act of writing made me feel very good about myself.

> *Dear Gran,*
>
> > *Today we arrived in Brest. The seminar ladies were waiting for us at the station. With flowers! Roses! Apparently they think that we are super important.* [I use "we" throughout. "We" are important. Not just my mother, but my mother and I together.]
> >
> > *Please, say hello to my dear hamsters.*
> > *Love, K.*

See, Len, see? See how happy I was?

And in the winter months, when there were no teachers' seminars, the fun continued. My mother took me everywhere with her, even to all kinds of grown-up places, to see serious plays, and operas, and ballets. She could've taken anybody: my grandmother, Grisha, Rita, but she picked me. Because I was unusually smart and mature for my age. Or at least that was what I thought when I was a child. Later I came up with another, less flattering, explanation. All of these other people had their own lives, their own partners, their own interests, and I was the only one truly eager to accompany my mother everywhere, listen to her, get excited by whatever excited her.

Our favorite outings were to see ballets at the Kremlin Palace of Congresses. The morgue-like palace was specially built for Communist Party conventions, but between the conventions, the space was used for various performances, usually ballets, usually set to music by Tchaikovsky. I loved walking toward the Kremlin down the chilly and brightly lit street, and then across the square paved with special stones that had ears.

"Mom, why does Uncle Grisha always say that our country is sick? How can a country be sick?"

"Shh! These stones can hear!"

What a thrill it was to enter the palace and catch a glimpse of myself in the enormous mirror, in the crowd of smartly dressed, loud, excited people. I was the smallest, the youngest, the brightest. I was in the theater while all the other kids were home watching *Good Night, Kiddies*. Everybody was looking at me, everybody was impressed.

Next we would go to the festive cafeteria with all those wonderful items normally reserved for big party bosses, like smoked fish sandwiches, and mushrooms in cream sauce baked in individual metal cups, and whipped cream. By the time the performance was about to start I would have gorged myself silly. I didn't see the point of watching the ballets, but I loved to scan the space through the tiny theater binoculars and hunt for things to laugh about. "Mom, look, that violinist blew his nose!" I would whisper. "Mom, look, that dancer is about to fart." "Mom, look, that woman to the right is using her nose like a conductor's baton!"

My mother would take one look and start laughing like crazy. People would hiss at us, but we wouldn't be able to stop. This was like a disease that we shared—the lack of control over our laughter. We truly couldn't help it. My mother came close to losing her job because she started to laugh during a Marxism-awareness session at the ministry, when the presenter said "the great teaching of Kax Max." I came close to being suspended from school because I laughed during a news screening, when a classmate whispered that Brezhnev looked like an old iguana. (Well, he does. Check for yourself!)

The fun lasted until the middle of the first act, when I'd feel the first waves of nausea, which would grow stronger and stronger every time the music swelled. Those mushrooms and smoked fish refused to play nicely with the whipped cream in my stomach. I would try to hold it in for as long as I could, but by the end of the first act I felt that something heavy and unstoppable was rising up my esophagus, about to erupt. My mother and I had to squeeze past all those indignant music and dance lovers and run for the bathroom. The performance of *Swan Lake* was the worst, because that time I didn't make it to the bathroom and had to release half-digested whipped cream and cream sauce all over the beautiful red velvet carpet and my good shoes. It was still worth it though. You hear me, Len? Worth it!

The most annoying thing about these fights is that when your internal dialogue gets going, you can't stop it. You keep finding solid arguments to prove your points, hours, days, weeks after your partner has forgotten about the fight altogether.

"So you consider it perfectly normal that you went everywhere with your mom, that you didn't have any friends your age?" Len would ask in my head.

I was hoping to make friends when I started first grade. On the first day, the teacher asked us to count up to the largest number we knew. Most kids could barely count to three. I was the only one who counted to one hundred and stopped only when the teacher told me to stop. My triumph didn't last long. As soon as the teacher left the room, the boy sitting next to me knocked me off my little chair. And as I lay on the linoleum floor that smelled like modeling clay and pee, another boy whispered: "Don't be such a smartass!"

Soon afterward, I started going to an orthodontist who fitted me with the first in a series of scary braces, and then I had to conceal not only my intelligence but also my ugliness, so I mostly kept my mouth shut.

The orthodontist appeared in my life as part of the endless parade of doctors I had seen since I recovered from pneumonia. All traces of the disease were gone, but my mother's fear and guilt weren't. Who knew what other diseases lurked in the dark depths of my neglected body? Hadn't my father been perfectly healthy too, and he went and died? What guarantees did she have that I would be spared? My very health spelled danger, because whatever was wrong with me must be hidden. In the year before I turned seven, I was subjected to countless blood tests, EKGs, and endoscopies, until we stumbled on that orthodontist who finally found something wrong with me. In his opinion, the worst mistake you could make was to wait for baby teeth to fall out. They had to be extracted. He promptly discovered that all my baby teeth were the wrong size and shape, which spelled disaster for my permanent teeth and my overall health. I had twelve remaining baby teeth. Twelve extractions. Then my permanent teeth started to grow, and it was getting obvious to him that my mouth was too small for so many teeth. So there were more extractions. Followed by years and years of highly experimental braces.

Note to a concerned reader. Now, before anybody decides that the guy was a crook, I have to say that in the Soviet Union, orthodontic services, like all medical services, were free, so he couldn't have been after our money. His interest in me was purely scientific. A tad sadistic, but mostly scientific.

Years later, my mother confessed that my orthodontist's ordering extractions made her feel relieved. There was something wrong with me after all, and it wasn't something truly awful, it was just my baby teeth, and she was eager to offer them up as a necessary sacrifice. I was eager to offer them up as a sacrifice too, not for the sake of my health, but for the sake of having my mother back.

So you see, Len? It's not true that my mother treated me like a guinea pig. She was simply overcompensating for the months of neglect that followed my father's death. And she would always let me pick out a small toy after a visit to the orthodontist. I loved that, Len!

There was a store ten minutes away from our house, belonging to a chain called Cult Goods, which didn't have anything to do with cults, but possibly something to do with culture. They sold everything from lightbulbs to notebooks to musical instruments, and they also sold toys. "Something that is priced under a ruble, please," I would tell the salesperson. "You see, I'm having many many extractions, and we can't afford a toy for each tooth, if they are over a ruble." The salesperson would react with a stunned expression, which I took for her being impressed by my grasp of math and economics, when she was clearly taken aback by my slurred speech and the pink saliva trickling from my mouth.

Making friends while trying to keep my mouth shut was very difficult, if not impossible. Sasha, Rita's youngest boy, was the only one who didn't make fun of my braces, but I refused to see him as a friend. I didn't choose him as a friend, he was forced on me by circumstance, so that made him more of an unwelcome family member. He was getting bad marks in math in his school, and Rita begged me to tutor him. At seven years old, I was a patronizing, dogged, and cruel teacher. "No, Sasha," I would say. "Not even close." Or, "Okay, fine, your answer is correct. But look how long this problem took you. I would've solved it in seconds." Our lessons often ended in tears, the tears streaming down Sasha's long twitchy face onto his scrawny chest.

Not that I needed any friends, Len. I had my mother!

I was about to put the "evidence" box back when I happened to see a thin stack of my childhood photos buried on the bottom of the box under the letters. I hesitated before taking them out—I had an inkling that they might ruin the happy version of my childhood, but I couldn't resist.

I would hate to admit this to Len, but both my mother and I do look a little crazy in the photos. My mother with her white hair framing a young face, sharp features, thick, pitch-black eyebrows, and an expression changing from cagey to murderous. And I, dressed as a boy, with a boy's hairdo, squeezing my lips so tight because of the braces that they look glued together.

My mother told me that long hair was too much trouble and a breeding ground for lice, and buying girls' clothes was a waste of money because I could have Rita's boys' hand-me-downs for free. I wore boys' clothes all the time, except to school where I wore the girls' uniform—a brown dress with a black pinafore. But my mother always insisted that I wear pants under my dress during the cold months. "You don't want to chill your ovaries," she said.

Outside of school, people often assumed that I was a boy, but that didn't bother me. I think I even enjoyed it. Once, when we were riding a train from Moscow to Saint Petersburg, and I stuck my body out the window too far, the conductor yelled: "Ma'am, get that boy off the window right now!" I didn't mind. I thought that concealing my gender was part of an adventure, that my mother and I were fooling everybody. Kind of like the way we did when people took her for my grandmother.

"You have to listen to your grandma!" some lady would say, and my mother would snap at her: "What? No! I'm her great-grandma!"

"That'll shut the bitch up!" she would whisper to me and then give the woman a glowering stare.

The thing is that even though my mother came back to me, she never regained her old Sevastopol self. At work, she seemed to be fully together. She resumed working on her textbooks, she had a good standing at the ministry, and a few years after we arrived in Moscow, she was offered a great teaching position at the university. She took me with her a couple of times, and I was in absolute awe of the power she projected. She stood at a podium addressing hundreds of students, brimming with confidence. From my seat in the back of the room I could see them eagerly following her with their eyes, trying to catch every word so they could write them down with their scratchy pens, laughing at her jokes. The girls sitting next to me in the back would sometimes turn and say: "Your mom is amazing!" and I would nod at them, polite but reserved: "I know." And they would laugh and say: "You are just like her." Which was the greatest compliment anyone could give me.

Outside of work, however, my mother revealed a less stable side. Every time we traveled somewhere together, she would push through a subway crowd like a torpedo, she would snap at strangers. One time she squeezed by a large woman and said in a deliberately loud whisper: "She should pay double fare with that ass!" Another time she pointed to a sweating man in a fur hat and said to me: "Hey, doesn't it look like that cat on his head just peed itself?" Moscow commuters were a tough crowd, you couldn't assault them without expecting retaliation. My mother's behavior was dangerous. Once, as we were running down a subway platform, I tripped on a huge duffel bag being dragged by a huge gloomy man. My mother helped me up and kicked the bag. "Watch it!" the man yelled, but my mother only laughed and asked: "Why? What do you have in there? Your chopped-up parents?" The man swung his arm as if about to punch my mother, but managed to stop himself. It was probably my presence that stopped him, but back then I thought it was my mother's glowering stare, which revealed the real magnitude of her meanness. I felt both frightened and protected by that stare. I thought that meanness was my mother's source of power, and wanted to draw up some of it for myself.

Perhaps Len was right, and I ended up extracting too much.

I shoved the box back into the drawer and didn't open it again until three years later, when B. asked me to show him my childhood photos. This was about three months into our affair, when the headiness of the first weeks had gone, we weren't "kissing like mad" or "talking like mad" anymore, we became clearheaded enough to see the wrongness of what we were doing and to feel a premonition of still worse things to come, but our interest in each other remained as intense as ever.

I took a few of the photos out of the box, put them into a manila envelope, and brought them to our next date in the park by the river. The day was uncomfortably cold and we were both shivering in our coats.

I handed B. the envelope, but as he reached inside, I felt a surge of panic. I had already told B. all kinds of stories about my relationship with my mother, but hearing all that was one thing, and seeing was another. I was about to find out whether B. would see my mother and me the same way that Len did, as a witch and her guinea pig.

He squinted his right eye and peered into the photos. A wisp of graying hair fell over his eyebrow and he blew it away. His eyes were brown, but much lighter brown than either mine or my mother's. His stare was devoid of meanness. I wasn't sure yet if he was kind or only appeared to be.

"Were these hand-me-downs?" B. asked about my clothes.

I was relieved that he offered a simple practical explanation for my wearing boys' clothes and told him that my mother's friend Rita had two boys, so naturally the hand-me-downs were boys' clothes. It was harder to account for the shorn hair. I didn't think B. would buy the "lice-protection" version.

B. sensed my anxiety and said: "I'll bring you my pictures next time. You should see what I wore. My grandmother claimed to be the best seamstress in Vilnius, and fuck, was she creative!"

I asked about the very worst thing he had to wear.

"Lederhosen!" he said with great certainty. "I was the laughingstock of my entire preschool."

We both laughed, then B. turned serious again and went back to my photos.

What looked cute in my early childhood photos started to seem more and more bizarre. There was a rare photo of me with my mouth open—somebody must have caught me unaware. The enormous braces were probably the first thing that jumped out at B., but the rest of me didn't look much better, what with the boy's hairdo accentuating my painfully thin neck, and that short brown dress with the pinafore bunched up over my wide woolen pants.

"You went to school dressed like this?" B. asked.

I nodded and hurried to say: "Sometimes I wonder if my mother consciously wanted to make me look ugly." B.'s expression told me that this thought had already crossed his mind, and he'd thought it would hurt less if I were the one to say it out loud.

B. looked at that picture for a moment or two, then switched to the one of my mother and shook his head.

"Could it be that she wanted to protect you?" he asked. "From love. So you wouldn't be hurt like she was?"

This explanation had never occurred to me. And even though I knew that it was too sweet and simplistic for B. and that he couldn't believe it, I was still grateful to him for this kindness.

B. reached for me and wrapped his arms around my back, and it felt so good that we stayed like that for a long time, not caring about our students or colleagues.

Don't push too
much math on
a child.
Or she might
rebel!

FIVE

Don't push too much math on your child? Really? By the time I was fourteen, it was certainly too late.

Anyway, I didn't rebel because of math, I rebelled because my mother betrayed me.

The first disturbing signs of something amiss came in the form of books. Once my mother came home with a book—she said a colleague had lent it to her—went straight into our bedroom, plopped onto her bed, and proceeded to read it. Didn't even come out for dinner.

I asked her what the book was. She said: "It's a novel."

But hadn't she said that she hated novels? Hadn't she said that novels that dealt with either love or death were unbearable, and all the others weren't worth reading? Hadn't she made a point to scoff every time she saw my grandmother with a novel? Hadn't she chuckled approvingly when she caught me scoffing in a similar way?

A perfect product of this upbringing, up until I turned fourteen, I hardly read anything except for math textbooks. I wasn't reading them for fun either—it was my job. Shortly after I turned ten, my mother received a huge and prestigious assignment to write a series of math textbooks for every single elementary school in the country. I was enlisted to help.

This coincided with me failing the so-called Gauss test meant to ascertain whether I was a mathematical genius. There was this problem that the great German mathematician Carl Friedrich Gauss solved when he was nine. Apparently, his lazy teacher wanted peace and quiet so he asked the kids to add all the numbers from one to one hundred. That'll give me a few hours for a nap, he thought. Well, he underestimated little Carl, who was done with the problem in minutes.

One day, my mother offered the same problem to me. For the life of me, I couldn't see a simple solution.

Finally, I said that I could add up all the numbers that ended with zero first, then all the numbers that ended with five. This must make the task somewhat easier, right?

My mother said: "Good, that's good," but I could sense how disappointed she was.

Note to a confident reader. By all means, go ahead and solve the problem. But please, don't offer it to your kids. There is a substantial chance that they'll fail, and your conspicuous disappointment will hurt them.

So here is what that obnoxious German boy did. He imagined all the numbers in a long row, snapped that imaginary row in half, and folded the right half over the left so it looked like this.

$$1 \quad 2 \quad 3 \ldots 47 \quad 48 \quad 49 \quad 50$$
$$100 \quad 99 \quad 98 \ldots 54 \quad 53 \quad 52 \quad 51$$

He saw that the sum of each pair would equal 101, and all he needed to do was multiply this sum by the number of pairs (fifty). The answer was 5,050. What a brilliant solution! Can't help but hate Carl Friedrich Gauss, even after all these years!

I told this story to my rich lover Victor shortly after we met. We were sitting across from each other in a bar, searching for things we might have in common. I wanted to get over B., so it was very important to me to find enough of those things, but the process of searching made me sad, because with B. I didn't have to search. B. and I matched so effortlessly that I would get a kick out of finding the points of divergence. Like his unquestioning acceptance of Christianity, or my passion for Alice Munro, who left him cold.

My conversation with Victor wasn't going that well, and it wasn't helping that I couldn't focus on what he was saying but instead kept staring at him, trying to persuade myself that Victor's slanted green eyes and wavy light brown hair made him more handsome than B.

But then Victor mentioned that before he switched to business he'd earned a PhD in physics (mathematical physics, to be precise). Math! I thought. How wonderful! Now we would have something to talk about.

I brought up the obnoxious Carl Friedrich Gauss.

"Of all the Germans to hate, you pick Gauss!" Victor said. He laughed for a long time, then told me that he used to be like the young Gauss, when he was a child. He was a rude, smart-alecky little prick. He grew up in a small village, where nobody cared about math, not his mother or his older brother—least of all their high school math teacher, an old drunk with digestive problems that made him belch all the time. Victor liked to correct him, which made the teacher shake with rage. There were times when Victor would raise his hand and the teacher would yell: "Shut the fuck up!" That teacher did a noble thing, though: he pulled a lot of strings to get Victor into a great boarding school for mathematically gifted children. Victor was positive that he wouldn't have become what he became if not for that school. But back then, he wasn't grateful to his teacher at all. He assumed that he just wanted to get rid of his most annoying student.

"Did you like that school?" I asked.

"No, I hated it. I missed my mom."

It was this confession that warmed me to Victor.

"Was your mom proud that you got accepted?" I asked.

"I'm not sure," Victor said. "I don't think she understood the significance of that."

Well, my mother certainly understood the significance of my failing the Gauss test. I couldn't help but notice the immediate shift in her approach to doing math with me. Instead of focusing on complex mathematical concepts, she began to explain how textbooks worked.

Here is the most important thing I learned. All math textbooks use stuff stolen from older textbooks, which use stuff stolen from even older textbooks in their turn. Some of the problems date as far as antiquity, and textbook authors have used them again and again, going to great lengths to update or renovate them. Not in terms of the math, no. The math stays the same. They are simply making the subject matter more suitable to the needs of their time, adding humor or pragmatism or socialist fervor. The better the problem, the more reincarnations it has had.

Here is one example. A truly ancient problem about Brahmins counting gold disks.

The older Brahmin says to the younger: "Give me one disk from your pile. Then I will have twice as much as you do!" And the younger answers: "No, you give me one disk from your pile. Then we will have the same number of disks." The question is how many disks each of them has at the moment of speaking.

I found that problem in at least seven different books. The same exact problem. The characters were the only thing that was different.

In one book, the characters were shepherds counting sheep.

In another, peasants dividing potatoes.

Children arguing over candy.

Children arguing over berries.

Dogs fighting over bones. (Talking dogs, no less!)

World War II soldiers distributing missiles.

Astronauts allotting food rations.

The main part of my job was to pore over all of our textbooks and pick the problems that were good enough to be stolen for my mother's new book.

We had hundreds of math textbooks at home, old and new. The older ones were so delicate that I imagined their pages could turn into sand at any minute and slip through my fingers in little trickles.

Not all math textbooks were good though.

"You know who I hate?" I asked my mother once.

"Who?"

(No, not Gauss. I would have never admitted to my mother that I hated Carl Friedrich Gauss, because it would have revealed my disappointment at not being a genius.)

"Tolstoy!"

Our bookshelves were sagging under the weight of Tolstoy's prose, but back then I knew Tolstoy only by the thin volume filled with math problems and educational fairy tales specially designed for the children of peasants.

Note to a curious reader. Tolstoy believed that illiterate peasants possessed greater truth and wisdom, yet for some reason he was obsessed with educating them.

My mother agreed with me. Most of Tolstoy's math problems were convoluted and imprecise. His stories for children my teacher often assigned to us weren't much better—all so dull and moralistic. But then I didn't see the point in reading any kind of fiction.

Sasha, who was an avid reader, would always try to push one or another novel on me. "What's it about?" I would ask. He'd say "life" or "people" or "love." And I would go, "Urggh," and say, "Go do math."

I didn't tutor Sasha in math anymore, because Rita wanted him to pass the entrance exam to a school for gifted children, and they hired a professional tutor for that. I asked my mother if I should try and take that exam too, but she said no. "You don't need that stupid school!" I didn't know how to interpret her words. I didn't need that school because I was naturally smart, or I didn't need that school because I wasn't smart enough? Or perhaps I didn't need any extra work, because I enjoyed working on math textbooks so much.

My favorite of all our math textbooks was published in 1952, shortly before Stalin's death. It was so good that it won a Stalin Prize, which was obviously the most prestigious award of that time.

Most of the problems in the book were centered on acts of heroism committed by ordinary Soviet people. There were all these *udarniks* trying to do more than the daily norm at their factories, there were young trainees trying to outwork each other, there were eager collective farmworkers milking their cows dry to get the most milk.

But this wasn't why I cherished the book so much. I cherished it because it made me experience my first orgasm.

The problem that did it for me was about two Soviet schoolchildren eager to do extra schoolwork.

Here it is. See if you can resist its erotic power.

A boy and a girl went to the outskirts of their town to take meteorological measurements. After they were done with their measurements, the boy and the girl took a rest on a grassy hill. There was a factory in the distance, a steam engine going past the factory, and a steamboat going down the river.

"What was the speed of the wind in our measurement?" the boy asked.

"Seven meters per second," the girl said.

"That gives me enough to calculate the speed of that train," the boy said.

"How is that possible?" the girl asked.

"Just look," the boy said.

"Right!" the girl said. "Now I see it too!"

Looking at the picture below, calculate the speed of the train.

Getting under that spell yet? No? Really?

Here is how it worked for me.

"A boy and a girl went to the outskirts of their town to take meteorological measurements."

A Boy and a Girl. Went alone together. To a remote deserted place. Were they holding hands? Maybe they weren't holding hands in the beginning, but then the girl stumbled and grabbed the boy's arm to keep her balance.

"After they were done with their measurements, the boy and the girl took a rest on a grassy hill."

Rest on a grassy hill? Were they sitting, were they lying? Probably lying. Lying in the grass. Was it warm? Was it dry? Grass could stain your clothes. The girl must have thought of that. She must have spread something on the grass. She must have spread the *Pravda* newspaper. Or perhaps, the *Young Pioneers' Pravda*. And so they were lying alone together, in the soft grass, on top of the rustling *Pravda*. They must have used something to prop up their heads, or they wouldn't have been able to see the factory and the river. Most likely their schoolbags. Their heads were very close to each other and inching still closer. Until their faces were so close together that they were afraid to breathe.

Up until I turned thirteen, I thought the pinnacle of sex was a kiss, and was too scared and excited to imagine what happened during the kiss. I didn't have any opportunity to practice, because I had a chastity belt attached to my teeth.

But that didn't prevent me from fantasizing.

I was the girl resting on that grassy hill with a boy. With Sasha. With Sasha's older brother, Misha. Or better yet various men who pressed against me on buses and trains.

I had begun touching myself a few months before that. I would lie down with a book but soon enough feel distracted by a certain disturbance brewing inside me. Then I would put my fingers inside my panties and stroke the external parts to quiet that disturbance down. But those attempts never culminated in something explosive and were usually terminated when I heard my grandmother's shuffling in the adjacent room.

That time, after reading the math problem, I found that I couldn't stop, and soon I felt that something irreversible was happening, that I lost control over my body, and I was being carried away to the place of no return. And when I did return from that place, and lay on my bed with that textbook facedown on my chest and my puckered fingers still inside my panties, trembling and counting the remaining spasms, I was completely overwhelmed by the terrifying power of what had happened.

Meanwhile, my mother's reading craze was getting worse and worse. More novels made an appearance, along with several thick magazines. She would spend whole evenings reading, and sometimes when I woke at night, I would see her reading. And sometimes I would even catch her reading when she was supposed to be working on her textbooks. She was neglecting our work for the sake of what, exactly?

I also noticed that she'd started spending more time on the phone, usually with Rita, talking about someone named Sergey, with a stupid dreamy expression on her face.

The next piece of reading that made an appearance at our house was a bunch of typed pages fastened together by a long rusty paper clip. My mother would read them again and again, every time with the same delirious smile on her face. One time she fell asleep while reading. I found the pages lying by her pillow after she left for work.

These were poems. By Joseph Brodsky—I'd never heard that name before. And they weren't clean and easy to understand like the poems we had to recite in school.

One was especially baffling. A man started by embracing a woman and went to list all the furniture in the room. The last stanza also mentioned a moth and an apparition, probably to suggest that the entire poem had a deeper meaning, which I didn't get. Another thing that I didn't get was the power the poem seemed to have over my mother.

I summoned Sasha for help. He took the pages from me with piety and whispered: "Brodsky. I've heard about him." This annoyed me to no end. Sasha had been accepted into that fancy school, and had immediately acquired a new haughtiness that I hated. He read the poems in silence, then out loud in a half whisper, following the lines with his long nose, nodding now and then. He spent the longest time on the poem about furniture, moth, and apparition. Then he asked if he could borrow the pages. I said no. Sasha sighed and told me that even though he felt like he understood the poems, he couldn't possibly explain them to me.

"Well, at least tell me what they are about!" I said.

He looked at me with pity, as if my inability to understand poetry made me some sort of mental invalid. (I understood math, math was tougher!)

"They are about love," he said.

"They are not!" I screamed, and kicked him out of the apartment.

A few days later I spotted tickets on my mother's desk. To Taganka Theater. For the new play based on Bulgakov's *Master and Margarita.* I hadn't read the novel, but my classmates talked about it all the time, and this Taganka Theater was supposed to be amazing. I yelped in delight.

My mother blushed and said that she was going with her colleague. "They're promising nudity, so it's hardly suitable for a child."

Oh, so now at fourteen, I was suddenly a child!

My mother took great pains to look good for that performance. She dyed her white hair a creepy silver-gray color and she bought a button-down shirt, clingy and pink.

She looked ugly in that shirt, white as a ghost. "I look awful, don't I?" she asked me. I confirmed with a little too much eagerness.

She ran into the bedroom and kneeled in front of our wardrobe, trying to find something buried under the pile of discarded shoes. She emerged with an old purse that she hadn't used in a very long time. She shook its contents out onto the floor and proceeded to rummage through a small pile of sticky coins, crumbs, and old pills. Then she found what she was looking for. A lipstick tube. The last time my mother had used lipstick was seven years earlier, so that tube must have been at least that old. My mother removed the top from the tube and twisted the bottom part to the right until a scuffed column of bright pink was revealed. She rushed to the mirror and swiped the lipstick forcefully across her lips. The rancid smell filled the room. I made loud gagging sounds. My mother threw the tube to the floor and wiped the stinking lipstick off her mouth with both hands. She looked like she was about to cry, but I didn't feel any pity for her. I felt anger, lots and lots of anger, and also shame, so much shame that I found it physically unbearable. I wanted to kick her, but instead

I started to laugh. My mother pushed me away and ran out of
the apartment.

As soon as she left, it occurred to me that I had a chance to
see with my own eyes the man who was stealing my mother from
me. He would have to see my mother to the door after the show,
because that was what lovers in Soviet movies always did.

The play was to end at 10:00 PM, and I estimated that they
would arrive between 10:50 and 11:15. My grandparents were
asleep by 10:30, so at exactly 10:50 I went to the kitchen, moved
the stool to the window overlooking the entrance, sat down, and
pressed my face to the glass. The kitchen was dark, and I could
see our street all the way down to the bus stop. This was early
March, and there was still plenty of hard dirty snow covering the
ground in ugly patches. At this time of night, the buses were rare.
I saw our drunk plumber, Uncle Pasha, get off one and stagger
down the street. I saw a woman I didn't know run toward the
stop. I saw a couple of stray dogs making sad circles in the snow
around the tightly closed garbage bin. Our window frame was so
rusty and old that it didn't close all the way. I was getting cold
and I wanted to pee, but I didn't want to risk missing my mother.
I kept my face pressed to the glass. Another bus pulled up to our
stop. A short, stocky man with a briefcase got off, turned toward
the bus, and offered his hand to a woman in a fur hat with long
flaps. My mother had the same hat. Then I saw that the woman
was my mother. The man took her under the arm and they started
walking toward our building. The closer they got, the fatter and
older the man appeared to be. He looked almost as old as my
grandfather! He wore a felt hat. At one point the wind made his
hat fly away, and I saw that he was almost completely bald. He

LARA VAPNYAR

couldn't possibly be my mother's lover! Why would I even think
that? I must have read too many romantic math problems.

The man was clearly a mere colleague, like my mother had
said. I felt like a fool. I was about to run back to bed, but I
decided to watch to the end, just in case. They stopped by the
entrance. The man was speaking, making wild gestures with his
hands. He must have been telling a joke, because my mother
started to laugh. She laughed hysterically for quite a long time,
until the man grabbed my mother by the flaps of her fur hat
and pulled her close and kissed her. The shock was so great that
I had to grab on to the edge of the windowsill to keep my balance. Everything around me was unbearable, from the chipped
windowsill to the greasy linoleum floor to my mother's slippers
I had on my feet. I kicked them off and ran barefoot to the
bedroom, where I climbed into bed and turned to the wall or
rather to the bookcase.

My mother walked in in about ten minutes or so. I pretended
to be asleep. She climbed into her bed but kept the night-light
on. The rustling of pages told me that she was reading. I guessed
that the book she was reading was another gift from the bald
man, and that he must have carried it in his ugly briefcase. Then
she fell asleep, but I couldn't, because as soon as I closed my eyes
I imagined my mother with her lover. By the age of fourteen I
was slightly better informed about the sexual act. I had read
my share of the greasy, poorly copied pages that my classmates
passed under the table in school. The thought of my mother
doing those things with her lover was intolerable. It made me
nauseous from disgust. I was afraid that if I fell asleep I would
dream all of that, so I forced myself to keep my eyes open. I

lay facing the book spines, as I did when I was little, and they reminded me of my silly prayers: "Bunny, mouse, doggy, cat. Make my mommy love me back." The memory was so embarrassing that I started to cry.

But even that wasn't enough to make me rebel. What did it for me was the teeth exercises.

This was a recent thing the orthodontist had added to my orthodontic treatment. We did the exercises as a group, ten kids ages seven to fifteen. We sat on the floor in front of a large mirror with our mouths open. All of us had two rows of braces, one each for the upper and lower teeth, connected by a tight rubber band. The band made moving our jaws painful and difficult, which was the point of this technique, I guess. I was so close to the mirror that the glass got clouded from my wet labored breathing. I was the oldest and the tallest in the group. I still had closely cropped hair, my pale thin face made inexplicably ugly by my open mouth.

I was suddenly very angry with my mother. She had made me ugly, she had made me friendless, she hadn't let me go to a good school, and then she had betrayed me! Abandoned me for the sake of her ugly old lover! I jumped to my feet and stormed out of that room. I ran all the way to the subway, the rubber band still bonding my teeth. There was a row of kiosks by the subway entrance. I hid behind one of them, in bushes smelling of old snow and dog and human urine, removed the rubber band, and unfastened my braces—it took me a long time, because of all those little hooks and bolts. Then I threw them into the garbage bin on top of crumpled pages of *Pravda* and half-eaten ice cream cones.

I was trembling all the way home, imagining the fight with my mother, but when I came in, she wouldn't even look at me.

She was screaming into the phone, her face streaked with tears. I tapped her on the shoulder, but she angrily waved me away. I thought that she was on the phone with my orthodontist, who'd complained about my behavior. Then I heard her screaming: "You know what you are, Sergey? A traitor!" and saw that the conversation had nothing to do with me. I felt relieved, but mostly mad at her.

When she finally hung up, I told her that I wasn't going to see the orthodontist anymore. She regarded me with a blank expression. I needed something stronger.

"I will grow out my hair and I won't do math with you anymore!" I said.

"Okay, fine," she said.

Her reaction was deeply discomfiting. Was she letting me know that I could do whatever I wanted? That I was on my own now? That I was the one in charge?

Years later, my mother told me that the day I quit my teeth exercises happened to be the day when she found out that Sergey was married. My teeth and my hair were the last things on her mind.

Note to children of parents. Parents do have their own problems. More often than not they trump yours.

It took me four months to grow out my hair enough for a tiny ponytail, and about the same time to learn to smile and relax my jaws so that my expression was more or less normal.

I believed that my new ponytail and the absence of braces changed my appearance to the point of exquisite beauty, but strangely enough nobody seemed to notice that. My classmates continued to ignore me, and people I saw in public places like the subway or the supermarket barely looked in my direction. But occasionally there would be moments when a man would give me an appreciative look, which would send me into a state of an extreme crazy high.

I decided to test my newfound powers on Sasha, who came to our place all the time, even though I didn't tutor him anymore. He had grown a few inches, and his hair was longer and fell over his eyes, which made him look spirited if not handsome. He was sitting on my bed, gushing about the new book he held open in his lap. I moved very close to him under the pretense of wanting to see the book better. I imagined what it would be like to kiss Sasha. I saw the pores on his skin and the spare reddish hairs growing from his ears down to his jaw, and I felt the faint smell of dill pickles gone bad emanating from his body. I didn't want to kiss Sasha, and he seemed to intuit that too, because he moved away.

I wished I knew how to make friends. But I found that, even if without braces and with longer hair I was significantly less ugly, the lingering sensation of ugliness was still there, and I was anxious about imposing myself on people. I would come home after school, do my homework, and sit there pondering my boredom.

Often, there would be one or another of my mother's students sitting in our bedroom, doing my old job, looking at my mother with canine deference.

"Why are they here?" I would ask.

"Well, you won't help me anymore," she would say, "and I have a deadline."

Her students were shy, homely girls in ill-fitting glasses. Most of them were married, a few of them were pregnant. I was insanely jealous of them, of their having had sex and of their taking my place with my mother. One of them said: "Professor Geller, you're my hero!" Her hero? *Her* hero? My mother was *my* hero! Still my hero, even if she had betrayed me.

I would walk into our room without acknowledging the students' presence and plop right onto my sofa with my homework and a bologna sandwich, to show them how little they mattered, that this was my space, my room, my mother. The bad thing was that homework at my school took me very little time. I had to be busy with something, so I'd pick a thick book from our shelves and pretend to read it. The thickest was *War and Peace*. By that time, I had read a few of Tolstoy's stories as part of my school curriculum. In my view, they weren't much better than his math problems. I found the first couple of chapters of *War and Peace* equally dull. But then I came to the scene of Natasha's first ball.

The handsome and brilliant Prince Andrei asks Natasha to dance, and Tolstoy shows how "that rapt expression on Natasha's face, ready for despair and for ecstasy, suddenly lit up with a happy, grateful, childlike smile."

Natasha is ready for despair and for ecstasy. For either despair or ecstasy. She isn't ready for any bland state in between. I wasn't ready for any bland state either. How did Tolstoy know that? How could he possibly know something about me that even I hardly knew?

I spent the next couple of weeks reading *War and Peace*, oblivious of my mother's pathetic students who couldn't possibly understand either ecstasy or despair, and once I finished, I went to our bookcase and picked up another book, then another, then another, then all the issues of the *Reading World* my mother kept on her shelf, until I earned the title of "avid reader."

And that was how my mother introduced me to her lover when he came for tea.

My grandparents refused to meet him and were adamant in their refusal. The man was cheating on his wife—it was disgusting.

"Serezha loves me!" my mother insisted. "He's only staying with his wife because they wouldn't let a divorced man attend foreign conferences!"

"Oh, really?" my grandmother said. "Is that what his wife thinks? Does she think that her husband is sleeping with her for the sake of the conferences?"

My mother ran into our room and slammed the door.

On the day Sergey was supposed to come, my grandparents went to visit Uncle Grisha. But I stayed. I was curious to see him up close.

He turned out to be just as old and ugly as I remembered, with shrewd little eyes made even smaller by thick glasses.

"Serezha," my mother said, "meet Katya. She's an avid reader, like you." She was all sweaty and flushed and unnaturally friendly.

"Oh, really?" Sergey said with a smirk. "Read anything interesting lately?"

I wanted to say *War and Peace*, but I had the sense that this wouldn't impress Sergey. I decided to go with the *Reading World*, and pick a piece that I found the most bizarre.

"There was a very funny piece about Gogol in the *Reading World*. Some Nabokov guy wrote it."

That made Sergey choke on his tea.

"Excuse me? Did she just say 'some Nabokov'?"

I blushed and looked at my mother. She was staring at me accusingly.

"I can't believe you don't know who Nabokov is!" she said.

And Sergey said: "An avid reader, huh?" After which they *both* started to laugh. Not only did my mother refuse to stand up for me, but she offered me like a sacrifice for her and her lover to mock and ridicule.

Note to parents (myself included) who mock their children for ignorance. Are you fucking serious? Isn't it 100% your fault?

For the first time in my life I felt true undiluted hatred for my mother. I wished the worst for her. Not her death or illness because that would be the worst for me, but something that would be awful for her, like Sergey dumping her, for example.

Which he did. Three years later. Sergey's wife found out about their relationship and demanded that he stop seeing my mother. Sergey broke the news to my mother in an especially cruel form. "It's not that I'm afraid of my wife," he chose to say. "We have to stop because I'm afraid of causing my wife pain."

My mother didn't tell me about this until years later. Back when Sergey broke up with her, I didn't know anything. I didn't even notice that he was gone. I had just fallen in love for the first time, and the rest of the world ceased to exist.

Reading Scales

SIX

In the seven months between my mother's diagnosis and her death, she was asked to assess her pain countless times. Every week, sometimes twice a week, sometimes even twice a day.

More often than not, there would be a startlingly bright pain scale poster on the wall.

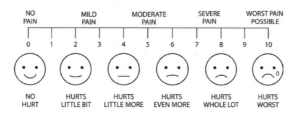

"Please assess your pain on a scale of zero to ten," a nurse would ask my mother, while pointing to the poster. "Zero is no pain at all and ten is the worst pain you can imagine."

"Nine," my mother would say in the beginning. This was the truth. Her pain was about as bad as anything she had ever experienced or could imagine.

But when they asked her the same question closer to the end, she would say, "Five? Six?" even though her pain at that time was much greater than in the beginning. This disparity wasn't caused by any increase in stoicism but by her newly acquired knowledge of what nine and ten truly felt like.

That's why I think being asked to assess pain on a scale of zero to ten doesn't make any sense. The value of ten is always the worst a person has experienced *so far*. We have no idea how much worse it can get.

The same goes for the pain of heartbreak. When your heart gets broken for the first time, you think that what you're feeling is a ten, and it could be true, but it could turn out to be a two or three compared to your future breakups. Just as with physical pain, you can't possibly imagine how much worse it can get.

I fell in love for the first time in the dark, half-empty auditorium of Sasha's school, at a screening that I attended with Sasha and my new friend Yulia. Yulia transferred to our school in the beginning of my senior year, after her family moved to Moscow from Saint Petersburg. She was a tiny redhead who came to school wearing adult pumps that made her gait unsteady and cautious. I struck up a fragile friendship with her, because she was the only other girl in our class who loved to read. She knew who Nabokov was.

Yulia's parents worked as stage designers in one of the Moscow theaters and they had ways of getting their hands on any book, prohibited or not. She promised to bring me a copy of *Lolita*, which was her favorite book. She told me that it was about this smart, free-spirited thirteen-year-old girl who was traveling across America with a grown man. The man was madly in love with her, so he paid for everything, for hotels and candy and beautiful dresses and shoes. And they were having really hot sex too!

Yulia was almost unbearably cool, but I was afraid that she was spending time with me by mistake, only because she was new at our school and didn't know any better. I desperately wanted to impress her, but I didn't know how. I thought of mentioning my mother the famous author of school textbooks, but math seemed too boring to impress Yulia. I tried to brag about my uncle Grisha who lived in New York and sent me American clothes, but Yulia only shrugged and said: "Who doesn't have an uncle abroad nowadays?" Finally, I told her about Sasha—a boy who had been hopelessly in love with me since we were three and who attended the best school in Moscow. They had these amazing screenings of art-house films, and perhaps I could even try to get us in. "Yes," Yulia said. "Yes! Please, try!"

The screenings were hosted by Sasha's favorite teacher, Boris Markovich. Sasha talked about him so much that if I hadn't known any better, I would've suspected that Sasha was in love with him. Boris Markovich was only twenty-four, but already finishing his doctoral thesis on twentieth-century Russian poetry. He read Mandelstam and Brodsky in class and he screened his favorite movies for his students in the school auditorium. The wife of Boris Markovich was very pretty and an aspiring actress. Sasha showed me a tiny photo of her in a theater program for a show in which she had a small role. Oh, and they had a baby, who was only seven months old. Sasha had gone to his house once—Boris Markovich lived right across the park from us. The wife hadn't been there, but he'd gotten to see the baby and even hold his little hand.

I would usually refuse to go to the screenings, because I knew I'd feel awkward in the company of fancy kids from a fancy school. But for Yulia's sake I was willing to do anything.

"Just don't tell anybody and don't be late," Sasha said. "Boris Markovich hates that." I promised that we wouldn't.

Yulia and I kept the first promise, but broke the second. Yulia asked if she could borrow any of my American clothes. I told her she could pick anything except for my favorite red T-shirt, and she took forever picking.

My mother was right there in the room, sitting cross-legged on her bed with the pile of manuscript pages in her lap, wincing at the noise we made.

"I don't like this girl," she whispered when Yulia went to the bathroom. "She's got shifty eyes." I waved her away.

"Your mother is so old," Yulia said when we finally left. "I thought she was your grandmother."

We missed our bus, then we ended up taking the wrong bus and got off at the wrong stop, then the guard at the school wouldn't let us in because I stupidly admitted that we weren't the school's students, we just came for the screening.

By the time we made it past the guard and into the auditorium, the film was already playing. It was black and white. There were two people on the screen. A boy around my age with long hair falling into his face, and a woman in a white coat, a doctor, urging him to do something with his hands. The auditorium was perfectly dark. We couldn't see anything or anybody, we weren't even sure that there were people there. There was a medical chemical smell in the room that matched the visual on the screen. Then I heard the teacher's voice. He said: "Shut the door! Shut the door tight and sit down!" His voice was high and strained. We shut the door and tiptoed down, groping at the backs of the seats, Yulia grabbing on to my arm, finding our way by the thin strips of light coming through slits in the heavy drapes on the windows. When my eyes adjusted to the dark a little, I saw a small group of people. Five or six kids were sitting in a single row in the middle, and the teacher was sitting alone in the row in front of them. I located Sasha and dragged Yulia there to take the two seats directly behind him. He said: "Shh!"

"Loud and clear!" the woman on-screen was saying. "Loud and clear!"

And the boy looked at her as if he had just woken up and said: "I can speak!" He was loud and clear.

Then the screen went black and there was the long queue of opening credits accompanied by heavy classical music.

"Shit," Boris Markovich said, "I've seen the opening scene at least three times and it still gives me goose bumps."

There were notes of anxiety in his voice. It seemed to be important to him that his students like the film. I found it moving, even if I wasn't moved by the opening scene itself.

Then there was a different scene, this time in color. A long-necked woman wearing a skirt and thick cardigan was sitting on a low fence, her eyes trained on a small figure approaching along the path on the edge of a field or a meadow. She was smoking nervously but gracefully, as if she wanted to hide her disquiet even from herself. The soft male voice-over told us what the woman was thinking. That if that figure made a turn toward the hedge, it must be her husband, but if it didn't— it was not her husband, and her husband would never come back. And it was then that I felt the goose bumps for the first time. There was something deeply familiar in the woman's expression and posture. She was guarded yet hopeful, proud but intensely vulnerable. I had a premonition that her husband wouldn't come back, and he didn't. The only way he would appear in the film was in the form of memories and dreams and lines of poetry.

There were many strange and disjointed moments in the film that I didn't understand and didn't enjoy. I couldn't follow the story or even see what the story was. I couldn't stand the imposing classical music that reminded me of all those concerts at the Kremlin Palace that had made me sick as a child. But I was still gripped by the power of the film. I was watching it in a way similar to how I used to watch movies when I was a child. Back in Sevastopol times, my mother would often sneak me into a theater to watch a grown-up movie with her, and even though I hardly understood the story, I was fascinated by the enormous figures moving on the screen in the dark. They looked and acted like regular people or regular animals, but they were magically beautiful and magically large, larger than anything life had to offer. My mother once showed me that all those enormous creatures reached the screen through the ray of light streaming from the tiny hole of the projector, but that didn't diminish my awe.

And then the movie arrived at the last scene, and Boris Markovich whispered: "*Stabat Mater*, here we come," and his voice broke.

There was the shot of the same field or meadow that we saw in the beginning. The long-necked woman who was smoking on the fence in that scene was now lying in the tall grass with her husband. The husband who wouldn't come back. But this scene was a flashback, and he was there, and he was asking her if she wanted a boy or a girl. There was a close-up of her face. She was happy, absolutely, unbearably happy, but she also knew that happiness like that could not last, it was too much, it wasn't allowed, it would be taken away.

I was suddenly struck by something that my childish egotism had obscured from me before. I had always thought of my father's death in terms of what *I* had lost (a father, a warm and happy mother, a perfect childhood by the sea). I had never considered what my mother had lost, which was incomparably more. And at that moment the music came out from the background, and rose—loud and clear and devastating—to crush me with shame and grief.

I spent the remainder of the film sobbing, until I felt Yulia tapping me on the arm. I saw that the light was on, the screen was blank, and everybody was staring at me. Yulia, and Sasha, and Sasha's classmates, and Sasha's teacher, Boris Markovich. I could hardly make out his features through the screen of tears. I only saw that he had dark long hair and a beard. He said something to me, I didn't understand what, but it sounded like something kind. Then I remembered where I was and bolted out of the auditorium.

I didn't want to take the bus, so I walked most of the way home. I continued walking even after it started to rain. I was thinking about my mother. This was her day off. I imagined her either sitting behind her desk or curled on the bed in a whirl of manuscript pages. I thought that I'd rush to hug her the second I made it home. But the closer to home I got, the harder it seemed. I couldn't just hug her, could I? I would have to explain, and I knew that I wouldn't be able to explain. I couldn't possibly put into words what I'd understood while watching *The Mirror*. It would take me many many years to learn how to put things I felt into words.

"You're dripping wet!" my mother said. "Go change or you'll catch a cold."

I nodded and went to change.

For the next few weeks after watching *The Mirror*, I avoided both Sasha and Yulia. I hated the fact that they had witnessed my embarrassment. What was even worse was that they both knew why I was avoiding them. "Hey," Yulia said, "it's not like you pooped your pants!" And Sasha said that his mom cried over movies all the time. A week later he told me that Boris Markovich was asking about me, that he actually said in class that I was the only one who truly got the film. This made me feel even worse. Not only did they still remember the incident, but they were talking about it, bringing it up in classroom discussions.

In order to dodge Yulia after school, I started walking home through the park, making a huge detour. These walks relaxed me. The farther into the park I'd walk, the fewer people I'd see, the more detached I'd feel from the incident, the easier it was to think about something else. Once I even made it to the farthest end of the park. I saw the light at the end of the tunnel of oak trees and the tops of the high-rises framing the park on the other side, and

I heard the sounds of traffic. I was about to turn back when I heard somebody speak to me.

"Hey, is it you? Sasha's friend? Yes, it is you!"

There was Boris Markovich sitting on a bench with a book in his lap, a baby stroller pushed against a tree, and a large fidgety dachshund by his feet. I considered running away, but his eyes were so kind and bright and he appeared to be so happy to see me that I smiled and confirmed that I was Sasha's friend.

"Sit down," he said. I sat down. "That's Max," he said, pointing to the dog. "We named him Max because he is big for a dachshund." Then he pointed to the sleeping baby and whispered that this was Mark, his son. "I still can't believe that I have a baby," he said, "a real human baby. So, what's your name?"

We sat and talked for a long long time, ignoring the fussing Mark and the persistent Max, who kept nibbling on my shoes. We talked about *The Mirror*, and about his favorite books, and my favorite books, and about all the amazing exciting things that were happening around us. The country was changing. There was no going back. We could do whatever we wanted. We could be whatever we wanted. We talked about what it was that we wanted to do. Boris Markovich wanted to start a magazine or to have his own radio show. He would invite people to discuss politics and art and life in general. In an honest open way. It would be unlike anything we had known before. And it wasn't an empty dream either. He had friends who were eager to do this with him. Then he asked what I wanted to do. I surprised myself by saying that I wanted to be a writer. He said that he was sure I would become one, he knew, he could feel it. I had cried over a movie, that meant I had a tremendous amount of empathy. People rarely talked about empathy, but he personally thought that this was the most important quality in an artist. Then he grabbed my hand and shook it as if congratulating me on my choice of profession. I didn't say anything. I couldn't speak. I suddenly felt as if I had a fever. I was nauseous, light-headed, and hot.

There was a moment in *War and Peace* that I hadn't understood until that day. Tolstoy is describing how the dashing Anatole seduces Natasha, even though she's betrothed to far-superior Prince Andrei.

> And, blocking her way, he brought his face close to hers.
>
> His shining, big, masculine eyes were so close to her eyes that she saw nothing except those eyes.
>
> "Natalie?!" his voice whispered questioningly, and someone squeezed her hands painfully. "Natalie?!"

Someone squeezed her hands painfully. There was nobody else in the room, just Natasha and Anatole. So why "someone"? I used to think this was a glitch, a mistake that crept into the manuscript and somehow escaped the attention of the editors of all the later editions of the novel. But then I understood that this wasn't a mistake. Far from it! This was Tolstoy's way to show that Natasha had lost her head. Because of sex, the promise of sex, the deep dark power of the sexual touch. This was exactly what I felt when Boris Markovich took my hand. And Tolstoy knew it—he saw right through me.

I came to my senses only when little Mark started to whimper, and Boris Markovich let go of my hand and said that he had to go home and give him a bottle.

Later that day I did something that I'd never done before and would never do again. I made a diary entry. I took one of my mother's pristine notebooks, opened it to the first page, and wrote: "I think I'm in love with B."

learning to
arrange things
in a certain
order.

SEVEN

It would be tempting to say that I fell in love with B. when I was seventeen and carried that love throughout my whole life. But I know that this is not true. I stopped loving B. shortly after I turned eighteen, and hardly felt anything toward him up until we started seeing each other almost twenty years later. I had become a different person by then, and so had he, and what happened between us then was an entirely different story.

Back when I was seventeen, the only love that I had witnessed was the love between my parents, which was all-consuming and absolute, and I thought that it was only natural that my love for B. should be the same. What I didn't know then was how quickly all-consuming and absolute can turn into obsessive, strip you of sanity, and make you do crazy embarrassing things.

I shared this with Nathalie after she experienced her first heartbreak. This was five years after my mother died. Nathalie had just turned eighteen. We were cuddled together in my bed, trying to sit very still, because we knew that if we didn't, the bed would start to shake and slide back and forth across the barren wooden floor. The thing was that the house had gotten infested with bedbugs. We had tried most of the conventional bedbug remedies, we had thrown out all of the rugs, we had scourged the furniture with poison— Danny had driven from college to help us—but so far nothing had worked, or not completely. The bedbugs would still come to bite us at night. That was when I became an addict of countless bedbug forums, willing to try things that were thoroughly insane. In that sense, bedbugs act just like unhappy obsessive love. They strip you of your sanity in a matter of weeks.

So here is one of the craziest suggestions for how to fight bedbugs. You have to pour an inch or two of cooking oil into small plastic containers and fit the legs of your furniture inside the containers. That way the bugs won't be able to make it off the floor and up the legs—they will end up drowning in oil. I'm not sure if it works (we still had bite marks, but perhaps they were imaginary), but I do know that it makes the furniture wobbly and prone to sliding back and forth. So you can cry but you can't sob while sitting on the oil-supported bed. You can't even blow your nose—or you end up on the other end of the room.

I explained to Nathalie my "pain-scale theory of heartbreak," but it didn't go over well.

"So you're basically saying that there are worse things to come?" Nathalie said. "That's not very comforting!"

And anyway, pain wasn't the problem, she could handle the pain. What she couldn't handle was the embarrassment. She was very close to sobbing now, so I offered to tell her about the embarrassing things I did when I fell in love for the first time.

"Yes," she said. "Yes!"

Nathalie loved it when I told her stories about myself at her age, especially stories about my failure. I couldn't help but notice that she was subconsciously competing with the main character of my stories, as if that girl were her sibling rather than a younger version of her mother.

But perhaps it was I who tried to distance myself from that younger version of me, because it made me feel that all the pain and embarrassment of love was far in the past.

So I took a piece of paper and listed the top five embarrassing things that I had done under the influence of love.

1. Stalking B. for days.
2. Confiding to Sasha and Yulia that I'd do everything for B. Which included sucking his dick (a taboo in Russia at that time) and ruining his marriage (less of a taboo).
3. Screaming that B. was stupid in a room full of his relatives and friends.
4. Spitting half-chewed hamburger into a sweet old lady's purse.
5. Leaving my grandmother at the store with twenty pounds of frozen chicken thighs and completely forgetting about her.

"That's all?" Nathalie asked.

I nodded.

"Aren't you forgetting something?" She was looking at me with panicky concern, the way she used to look at her grandmother when she started to lose her mind. I didn't understand.

"What about the chair?" she asked.

"What chair?"

"Remember how you threw a chair at him?"

And then I remembered. I did throw a chair at B. Across a crowded room. In front of the kids, in front of Len, in front of everybody. At my mother's funeral. And this didn't happen to that stupid seventeen-year-old all those years ago. It happened to me just five years ago. My whole body contracted with the pain of embarrassment. Now it was Nathalie's turn to comfort me. She reached to hug me, but her movement made the bed move to the left. She sat back, and the bed moved to the right. Its little legs soaked in cooking oil squeaked under our weight. We both started to laugh.

"You know what the best cure for heartbreak is?" Nathalie asked.

"What?"

"Bedbugs."

Note to a skeptical reader. Just try it!

Even though I didn't confide in my friends about all of the embarrassing things I had done, I did nothing to conceal my feelings, and both Yulia and Sasha soon became aware of my obsession. Sasha reacted with persistent "Urghs," but Yulia was riveted. She had read about the insanity of passion in one novel after another, and here it was, up close, and just as crazy as those writers described, or possibly even crazier. She'd be trembling with excitement every time she talked to me about B., and her pale freckled skin would turn glowing pink. I hated her interest, but I couldn't resist talking about B.

"Would you let him do all sorts of things to you?" she would ask me with cautious fascination, as if I were a dangerous animal in a zoo.

"Yes!" I would say.

"Even that thing?"

"Yes, even that!"

We had recently discovered descriptions of oral sex in a dirty hand-typed pamphlet somebody brought to class, and it seemed more frightening and disgusting to us than any other version of the sexual act.

"Would you run away from home with him?"

"Yes!"

That last question she asked in Sasha's presence, making him utter the loudest "Urgh!" so far.

"What are you talking about?" he asked. "Boris Markovich is married. He has a baby!"

But this didn't deter me at all. I didn't see little Mark as a child, as an important person in B.'s life, but rather as an accessory—something to take with you on walks, along with Max the dog. And B.'s wife didn't seem real to me at all. I couldn't imagine her sharing a home with B., eating breakfast with him, going to bed with him, or even giving him a kiss. He couldn't possibly love her. And she couldn't love him either, because I loved him so much. I thought that the amount of love directed toward one person by all the other people couldn't be unlimited, and I definitely used it all up.

Just like Tolstoy's Natasha, I was ready for *either* ecstasy or despair. What took me by surprise was that love turned out to be a constant back and forth between these two states.

Since meeting B. in the park, I never missed a screening, and there were times when he lavished a lot of attention on me, each word of praise making me deliriously happy. But there were also times when B. wouldn't even look in my direction. Or worse—he would ask me a question but ignore my answer, and turn his attention to somebody else, and my heart would sink, and I would experience it in a physical way. My heart grew heavier, bulkier, weighted down by disappointment.

The thing was that I was completely ignorant about world cinema. I would intuitively understand certain moments in the films we watched, especially if those moments were emotional, but every time a little bit of hard knowledge was required I would be lost. "Isn't this a homage to Fellini?" Yulia would ask, squinting at B. from behind her glasses, licking her lips. And I would think: Who's Fellini? And also think: I want Yulia to die.

Another thing that amazed me about love was how quickly it could turn from something bright and bubbly into a destructive and exhausting force. Within two months of meeting B., I stopped doing my homework. Instead, I devoted myself to reading every book that B. ever mentioned and searching for the films (by Bergman and Bertolucci and Pasolini) that he recommended. Finding those films was a Herculean task. Nobody I knew had a VCR or a movie projector, and even if they had, it would have been impossible to find the movies themselves in the Soviet Union of that time. Perestroika had just started, and huge stores of information, from historical facts to previously forbidden movies and books, were being unlocked for us, one by one. The process seemed overwhelmingly fast to older people. My grandmother, for example, who had abandoned novels and inherited the newspaper-reading business after my grandfather died, would spend her days buried under the fresh spread of periodicals, gasping and moaning and screeching: "Nina, look! Look what they're writing about Stalin! Are they crazy or what? Oh my God, these poor stupid writers are all going to die!"

But for younger people, the process was maddeningly slow. You could read *Gulag Archipelago*, but you still couldn't see any of the Western art-house classics. I had to resort to going to the Theater Library, which had a great collection of Western plays, as well as screenplays and even film magazines. You couldn't check out any of that, so I spent hours in the reading room, trying to collate the script of, let's say, *The Passenger* with the photos of Nicholson and Schneider in film magazines, so I could imagine the whole film in my head.

Only once did I get to see one of these films on a large screen. They were screening Pasolini's *Salò* in the brand-new Artists Palace, which boasted the largest movie screen in Moscow. B. said that *Salò* was one of the most provoking films of all time. Such a stunning metaphor of Nazism! So exquisitely made that B. had a perfectly visceral reaction when he saw it. I absolutely had to see it so I could tell B. that I had a visceral reaction too. Everybody knew that it was impossible to buy tickets, but Yulia hinted that her parents had an in. "If you get me the ticket, I will give you my red T-shirt!" I said.

Yulia got us three tickets, for herself, Sasha, and me. We came to the Palace early and went to the cafeteria, famous for serving exotic foreign foods like pizza and hamburgers. We ordered three hamburgers, which took a crazy long time. When we made it to the theater, the film had already started, and we had to squeeze to our seats past some very indignant people. I think I even stepped on the foot of a neat gray-haired lady sitting next to me. I apologized, and she was sweet enough to tell me that "it could happen to anyone." We finally settled in our seats, impatient to sink our teeth into those huge hamburgers that smelled better than anything I had ever smelled in my life. Mine was too big for me, so I had to remove the top bun, which made the patty slide out and onto the floor. I bent to retrieve it from under my seat (this was my first hamburger—I couldn't let it go!), put the patty back on top of the bun, took the first juicy bite, sat back, and only then looked at the screen.

I saw a group of naked boys and girls being led on leashes by grown men, made to bark and pant and eat off the floor like dogs, while the men groped and tortured them.

I turned to Yulia and Sasha. Sasha sat as if paralyzed with his hamburger suspended in his hands, dripping warm grease onto his pants, but Yulia was nonplussed. She was taking neat tiny bites out of her hamburger, chewing it carefully, an appreciative smile on her face. The gray-haired lady to the right of me had the same smile, only hers looked more genuine than Yulia's. I couldn't believe people could actually enjoy the film. As for me, I sat there with my mouth full of meat and bread, gathering more and more saliva, but unable to swallow, because I knew that as soon as I swallowed I would immediately throw up, as I had during ballets at the Kremlin Palace. Luckily, I had my mother's large purse with me, right there on the floor by my seat. I leaned in, opened the purse, spit the contents of my mouth into the purse as discreetly as I could, dropped the rest of the hamburger there as well, and shut it closed. I'd clean it out later, I thought.

We sat through ten more minutes of rape and scatology, then Sasha stood up and headed out, and I stood up too and reached for my purse. The gray-haired lady shook her head, smiling. This was her purse. I remembered that I had pushed mine under the seat. I said "Sorry," retrieved my purse, and started squeezing toward the exit.

It was only when I made it outside, and stood on the steps gulping fresh air, that the horror of the situation got to me. I opened my purse—there was nothing there, except for my loose change and my mother's stomach pills. No hamburger. I must have spewed my half-chewed hamburger into the purse of that sweet lady in the adjacent seat. The image of her reaching into her purse for the subway fare and finding the wet, greasy, gooey, stinking mess haunted me for weeks. It would've probably haunted me even longer if I hadn't received this devastating news, which made me forget about everything else.

"There won't be any more screenings," Sasha told me. "Boris Markovich quit."

"Why?" I screamed.

"He's leaving for America next month. For good. Like your uncle Grisha."

I couldn't, wouldn't believe him.

"How do you know this?" I asked.

"He told me himself after class. They are all leaving. His wife and his baby too," he added with a nasty smile.

So this was it? I would never see him again? He would leave just like that? Without talking to me? Without saying goodbye? This was inconceivable.

I begged Sasha to give me B.'s phone number, but he wouldn't. He said he didn't know it himself, and I didn't know whether to believe him or not.

I started skipping school and going to the park every day, hoping to see B. as I had that one time, with his baby and his dog. This was the end of March, a strange month, when you're so tired of winter that you want to pretend it's spring, and you go around shivering in your light coat and thin boots, hoping for a bit of sunshine to fall on your face, to at least warm up your nose a little. I would walk and walk and walk down the barren alleys, the thin soles of my boots slurping in the slush covering still-frozen ground, until my toes started to feel numb. Sometimes I would exit the park and walk around B.'s neighborhood, circling the streets, entering random stores to warm up, hoping that B. would happen to be shopping there at that precise moment. Once I spotted little Mark's stroller at a fish store called the Ocean. It wasn't B. pushing the stroller, though, but an imposing older woman wearing crimson lipstick who must have been B.'s mother or mother-in-law.

Around that time I got a school report card that was so bad that I had to fix it before showing it to my mother. I did a rather crude job of it, with razor scratches and ink stains all over it, but my mother, who had broken up with Sergey, was morose and distracted, and didn't notice.

"We need to talk about your future," she said.

"I'm applying to the university with Sasha and Yulia," I said.

"Don't you need to study a lot?" she asked.

"I do."

She said, "Okay."

I prayed to God, or rather to Something, that I'd get to see B. I begged and begged and begged, and I finally got my wish.

I saw B. at the large supermarket somewhere in between our two neighborhoods, in the long line to get so-called Bush's thighs.

The year was 1990, perestroika was in full swing, and the enormous slow country couldn't keep up with the speed of the changes, political as well as economic. One of the changes that was hard to ignore was that food had started to disappear from supermarket shelves. The late Soviet Union couldn't boast of a food bounty either, especially in the remote regions. But in Moscow, we could always count on the staples, like bread and meat, and dairy products, and basic seasonal vegetables and fruit. We were used to standing in huge lines to buy delicacies when and if the supermarkets had them in stock, but the bread lines were something new. As were the lines to buy vodka. My mother had to spend hours to buy two bottles of vodka—they wouldn't sell more than two. Nobody drank vodka in our household, but we kept a solid supply in the back of the kitchen cabinet, because it was precious currency in those times. You could ask a neighbor to move heavy furniture for a bottle, or to fix a leaking faucet for two.

Flooding the struggling Soviet Union with American chicken thighs was a brilliant idea. We liked to believe that the idea belonged to George H. W. Bush himself. It was a win-win situation. The US could unload unpopular chicken parts, help stabilize Gorbachev's West-friendly regime, and display the patronizing generosity of Cold War winners. And we—we got the thighs. Bush's thighs. Dream thighs. Twice as big as the thighs of underfed Russian chickens, plumped up with antibiotics and hormones, with buttery fat pushing through their pale skin, promising gastronomic delights of an unprecedented degree.

People hunted for them in stores all over the city and stood in long lines to get them. My grandmother established a whole network of friends who promised to tell each other whenever they spotted Bush's thighs on sale.

"They are selling Bush's thighs in the big store!" my grandmother announced one morning in April.

"I'm busy," my mother said. "Take Katya."

I groaned. The big store was far away, way outside of our neighborhood, and I had just come home after fruitlessly roaming the streets in search of B.

"I'm busy too," I said.

"But Bush's thighs!" my grandmother repeated, and my mother glared at me. Everybody knew that missing the chance to buy Bush's thighs wasn't just insane, it was criminal.

I had to go. My grandmother insisted on coming with me, which would make the trip twice as long, but I couldn't say no. Ever since Grisha had left and my grandfather had died, my grandmother had been getting progressively weaker. Recently she had developed bouts of dizziness and my mother wouldn't let her go to the store alone anymore, stripping her of her favorite activity.

We walked very slowly, making frequent stops so my grandmother could catch her breath. By the time we finally made it to the store, the line had spilled out onto the street and was stretching along the entire length of the store. People kept peeking into the glass window, trying to get at least a glimpse of the Bush's thighs. It took us a while to make it inside the store, and it was then that I saw B. He was approaching the cashier with a large block of frozen thighs in his arms. At first, I couldn't believe my eyes. I'd been searching and searching, and there he was, at the same store, in the same line, buying the same thing. He paid, put the thighs into a large shopping bag, and headed to the exit.

"Grandma, I'll be right back," I said and ran after him.

"Boris Markovich!" I yelled. He stopped and looked at me in surprise.

"Katya?"

I said that I needed to ask him something.

"Go ahead," he said.

"Is it true that you're going to America?"

My heart was beating so hard that I wrapped my coat tighter as if it could help to hide it from B. He looked at me for what seemed like a very long time, then asked if I had some time. He knew a café nearby where they served hot chocolate.

Yes, he said after we sat down at the café, it was true. They were leaving in two weeks. They had the tickets and most of their things were packed. There were six duffel bags on the floor of their living room, of the exact size and weight allowed by the airline, two for each of them. His wife and her mother kept repacking them. They would think of something essential to add, but that would wreck the weight balance, so they would need to remove something of equal weight to restore it. And they kept arguing, and fighting, and crying. And every time he looked at those bags, B. would be paralyzed with dread. Because he knew something now. He knew that it didn't matter what they packed, because the whole idea was a mistake. It was a mistake to leave. He had wanted to go for a long time, he was the one who had to talk his wife into going. And now she was so excited, and he now knew how wrong this all was. How unhappy they would be there. And to leave now, at the peak of perestroika, when so many exciting things were happening in Russia? This was insane, right? A friend had just offered him a job at a brand-new TV channel. He would be a producer. He would have a license to create his own show. Something modern and cool about film. Instead of the old and tired Kinopanorama. He kept thinking about his show, fantasizing about possible topics and guests, coming up with witty lines of dialogue in his head, even as he knew that he was leaving. Leaving in two weeks!

I got hot chocolate on my nose, and B. flicked it with his fingers, making me laugh. This was real hot chocolate, not the weak American version. It was silky and dark and viscous and so sweet that it made me high. We drank two large cups each.

"Stay!" I said.

And B. looked at me as if I had just offered a simple solution that hadn't occurred to him before.

"Stay? Just like that?" he asked.

I eagerly nodded.

"Because nobody can make me go, right?"

I shook my head.

"You know what, Katya, you're right. They can't make me!"

Before we parted, B. kissed me on the cheek and told me that I was his favorite girl in the world!

I walked all the way home with a delirious smile on my face.

"Poor Mamochka!" Nathalie said. "So, so stupid."

This was the point of telling the story, to make Nathalie feel smarter, more together than I was at her age. But still, her words hurt me a little bit.

"What about your grandmother?" she asked.

"Who?" I asked. The thing was, I completely forgot about her. Both now, as I was telling this story to Nathalie, and then, when I left her at the store.

I remembered about her only when my mother opened the door for me and asked where my grandmother was.

"Oh, no!" I said. I looked at the clock. Almost three hours had passed since I left my grandmother at the store. My mind was flooded with all these scary images. My poor grandma waiting for me in vain, starting to walk, bending under the twenty pounds of Bush's thighs, trying to make it through the slush, down the slippery path, getting dizzy, slipping, falling, lying on the ground, moaning and crying for help, whimpering, panting, dying. Dying because of me.

Fortunately, we didn't have to worry for long. The doorbell rang, and my grandmother walked in. There was a quiet drunk by her side, dressed in a filthy overcoat, smelling of either urine or pickled cabbage, holding the bags of chicken thighs in both hands. My grandmother sat down on a little chair and began removing her boots. She was breathless, but she sounded victorious. Apparently, she had waited for me for a long time, before figuring out that she was waiting in vain. Then she spotted this wonderful man, Stepan. "Semyon," the drunk corrected her shyly. She had promised him a bottle of vodka to get her and the thighs home. My mother groaned, but went to get the bottle.

"Here!" she said to the drunk. But he wasn't leaving.

"What?" my mother asked. He cleared his throat and whispered without raising his eyes: "The dinner?"

"What dinner?"

"The woman said the bottle of vodka and a dinner 'worthy of the tsars.'"

My grandmother nodded with a guilty expression.

"Wait here," my mother said. She went to the kitchen, cut a thick slice of rye bread, spread it with butter, slapped bologna on top, and gave that to the drunk. "Many thanks!" he said. He was almost out the door when he suddenly stopped and took a long, skeptical look at his sandwich. "Would a tsar eat that?" he asked.

"Oh, yes," my mother said. "That's exactly what they served Nikolai II on special occasions."

How she yelled at me afterward!

I didn't really care. My grandmother was fine, and my mother could yell all she wanted. I was so happy that B. was staying that I was invincible. I shut the door on my mother and called Sasha to tell him the good news.

My happiness lasted for the entire week following the Bush's thighs episode, until Sasha dropped by and told me that B. had called to invite him to his going-away party.

"You must have misunderstood!" I said.

"Do you want to come with me?" Sasha asked. "Yulia's coming too."

"Did you go?" Nathalie asked.

I nodded. She cringed and said that she had a feeling she wouldn't like the rest of the story. Then she asked what I wore.

I didn't remember. I remembered what I wanted to wear—one of my American T-shirts—but I couldn't find any. They must have all made it to Yulia by that time, one by one. Then I remembered one of the photos and imagined that I looked exactly as I had in that photo. Dressed in a short checkered dress that made my legs look painfully skinny, hair gathered in a messy ponytail, eyes glowering.

I became deeply embarrassed for that girl, as if she were someone separate from me, as if she were my daughter. I had an impulse to warn her of what was about to happen, to shield her from the imminent pain even if I knew that it had already happened and there was nothing I could do, except maybe tell the story to my real daughter in hopes that it would warn and possibly shield her.

I walked into B.'s apartment together with Sasha and Yulia, but there were so many people that I lost them almost right away. I craned my neck, but I couldn't see B. anywhere. I made my way forward, cutting through groups of people I didn't know, tobacco smoke and noise. I still couldn't see B. I saw Max thrashing about the apartment, bumping into people, his voice all coarse from barking and excitement. I saw little Mark in the arms of the older woman sporting crimson lipstick, both looking terrified. I saw B.'s wife, whom I recognized because she was the only one who looked like an actress. She was sitting on the edge of a windowsill, fixing her long shiny hair into a braid, laughing at the jokes of all these men who crowded around her, shaking her head to undo the braid.

I finally saw B. on the small balcony, drinking in the company of five other men who barely fit there. There was no way for me to approach him except from the back.

I made my way to the back, which was a mistake, because while I was squeezing between all those people, the crowd shifted, cutting me off from the balcony. I found Sasha and Yulia though. They stood between a large buffet and a TV cabinet, giggling and sneakily drinking vodka from the same glass, Sasha's hand on Yulia's waist. I did register this as a betrayal, but an unimportant one, compared to the tumult of my feelings for B.

I had my eyes on the balcony door. Any minute now B. would emerge from the balcony and announce that he wasn't going to America. He had decided to stay. He was staying. And there wasn't anything anyone could do about it.

Here he is! Opening the balcony door, stepping into the room. Stumbling from all those vodka shots, grabbing the edge of the gleaming buffet to keep his balance, in an untucked shirt with missing buttons, smiling stupidly. His neck is so thin. He's so young.

He pushes past all those people, walks up to his wife, squeezes her in a big hug, and lifts her off the floor. She squeals, and B. lets her go, because she is heavy, and he is so skinny and weak and also very drunk. Somebody hands him a shot of vodka, B. raises it up and yells: "To Oksana and me! To our new life!" There is applause. Drunken yelps. Everybody cheers.

And I, I stand in the middle of the room, stuck among all those drunk sweaty bodies. I'm shocked, overwhelmed, gasping for breath. Nobody warned me that the pain could be that intense, that scary.

"But in fact it was a three or four on the pain scale?" Nathalie asked.

"Yes," I said. "As I see it now. But back then it was a perfect ten. Worse than my father's death, way worse than my grandfather's."

I didn't know how to handle this. What to do.

So here is what I did. I screamed: "Boris Markovich! You're a coward and a fool!" and shoved my way through the crowd out of the apartment.

I ran and ran and ran through the dark park. There was only one person I desperately wanted at that moment.

"Grandma?" Nathalie asked.

Her question startled me.

"My grandma," she said. "Your mom."

"Yes," I said, "my mom."

Bonus problem. List all the embarrassing things you have done for the sake of love and place them on the scale of embarrassment, where 1 is mildly embarrassing, easily remedied with a chuckle, and 5 is so embarrassing that you hesitate before committing it to paper.

    1.

    2.

    3.

    4.

    5.

What would be
a great example
to show how
calculating
percentage works?

EIGHT

In seventeen years of my marriage, I have spent 330 happy days with Len and 6,240 days ranging from desperately unhappy to simply uncomfortable.

I wonder if this math is terribly sad or if this is how most marriages work.

> Bonus problem. Please calculate the percentage of happy days in my marriage. Then do the same with yours

Len and I met in August of 1994 on the chipped slippery staircase of one of those old Saint Petersburg buildings that seemed to soak up history like a sponge. They had known tsarist-era splendor, the tumult of the revolution, the unspeakable horrors of the Nazi siege, and the quiet abuses of the stagnation period.

Len was climbing up, I was skipping down. He lived in Saint Petersburg. I had come to Saint Petersburg to visit. Len was twenty-two, a recent graduate of the Electronic Engineering School. I was twenty, a junior at the Moscow Pedagogical University.

We couldn't really see each other, because somebody had taken out the lightbulb a few days before. Len loved to say that he fell in love with the light and cheerful sounds of my steps.

"Do you live in the building?" he asked. I said that I was visiting from Moscow. He didn't live there either. He had come to fix his aunt's TV.

"Do you want me to show you around Saint Petersburg?" he asked.

He had a deep voice with occasional high nervous notes. He sounded protective and in need of protection at the same time. I liked him right away.

I had planned to go to Saint Petersburg with my mother— a distant relative had offered us her empty apartment—but my mother changed her mind at the last moment, saying that she was exhausted and the trains were too drafty anyway.

The past few years had been cruel to her, especially since my grandmother had died and my mother had gotten fired from the ministry. My grandmother had had a stroke at the peak of perestroika, and my mother had been too distracted by her illness and death to keep up with the changes at the ministry. She still had her university job, but she seemed to have lost both her confidence and her spark. She spent most of the time at home, either reading or composing long letters to Grisha, wearing a knitted hat and a scarf because it was "too drafty" and sipping tepid tea because hot tea "burned her throat." She was turning into this sad old woman right in front of my eyes. Her huge brilliant eyes had become dull and narrow, hiding behind bags of flesh. Her white hair had acquired a yellow tint.

I couldn't bear seeing her like that, because I suspected that I was pathetic too. Perestroika, along with glasnost and the sexual revolution, was raging on, and students everywhere, especially at the better schools like the one Sasha and Yulia attended (they had both chosen the psychology department), listened to exciting lectures, went to rock concerts and protests, experimented with sex and drugs, while I was stuck in a school where most professors were hopeless retrogrades still droning on about the many advantages of the socialist economic system. This was nobody's fault but mine. If I wanted to get into a better school, I should've studied instead of chasing B.

To be fair, Yulia and Sasha did try to involve me in their life. I would go with them to lectures and screenings, but they were officially a couple now, and I would always feel like the third wheel. Plus, now that I was free of my infatuation with B., I saw my behavior of the previous year as temporary insanity, and didn't want to be around people who had witnessed my humiliation. For the same reason, I would refuse to meet the guys Yulia constantly pushed on me. Her expression would turn suspicious and a little hostile every time I said no. She must have worried that I'd try to steal Sasha, but I had no such intention. Sasha had grown remarkably handsome, tall, wiry, with intense eyes and an interesting nose, but I still wasn't attracted to him. Anyway, after B., the mere idea of falling into another embarrassing love was too painful for me.

I preferred to stay home and read, or write what I called "sketches" or "notes." Just like my school essays, they were mostly about my mother. My mother and I felt close to each other, but in a different way now, as equals. We talked about everything. My obsession with B. had left me baffled about the concept of love, and I hoped that if I studied every detail of my parents' relationship, I would be able to crack love as if it were a math problem. It was then that my mother showed me my father's letters and the note scribbled on the yellowed corner of the *Pravda* front page.

This happened one evening when my mother and I were drinking tea in our kitchen. Ever since my grandmother died, my mother had taken to sitting in her old spot by the kitchen window. I sat across from her, where my grandfather sat all those years ago. My mother kept blowing into her tea, while I asked question after question about my father. "But how did you know it was love?" "When did you know?" Suddenly my mother stood up and pushed her chair back. "I need to show you something." She went out of the kitchen and returned with a shoebox full of old letters. My mother put the box in front of me on the table and I reached in, but she said, "Wait," and left the room. She couldn't look at the letters even after all those years.

Len and I ended up spending every day of my Saint Petersburg visit together. He took a week off from work, pretending to be sick. Len said that he liked every single thing about me. I was filled with so much gratitude and wonder that I immediately liked everything about him too. From his gawky frame, to his mop of light brown hair, to his pensive blue eyes, and especially his large mouth that curved downward in a way that made Len look either sad or skeptical.

At the beginning he dutifully showed me all the famous landmarks, but we quickly abandoned them for the sake of the parks with sagging benches where we could sit and talk and kiss. We spent my last two days in Saint Petersburg in my mother's friend's tiny apartment. The bedroom was crowded by boxes of sheet music and various musical instruments in cases covered with sticky dust. This gave me the strangest sensation—I couldn't hear it, but I somehow felt surrounded by music. To get to the bed we had to climb over the early works of Rachmaninoff and squeeze between two cellos and a double bass. We lay on that bed, in the exhilarating agony of fruitless touching, because I was too scared to go all the way.

On the day of my departure, Len came to see me off at the train station. We arrived early and stood on the platform for a long time, hugging. We exchanged "I love yous." I had my face buried in his neck and my eyes closed. He had his lips pressed to the skin above my ear. We were trying to imbibe as much of each other's smell as we could. We stood perfectly still. Meanwhile, everything around us seemed to move. It was as if we were inside of a huge complicated organism. The trains would arrive and depart on adjacent platforms, screeching and panting, blowing whistles, emitting their heat and the heavy smells of diesel and grease. And those people around us, dragging their suitcases, stomping their feet on the platform, running, squeezing through, chatting, yelling, groaning. And the rough Baltic wind making its way onto the platform in sneaky drafts. And Len and I were in the middle of it all, but not part of it. We were separate, we were complete and self-sufficient, we were invincible.

The boarding announcement made us shudder. I let Len go and walked up the steps into my car. Len hoisted my suitcase up. I took it and dragged it to my compartment, then ran back to the door to look at Len one more time. He stood in the same spot where I'd left him, craning his neck, searching for me. I waved to him. Then the platform started to move, carrying Len away from me. It took me a moment to realize that it was the train that was moving. Len said something, but I couldn't hear. He started running after the train. He yelled: "Will you marry me?"

I yelled: "Yes! Yes! Yes!" and kept repeating it while I still could see Len.

Later, on the train, some angry woman was moving past me on the way to the bathroom. She said: "Wipe that smile off your face!" and when I didn't, she shoved me hard on the shoulder. I hardly felt the blow. I was invincible.

I didn't really ponder what it meant to be married, or explore the idea of something being for the rest of my life. I thought of his proposal and my acceptance as the ultimate expressions of the love we felt at that moment. At that moment. At that precise moment. What we had was here and now, and it was mind-blowing. I couldn't imagine my life without it or beyond it. And I couldn't wait to tell my mother!

I found her in the kitchen, drinking tea by the window in my grandmother's favorite spot. She had my grandmother's old cardigan on, and she was blowing into her cup like my grandmother used to do. For a second, I thought that this was not my mother but my grandmother's ghost.

I told her about Len, she started to cry. I hugged her and said: "No! Please don't cry! You'll like him, you will really like him!" Len was sensitive, Len was intelligent. He had to work two jobs to make a living, as a TV engineer and as a computer programmer. Len loved music and Soviet comedies. He loved to laugh. He wasn't funny himself, but he laughed at my jokes. Oh, and he was good at math. He had learned computer programming on his own. Imagine that!

My mother said that these were tears of happiness and that she had a very good feeling about Len.

I said I was sure that he would love her. She was my mother, she was so much like me, it seemed impossible that somebody could love me and not love her.

Note to a cynical reader. I was twenty. I didn't know a whole lot about how life worked.

It wasn't until the following day that my mother asked me if I had told Len about America. I gasped.

The thing was that about six months before I met Len, my mother and I had applied for US visas. Uncle Grisha had insisted that we do that. Right now the life of Russian Jews might not be so bad, but nobody knew what would happen next. Hatred and anger that had been suppressed for years were emerging from under the ruins of the Soviet Union. Nationalism, along with anti-Semitism, was on the rise. And right at that time the United States government passed the provision that Soviet Jews (especially those who had relatives in the US) could get entry visas and even refugee status. Uncle Grisha said that it would be remarkably stupid not to use this opportunity. He started the process for us, and now our applications were slowly creeping through immigration offices to be considered.

Immersed in my new love, I had completely forgotten.

We called Uncle Grisha, and it turned out that it was possible to include Len in our application, but only if we registered our marriage before the end of the year.

I explained the situation to Len, and he said that it didn't matter to him whether we ended up in New York, Moscow, or Saint Petersburg, as long as we were together.

We got married four months later. At the Grand Wedding Palace in Saint Petersburg.

I have one photograph from the wedding. There are ten people in it, all standing on the marble staircase of the Grand Wedding Palace in Saint Petersburg.

Sasha and Yulia are on the top, laughing from the sheer shock of it. Len's father, who had just met me, is a bit lower, his expression a blank. Len's stepmother by his side, smiling tensely at something to the right of the camera. Two of Len's college friends looking stupefied. My sobbing mother on the second step, supported by Rita.

And there are Len and I at the bottom of the steps, holding hands. Len, wearing an ill-fitting suit, is gawky, shaggy-haired, squeezing my hand with a brave determined smile. I'm skinny and young, with messy dark hair, long strands falling all over my face and neck. My dress, which I bought for sixteen dollars including the tiara and gloves, is shapeless and stiff, and bunched up on the bottom so that the tips of my lavender pumps show. None of it matters, because I look ready to take a leap.

Twelve years after my wedding, the *Important Fashion Magazine* assigned me to write a piece about my wedding dress. I wrote it in about a week and attached a copy of my wedding photo. The editors loved my piece and especially my photo, but they asked for a couple more—recent ones of Len and me, so that they could prove to their readers that we were still happily married. I had written a beautiful fairy tale, so it was only logical that readers would demand their "happily ever after." No fairy tale should end with its characters taking a leap or plunging into the unknown.

The year was 2003—way before the era of digital. We kept our photos in large plastic boxes in the basement of our home on Staten Island. I opened the box with more recent photos and poured the contents onto the ugly tan carpet. The photos were dusty and sticky, some stuck together. Most of them were of the kids. Dan trying to feed a frog. Nathalie taking off her ski boots. Len and the kids lying in the hammock together. The kids and I going down a woodsy path. Dan and Nathalie performing in a five-minute-long, two-person ballet based on *The Hound of the Baskervilles*. There were very few photos of Len and me together, and we didn't look happy in any of them. Far from it. It was always one of three possibilities:

The too-tight hug and the forced smile.

Barely touching and visibly wincing.

Each taking up his/her own space in the photo, seemingly unaware of the other's presence.

I finally picked a photo that we took on a ski trip to Mont-Tremblant six or seven years earlier. It was ten degrees Fahrenheit and we were both wearing bloated ski jackets, so "barely touching and visibly wincing" could have been attributed to the weather and not the state of the marriage.

Note to Important Fashion Magazine readers. If you happened to read the piece about my wedding dress and were under the impression that my marriage was still happy twelve years later, I owe you an apology. Len and I had been happy for less than a year.

The wedding coincided with the start of the school break, so I got to spend the time in Saint Petersburg fully submerged in the role of a newly married woman. I went shopping with a big checkered bag, I bought bread, I bought onions, I bought rice and buckwheat—I'd never bought grains before. I got myself a wallet because I thought that keeping money in a crumpled wad in a pocket of my jeans like I used to do was unseemly for a married woman. Everything was exciting and new and not completely serious.

The prospect of emigration frightened me amazingly little, probably because I concentrated on arriving, not on departing—never stopped to think what I'd be losing. I thought of immigration as a great adventure, much like my marriage. I had jumped into marriage without thinking and it was working fine, so there was no reason to suppose that immigration wouldn't. In addition, I thought that I knew what emigration was all about. I'd immigrated from Moscow to Saint Petersburg. Every morning after Len left for work, I would choose a different route to walk toward the center, marveling at how the architecture was nothing like Moscow's, taking in all the wonderful foreign details, from the way the streetcars were painted to the way people dressed. After each walk, I would come back to the apartment and write. Sasha had recently told me that the *Reading World* had announced a competition for aspiring writers. The winner would get his story published in the magazine. Both he and Yulia were going to submit stories. I still didn't take my writing seriously, but I decided to try my luck anyway.

I would write a little every day, interrupting my studies to buy and prepare food. At the wedding, my mother had given me a recipe book her mother had given her when she moved to Sevastopol. The simplest and most successful dish was the fish soup. I threw diced potatoes, onions, and carrots into the pot, and when they were almost ready, opened a can of salmon packed in tomato sauce and added it to the soup. I guess it was similar to Manhattan clam chowder, minus the clams and Manhattan. The main advantage of the soup was that I had to spend very little time cooking it and so almost no time conversing with the neighbor in our communal kitchen. The neighbor, Alla, was a busty middle-aged woman who went braless, wore threadbare robes, and was kind to animals. She had a dog, saved from the street and adopted. Her name was Nusha. She was playful and dumb. She would butt her head into the door of our bedroom every morning and storm in. Once there, she would prance and jump around the room until Len threw a pillow at her and yelled that she must leave. "Nushka, now!" What she did was snatch used condoms we would throw under the bed in the course of the night and bring them to Alla. Alla made sure to comment on that in the kitchen. "I got another little gift from Nushka this morning." I pretended to be embarrassed, but I was secretly proud. We had lots and lots of used condoms. What better proof of a robust marriage!

Recently, I found out that Nathalie had the same idea of condoms being a marriage thermometer when she was a child. She told me that when she was ten or eleven, she and her best friend Masha went to raid the nightstands in my and Len's bedroom. Masha was a year older and vastly more experienced, because her parents had already gone through the divorce and had sex with other people. Among other interesting things, the drawer revealed a pack of condoms. "That's a good sign," Masha said. "That means your parents are still having sex." Nathalie felt relieved—she had always worried that Len and I would get divorced. Then something compelled her to check the expiration date. At that time Nathalie was spending about an hour a day doing math with her grandmother. She knew the importance of "doing math in your head ALWAYS." "They haven't had sex in five years!" she determined. Masha said that if that was the case, we were going to get divorced for sure.

What it actually meant was that many years ago I was in the process of switching birth control methods and we needed condoms for a few gap weeks. We didn't get divorced until many years after that raid and we were having sex up until the very end.

Note to children raiding their parents' drawers. First of all, don't! Nothing you find there will make it worthwhile. But if you do, know this: while the absence of sex is probably a good indicator of an impending divorce, having sex isn't proof of the opposite. Your parents can have plenty of acceptable or even pretty good sex and still be miserable.

But back then I couldn't even imagine ever being miserable with Len. Our love was so strong that it felt like a presence in that communal apartment, as if it were another tenant. It had an amorphous shape and weird density; it was less dense than an actual object, but denser than the air in the room. It felt as if I could touch it. I could move my hand through the air and feel resistance in places where love was. While Len was at work I missed him like crazy. When it was time for him to come home, I would come to the front door and listen for the sound of footsteps on the staircase. When I heard his I would rush to open the door. And he would walk in and hug me, and we would stay like this for a minute or two, while Nushka jumped and panted and wagged her tail.

I would describe all that to my mother, in our daily phone calls. I would be gushing about my happiness, but as soon as I put the receiver down I would be invariably overcome with panic. My mother and father had loved each other too, and look how it ended. My father had died just like that. What if they had loved each other too much, and that was why my father died? Wasn't it arrogant to dare to love each other that much?

I would lie in bed next to the sleeping Len, letting his hair tickle my nose, taking in the warmth of his back, and think of childish prayers. I couldn't pray like that anymore, could I? I was a married woman now. I had to come up with a more grown-up way of praying.

"Dear God [even though I still imagined God as Something]," I would beg, "I'm not arrogant. I swear I'm not. I know I don't deserve this happiness, but please, please don't take Len away from me, don't let him die."

God didn't take Len away. What he took away was our love.

Fun with graphs

If you can't determine the exact moment of the event, try to find the last defined moment before the event, and the first that comes after.

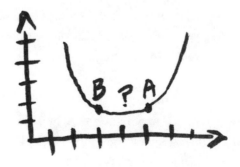

NINE

I wonder if there is a precise mathematical formula that lets you determine the exact moment when your love started to die. If you imagine love as a line graph, you can look for the last moment when it was definitely there, and the first moment when it was definitely gone. The moment when your love started to die would be somewhere between those points.

So what was the last moment when Len and I were happy? I remember one moment about a week before we left Russia for the United States. To my complete shock, I ended up winning the *Reading World* competition. The story I submitted took place during the stagnation period, and focused on a young woman who had to visit remote schools as part of her job for the Ministry of Education. I even included my mother's favorite anecdote about the Moscow man who wanted to poop. The editor had written me a gushing letter, but I couldn't really believe that my story was getting published until I received the magazine in the mail, opened it, and saw my name in the table of contents. Katya

Geller, "Math in the Sands," a short story. Len took the magazine from me and stroked its light blue cover, lovingly, as if it were a pet. He was so happy for me that there were tears in his eyes. His happiness touched me more than that of my mother, who was absolutely delirious. Mothers can't help but love their kids' writing, especially when they are the main characters in that writing. Husbands are a different story. Afterward, Len and I went for a walk in a park. The day was chilly and bright. We walked down the icy path, Len's hand on my waist so that I wouldn't slip on the ice, and my hand over his so that it wouldn't get cold. The love was still there then, definitely there, caught between our fingers like the flickers of warmth.

Finding the first moment when the love was gone is harder. There was emigration. Selling the apartment. Getting rid of our things. Saying our goodbyes. The going-away party. Seeing Sasha drunk for the first time. He was crying and saying that he and Yulia were getting married soon, and that he didn't want to get married, that he was sick of his life, that he would've given anything to be going somewhere too. His mother, Rita, gave my mother a pack of tea with the words: "Here, so you could have tea, if things get really bad."

Then there was the long flight over the Atlantic. My first time on a plane. I remember three things.

The clouds looking like the dust gathered in the bag of a vacuum cleaner.

Imitation crabmeat for lunch.

And the scary sound the toilet flush made.

Then there was immigration. Seeing Uncle Grisha for the first time in years—shit, he looked so bad! Exploring the new

place. The hot rush of strangeness. Len and I were beside ourselves with excitement, and it made me mad that my mother refused to share it.

Uncle Grisha had found a tiny one-bedroom for us, in a
cheap corner of Brooklyn, crowded with both Orthodox Jews
and Haitians. Len and I got the bedroom with no windows and a
huge crack in the wall, and my mother settled on the sofa in the
living room separated from the rest of the apartment by a greasy
yellow curtain. She spent her first weeks in the US sitting on that
sofa, drinking Rita's tea and holding one of our Russian books in
her lap, but not reading it. I was annoyed with her. I thought she
was just stubborn in her refusal to go out and admire all things
American, like skyscrapers, hot dogs, and free plastic bags.

It was only years later that my mother told me how scared
and lost she felt then, how thoroughly useless. She said: "Remember how we couldn't decide if we should bring our down pillow
with us?" I remembered. Some people had told us to leave it,
but others had insisted that they didn't have good down pillows
in the US and they were worth their weight in gold. Eventually,
we decided to ship it. We were shipping tons of books anyway.
All the Russian classics, all the math textbooks. Spent a fortune
on postage. The pillow arrived safely, but it turned out to be too
big for the American pillowcases, and anyway, it was lumpy and
fat and uncomfortable. We stuffed it in the back of our closet in
Brooklyn and it never saw the light of day again. "I felt like that
pillow," my mother said.

During those first weeks in New York, Len and I went exploring the city every chance we got. We'd take the Q train into
Manhattan and exit at a different stop each time. This way, we

thought, we would see the city at random, not as tourists but as explorers. It was such a thrill to go up the subway steps without knowing what we would see at the top, whether it would be a bunch of skyscrapers, a park, a Korean deli, or a fancy restaurant. We walked the streets hand in hand, choosing our direction depending on traffic lights. When the light was green, we walked forward; when the light was red, we turned. Sometimes we had to run across the street, and we ran, laughing, squeezing between people, jumping over puddles.

I described all that in my letters to Sasha and Yulia, especially the joy Len and I felt, the joy of having "made it," of belonging to this city that we had known only in movies.

Was our love still there then? I can't tell. The intensity of the first weeks in the US was too overwhelming to keep track of love. To keep track of anything, really.

Both Len and I felt buoyant with enthusiasm about our job prospects. Well, in Len's case our enthusiasm was perfectly justified. He was a gifted computer programmer, and computer programmers were in high demand. Len found a great job within three weeks. Bought a *New York Times*, circled ads in the help wanted section, sent out his résumé, had a couple of interviews, and got a job. Just like that. His salary was $38,000. Everybody said that the highest starting salary for a computer programmer was $35,000. Len got $38,000! He could barely speak English!

I was sure I would find a great, exciting job within weeks too. I was smart, I thought. I was a quick learner, I had an open mind, I didn't mind hard work. And my English was much better than Len's. I had studied it in college, and here in Brooklyn I had been supplementing it using my own system. Uncle Grisha had brought us his old VCR and a huge box full of VCR tapes with Hollywood movies he had recorded from TV. *Wall Street. Pretty Woman. Working Girl. Once Upon a Time in America.* I'd watched each of these movies hundreds of times, pausing and rewinding every time I couldn't understand a line of dialogue, until I finally got every word.

So strong was my willed optimism that it held against all odds for all of two months. Even as all of my job applications went unanswered, even as I was running out of ads to respond to, I kept reading and circling, reading and circling, steadily shedding my vanity and applying for less and less exciting jobs. "Oh, no," a woman said to me at one place, where I'd applied to be a receptionist. "We need somebody who speaks English."

This came as a shock. I had been very proud of my English, but apparently it wasn't good enough for working with people, or with animals, for that matter, as I found out after being rejected as a dog walker. And I'd applied to be a language arts teacher! I imagined how people had chuckled when they read my résumé, when they looked at the xeroxed table of contents from the obscure Russian magazine I always attached.

I couldn't bear to go to Manhattan anymore. I couldn't even bring myself to write to Sasha and Yulia anymore. I sent them a short postcard congratulating them on their wedding, but other than that I had nothing to say.

"She needs to learn a useful profession!" Grisha's wife, Bella, said. "That's what Americans do."

They would invite us to dinner and speak of themselves as "Americans," as opposed to immigrants who remained hopelessly Russian, including my mother and me. Bella even coined a term for people like us—"Ruswine." As in, "Look at the Ruswine hunting for furniture in the garbage."

"Why don't you learn computer programming?" Len asked. He promised to help me study, so we wouldn't need to pay for classes. This was the nineties, the time of the huge technological bubble. "Even the shittiest programmers are finding work," Len said.

I noticed that Len had changed dramatically in the weeks since he'd found a job. He used to be shy, skinny, and shaggy-haired. Now he was square and trim, with a new confidence shining from his blue eyes the way synthetic glow shone from his new Century 21 suits. He was twenty-four, but he looked almost forty.

I thought that the old shaggy-haired Len would've understood that I didn't want to be the shittiest programmer or the shittiest anything. He would've urged me to find something where I could shine, just like he did.

Then I noticed another change. The old Len used to love my mother. He felt more respect and affection for her than he did toward his own parents. The new Len wouldn't conceal how annoyed he was by my mother's mere presence, let alone the fact that she lived with us. He would engage in petty bickering with her that frightened and appalled me.

"Nina, why are you putting bologna in the freezer?" he would ask.

"It was starting to rot."

"Nina, if something is starting to rot, you have to fry it up, not put it into the freezer!"

Note to a practical reader. Try to determine the correct course of action with that rotten bologna. Keep in mind that we were recent immigrants from the former Soviet Union and throwing bad food into the garbage was out of the question.

My mother wouldn't argue with Len, but she would get back at him in some sort of sneaky way. For example, she liked to wait for Len to walk into the bathroom with the fresh issue of the *New York Times*, so she could tiptoe up to the light switch in the hall and turn the light off as if by accident. She knew that Len found it intensely embarrassing to talk to people while he was on the toilet. So it was pure torture for him to have to yell: "Hey, somebody! Anybody! Please turn the light back on!"

I think it was my mother's petty war with Len that helped lift her spirits. I would often overhear her talking to Uncle Grisha on the phone, laughing and boasting of her small victories. I remembered how after my father died, she would draw power from her meanness, and perhaps this was exactly what was happening now. Her mood was certainly better; she started to leave the house more, go and explore New York on her own, and one day she put her best textbooks into a plastic bag and went to the Jewish Immigrant Agency to ask them to help her find a job. The women at the agency weren't impressed by the textbooks or by the fact that my mother had been a university professor. "Perhaps I could tutor Russian kids in math?" my mother suggested. The women at the agency chuckled and explained that you needed to know the ins and outs of the American school curriculum for that. "How about cleaning houses?" one woman asked. "Or perhaps you have experience caring for the sick and elderly?" suggested another. "Yes! Yes, I have!" my mother said, feeling darkly fortunate that my grandmother's long illness provided her with a marketable skill.

Her first patient was a sixty-five-year-old widower with Parkinson's. His name was Elijah Ross. My mother liked him right away. So intelligent, so well-read, she would gush at home. He used to be an editor at the *Most Important Literary Magazine*, and yet he was so modest, so grateful for every little thing she did for him.

My mother's schedule was Tuesday through Saturday. She would get up every morning at seven, have a quick breakfast, and rush to the subway so she would be at Elijah's Upper West Side apartment by nine. More often than not, she would arrive too early, and then she would exit the subway a couple of stops earlier and take a little walk to Elijah's place, using a different route each time. She said that the best thing about finding a job was that it made her days structured again.

Bonus problem. Considering that Elijah's apartment was on the corner of Ninety-First Street and Amsterdam Avenue, and my mother got off the subway on Seventy-Second and Central Park West, calculate how many different routes she could use along that neat grid of NYC streets.

"Even your mother found a job!" Bella said to me. "And you're still wallowing in your specialness?"

I don't think Bella expected that her words would hurt me that much. But they did. They made me understand the meaning of self-loathing. You hate and despise somebody so much that you physically can't stand her presence, but you can't do anything to escape her presence, because that person is you.

I asked Len to teach me computer programming the next day.

Len bought several used C++ textbooks and made a plan of study. I was to read a certain number of pages a day and do several exercises. At the end of the day, Len would check my progress and point out my weak areas so I could study them more before the next day's assignment.

My days became structured too. As did my evenings. One of those evenings, I was sitting in our bed, leaning against the wall—the bed didn't have a headboard—with the *C++ for Beginners* propped against my belly. My mother was snoring on her sofa bed behind the curtain. Len was sitting with his back to me at our makeshift desk, playing *Tetris*. As far as I could see he was doing well. I wasn't. I was rereading the chapter that I had failed to understand earlier that day, and I still didn't understand it. Every couple of pages I would be seized by an urge to masturbate, out of sheer boredom rather than anything else. I could easily accomplish that without Len noticing, but I felt too lazy to do that. I kept dozing off, floating away from reality, until I was woken up by the victorious *Tetris* beeps. Then I went back to C++ and the circle repeated itself. I managed to maintain that routine for a couple of weeks. Then I started to cheat.

Elijah gave my mother a whole pile of old issues of the *Magazine* so she could improve her English. She would spend most of her evenings bent over our kitchen table. There was a magazine issue spread in front of her, and the huge English-Russian dictionary we had brought from Moscow, and a little notepad she used for writing down words she didn't know. Every word had a numerical value from one to three. One was assigned to words that appeared in the text only once, two to words that appeared several times, and three to words that appeared all the time. At the end of each session, she would memorize all the three words, some two words, and ignore unimportant one words altogether.

Note to a reader who wants to learn a foreign language. This method will do wonders for your reading skills. But only if you're naturally disciplined! If not, forget about it.

I started taking long breaks from studying computer programming to read the *Magazine* too, telling myself that I did it to improve my English so I could have better job prospects as a computer programmer. I admired my mother's system, but I didn't have the patience to follow it myself, so I would submerge myself in the text, skipping words that I didn't know, trying to either guess or imagine whatever I couldn't understand. This method didn't work for nonfiction essays, but I found that I could read short stories with growing ease. I hadn't read any fiction since we left Russia, and I was starved for stories.

There was one author that I especially liked, she would appear in the magazine again and again. I was hooked when I came to the following passage:

> Young husbands were stern, in those days. Just a short time before, they had been suitors, almost figures of fun, knock-kneed and desperate in their sexual agonies. Now, bedded down, they turned resolute and disapproving. Off to work every morning, clean-shaven, youthful necks in knotted ties, days spent in unknown labors. . . . What a lot they had to learn, so quickly. How to kowtow to bosses and how to manage wives.

The story took place in Canada decades ago, and yet I recognized Len right away, down to the image of his "youthful neck" sticking awkwardly from his discounted Kenneth Cole shirt. This writer, Alice Munro, captured him perfectly without ever meeting him. What was more, she captured how I saw him. She knew exactly how I felt. I wasn't alone in feeling that. I wasn't alone, period. I experienced a rush of overwhelming, almost embarrassing, gratitude.

"Do you like Alice Munro?" my mother asked when she caught me reading her story. "Her writing is too difficult for me, but Elijah likes her. He says she's the greatest living writer. He worked with her, you know."

My mother was definitely talking about Elijah too much. It was like she couldn't help but bring him up again and again, which could be a sign of what exactly? Attraction? Infatuation? Still, I didn't ponder their relationship much, until my mother came to me with a strange request.

She wanted me to translate my *Reading World* story for Elijah.
"Why?" I asked.

"Because it's about me," she said, blushing. "I want him to know me."

I found it flattering that my mother thought it was possible to get to know her through my story, but I doubted that I would be able to translate it well enough. "Something rough will do," my mother said. I said I'd try. That very night, I took out the copy of the *Reading World* and our enormous Russian-English dictionary and set to work, which turned out to be much more challenging than I'd expected. Some words didn't have an English equivalent; others had too many and my grasp of the English wasn't strong enough to choose the right one, and even when I managed to come up with a passable translation of one or another sentence, it would still lack something vital, something more important than the correct meaning. Those *Tetris* beeps were infuriating! I asked Len to lower the volume and he turned and asked what I was doing. "I'm translating my story," I said. He scoffed and turned back to the screen. He must have thought that self-translating was yet another expression of my vanity.

The next day, I decided to try something else. I abandoned my Russian story and started writing a new one, in English, from scratch. This one was about us: our trips to teachers' seminars, how we'd lived in empty schoolhouses, slept on piled-up mats, brushed teeth in school bathrooms, boiled eggs with the help of an immersion heater. Writing in English turned out to be easier, less constrictive, and much more thrilling than translating. It didn't require torturous attempts to find the single right word. The English words that I knew effortlessly rushed to my mind, and I found that I rarely needed the words that I didn't know.

And if I ever got scared or overwhelmed by the task of writing in a foreign language, I would tell myself that this wasn't a short story, this was more like a long sketch about my mother. I finished in two weeks, typed it up on Len's computer, printed out the pages, and gave them to my mother. "It's not the same story," I said, "but it's still about you." She took our English-Russian dictionary, which was even thicker than the Russian-English one, and went to her sofa to read it. "I didn't understand all of it," she said the next morning, "but what I did understand I liked." It didn't occur to me to show the story to Len.

A week later, my mother told me that Elijah wanted to see me. We both assumed that he wanted me to clarify something about the story. On Saturday, my mother and I took a long subway ride to the Upper West Side together, and exited onto the leafy street neatly framed with tall dignified buildings. "It will be like entering a Woody Allen film," my mother told me in the elevator, "you'll see," and once we entered I saw what she meant. We had watched a couple of Woody Allen movies on TV, and even though my mother couldn't understand what the characters were saying (they spoke way too fast even for me), she was quite taken with the interiors. Elijah's apartment looked exactly like the one in *Hannah and Her Sisters*, with its high ceilings, and large windows, and endless bookshelves, and a grand piano in the middle. Later, after I'd visited a lot of similarly furnished apartments on the Upper West Side, I realized that it was quite typical, but back then I decided that Elijah must be a huge fan of Woody Allen to build a replica of his movie set.

My mother opened the door with her key and yelled to Elijah that she was here with her daughter. He said something back. Then she told me to wait in the living room while she helped

Elijah get dressed. I noticed that my mother moved around the apartment with perfect ease, as if she lived there, moving chairs, fixing pillows, picking up stray items, while in our Brooklyn apartment she tended to keep to her corner, tense like an unwelcome guest. She even offered me tea.

I had imagined a tiny shriveled man, but Elijah was tall and broad-shouldered, made even bigger by his roomy corduroy pants and a cable-knit sweater. He was looming over my mother as if he were shielding her, even though she was the one who supported him as they walked. She led him to a chair that faced the couch where I sat, and sat down on a low pouf so that she was kind of between us. From that position, she kept looking up at him or at him, visibly anxious that we like each other.

Even sitting down, Elijah remained imposing, his knees spread wide, his large hands spilling over the polished armrests' edges. He reminded me of fairy-tale giants if you could imagine those giants unsteady and infirm and smelling of skin creams.

"Did your mother do all those things in your story?" he asked after my mother introduced us.

"Most of it, yes," I said.

"Did she really boil potatoes with the immersion heater?"

"Oh, yes," I said. "And she did write the indignant letter to the factory after it broke down."

"She is one hell of a woman, your mother," Elijah said in his slow slurred way.

My mother laughed and slapped Elijah on the knee. Then she mimicked him: "One . . . hell . . . oooff . . . awo . . . man."

This shocked me. My mother might have been mean, but it wasn't like her to make fun of a disabled person. What shocked me even more was that Elijah seemed to enjoy it. More than that, he mimicked my mother in his turn. Every time my mother mispronounced words (which happened fairly often), he would laugh out loud. My mother didn't seem to mind, which also shocked me, because she was usually very sensitive about her English. Just a few days ago, she had started crying when Len tried to correct her grammar. Both my mother and Elijah laughed at my shocked expression. Then my mother explained it to me. She said that when she first started working with Elijah, he told her that he couldn't stand talking to his friends anymore, because they all listened to him with squeamish pity. My mother didn't know what "squeamish" meant, but after Elijah explained it to her, she said that this was exactly how people reacted when she tried to speak English.

"So we decided to do away with pity," my mother said.

"Your mother and I are both verbal cripples," Elijah added with great satisfaction, "and we accept it."

I stayed with them for an hour or so, and it wasn't until I stood up to leave that Elijah started to talk about my story again.

He found it incredible that the English of my story was so much better than the English that I spoke. I said that this was because I read so much in English but hardly ever got to speak. He nodded and asked if it was okay to send my story to his friends at the *Magazine*.

I asked: "Why?"

"Because it's extraordinary," Elijah said. It took him a lot of effort to get the word "extraordinary" out, but this time my mother didn't laugh or mimic him, but stroked him on the back.

On the way out the doorman asked me if I was okay.

"I'm good," I said. "I'm happy."

He reached for something under his desk and handed me a tissue. It turned out I was crying, but if not for the doorman, I wouldn't have noticed.

When I came home, Len was in the bedroom, crouching in the corner with his back to me. He was trying to assemble a desk from a wide board he had found on the street and several large boxes to serve as legs. The trick was to make the structure sturdy enough so that it wouldn't wobble, and Len had come up with the idea to hammer the board right to the boxes with large nails.

We did have money, not a lot of it, just what my mother and I had gotten when we sold our apartment, but everybody said that we weren't to spend a cent, because we'd need it toward the down payment on our future house. Everybody insisted that we had to buy a house as soon as possible. Len would spend all his weekends building makeshift furniture so we could save money.

I said: "Len!" He turned to look at me. There was a hammer in his right hand, and a large nail in his left. There were beads of sweat on his forehead and a smudge of glue on his cheek. There was something in his eyes that startled me, or rather there was the lack of something in his eyes. The lack of affection? Interest? Care?

I told him that Elijah thought that my story was extraordinary. He was going to send it to the *Magazine*.

"Sounds like a long shot, don't get too excited," he said and went back to work.

That was when I knew that Len didn't love me anymore. I found my discovery upsetting but not devastating, which could mean only one thing: that I didn't love him either.

Back to my love graph. A few weeks before we left Russia, the love was definitely there. A few months after we arrived in the US, it was definitely not. We lost it somewhere between these two points.

I like to think that it didn't survive the transatlantic flight. There is something bitterly poetic about that. The love that crumbled in the altitude. Evaporated under pressure. Suffocated because of the lack of oxygen. Got vacuum-sucked down the plane's human-waste line into a two-hundred-gallon tank.

Human waste sounds about right. Isn't that what love leaving a person really is?

Money.

Some children cannot understand complex mathematical concepts, <u>unless</u> they are explained through oper<u>ations</u> <u>with</u> <u>money</u>.

Then they understand.

TEN

I don't know if it was Elijah's praise, my discovery that Len and I didn't love each other anymore, my growing, almost physical hatred of C++, or my mother's resurgence from her depression that made me veer away from Len's plan for me.

I wasn't really hoping that my story would be accepted by the *Magazine*; I wasn't even sure that Elijah had submitted it yet—he had said he wanted to wait until his friend there came back from a trip abroad. And anyway, I couldn't possibly imagine earning a living as a writer. But I was absolutely sure that I didn't want to be a computer programmer, and it seemed stupid to put so much effort into learning a profession that I hated. There must be something else for me. Something that I could do well. All I needed was more time to figure out what it was. And to buy that time, I needed to find a temporary job, any job at all. The jobs advertised in the *New York Times* turned out to be out of my league, so I went and bought *Our Brooklyn*, a Russian-language weekly that advertised temporary and often illegal jobs in immigrant businesses.

LARA VAPNYAR

Most of them required skills, experience, or some special quality that I didn't have. I had never painted a house, driven a cab,
cooked gefilte fish, baked meat pies, or assassinated people. But
after a while I found one ad that captured my attention: "CIN-
DERELLA SCHOOL. Learn English to find your dream. Fast, af-
fordable, flexible hours." And in smaller letters, "Russian-speaking
English teacher wanted." The ad also asked for a valid English
teacher's diploma, so I took out my diploma, picked up a black
pen, and carefully printed "and English" next to the words certify-
ing that I could teach Russian language and literature. Just a few
days before, Len had said that the only people who could make it
in immigrant businesses were dishonest and unprofessional. According to his theory, I now had a fair chance at success.

The next day, I put the diploma in my purse, took the Q
train down to the Sheepshead Bay stop, and walked up one of
the side streets. Once there, I had to double-check the address,
because the place didn't look like anywhere you'd go to teach or
learn. It was a regular two-story house, painted blue, with a gray
coating of dirt and a white sign in front that said "Alternative
and Holistic Medicine" in big Russian letters, and "Witchery
and Magic" in smaller ones. Inside, I found myself in an airy
waiting room adorned with many posters and framed clippings
from *Our Brooklyn.* The largest poster showed a woman in her
forties with wild blonde hair adorned with arrangements of
leaves and twigs. "Evelina, the authentic witch from the woods
of western Ukraine, will help you with your financial and romantic problems," it said. The other posters were devoted mostly
to the miracles performed by Dr. Solomon, a severe-looking
man with a mane of ginger hair. Dr. Solomon had, he claimed,

the ability to cure obesity, stomach ulcers, spine problems, and all kinds of anxiety. Penises in various stages of decline were depicted in a few of the posters. One of them was represented by a wilting daisy, another by a sad little mouse. I was about to check the address again when a blonde woman at the reception desk squinted at me through her heavy makeup and asked me what I wanted. I showed her the ad. She studied it for a moment, during which I couldn't help but stare at her enormous breasts pushing up from the dark depths of her purple sweater. She gave me a glare and it was the glare that made me recognize her as the woman from the poster, the "authentic witch from the woods of western Ukraine." She pointed at a door to her right. "Solomon will see you there."

This room was small and dimly lit. The wall to my left was painted red, and a huge poster for the Kieślowski movie *Blue* hung in the middle of it. The wall to my right was painted blue and had a poster for Kieślowski's *Red*. I took this for a good sign, because I'd watched each of these movies at least five times. Almost every other object was black (the leather lounge chair, the massive desk by the window, the small file cabinet, the exercise equipment), except for the collection of plastic penises on the desk. These were mostly pink, although one was cream-colored, and two or three were purplish red. I did my best to ignore them.

Ten minutes later, the door opened with a bang, and the man from the posters marched in. He wore a tweed jacket that was a little too long for him. He was stocky but short, an inch or two taller than me, and a lot shorter than Len. He was also bald. The bouncy mane he had in the posters wasn't there.

Dr. Solomon asked if I had brought my diploma. I took it out of my bag. He put on his glasses, glanced at the diploma, then peered at me.

"I see everything that's going on inside you," he said, and I thought that he meant the lie I had printed on my diploma.

"Okay, tell me," he continued in English with the thick, tense accent of someone who was trying too hard to hide it. "Have you seen *Red* and *Blue*?"

"Yes, I've seen them," I said.

"Who is more beautiful, Juliette Binoche or Irène Jacob?"

I turned my head to the right, then to the left.

"Juliette Binoche," I said.

"Why?"

"Because Irène Jacob is pure soul. Pure soul cannot be beautiful."

He took his glasses off and stared at the posters.

"You know what?" he said, switching into Russian again. "That is an absolutely brilliant answer—a professor from an Elite University wouldn't have answered better."

I wanted to appear skeptical. I tried to master a look of ironic detachment, but instead I felt a smile of pure delight spread over my face.

He then told me that the system of payment was more than fair. I would get 50 percent of what my students paid, so the more lessons I gave, the more I would earn. And I could start as early as the next day, at nine.

Len didn't like it when I called him at work, and I usually didn't. But that day I couldn't wait. I couldn't even wait until I got home. I fished a sticky quarter out of the pocket of my jeans and dialed his number from a pay phone. "Do you have a minute?"

I asked. He said that he didn't. "It'll only take a second," I said. "Okay, I got a job, and I'll tell you all about it when you come home. Bye." But as I was about to hang up, I said, "It's a very good job. Really. Bye." We hung up. I started to walk toward the subway, but a minute later I returned and fished another quarter out of my pocket. This time I dialed Elijah's number. "Good afternoon," my mother said.

"Mom, it's me!" I said. "I got a job!"

My mother actually screamed.

On my first day, I had a group of four women between the ages of thirty and sixty. They said that they liked the idea of flexible hours, because they worked as live-in nannies for other Russian families, and couldn't attend classes with a strictly set schedule. None of them had come to the US to stay. Most were immigrants in a precarious legal situation, with husbands and children waiting for them back home. They had come to the US to earn money for their struggling families. They needed English so that they could defect from their Russian employers to American families, who allegedly paid more and lacked the guts to abuse their nannies. We spent the first lesson studying basic introduction skills, and their stories all sounded more or less the same. "My name is Marina. I'm from Moscow. I'm forty-seven years old. I have a husband and two sons. My youngest son won the interschool model-building contest. I used to work as an engineer. I sleep on a mattress on the floor of the baby's room. I have high blood pressure. I'm going crazy with the baby's screaming all night long. The little shit gets his rest during the day, but I have to cook and clean the house."

These women paid eight dollars each, so I ended up making sixteen dollars that day. Len earned $140 per day, but the disparity didn't discourage me. I was sure that I would find a way to get more students.

As I was leaving, I heard a muffled conversation coming from Dr. Solomon's office. "Your penis becomes big and hard . . . and stays that way," he was saying. "You're strong. You're powerful. Nothing frightens you. Nothing intimidates you. Big and hard. Big and hard." I stood and listened, hardly breathing, until Evelina spoke to me.

"Here is your money," she said. I saw that she noticed that I fell under the spell of the penis mantra and despised me for that.

I spent the next couple of days preparing a special course for the nannies. We studied the names of body parts, children's toys, cooking utensils, cleaning products, and, most importantly, ways to ask for a raise. At the end of each lesson, we watched a scene from a movie. I brought in a large box of videos and asked the nannies to choose. They picked *Working Girl* and *Pretty Woman*. This was their favorite part of the lesson. I asked them to listen to the dialogue and try to repeat the lines, and sometimes they even improvised. Where the Pretty Woman said simply, "You work on commission, right?" Marina said, "You bitches work on commission, right?"

Thanks to word of mouth, by the end of the month, I had four groups of nannies and eight students who came for private lessons. On Mondays, my first class started at eight thirty, and Len and I left for work at the same time. We ate our cereal leaning against the kitchen counter, dressed in a hurry, and ran to the Q stop together. Len took the steps down to the platform for the uptown train, and I crossed the street to get to my downtown Q. Often, if the trains didn't come right away, we'd wave to each other from opposite platforms. It felt great to be going to work at last, just like Len, just like everybody else.

Gradually, I was getting to know the inner workings of our office. Evelina was the first to arrive, and the last to leave. She usually sat behind the reception desk, but sometimes she would retreat to a special room to see her clients. She had a long dark room, decorated with a human skeleton, black candles, a crystal ball, and a large Orthodox icon. I knew this because she would sometimes invite me there to have lunch with her. We would eat our sandwiches right at her "magical" round table and gossip about people in the office. Or rather she told me stuff and I listened, because I didn't have anything to share.

Most of Evelina's clients were women with love misfortunes. Some asked her to find them a man; others asked for help keeping the one they'd already found. One woman asked for help getting back the husband who had beaten her unconscious and run off. The men who came to see Evelina looked down on her female clients. They were serious and pragmatic, and couldn't care less about the problems of the heart; they paid Evelina to take care of their businesses. They'd ask her to come and bless their new office space, or to put an evil eye on the competition, or to get rid of the evil eye that somebody else (or possibly Evelina herself) had put on them.

The men who came to see Solomon were different. They were shy and compliant, and seemed plagued by either guilt or shame. They all complained about spine problems when they called. "Spine problems. Right!" Evelina would say after she'd hung up the phone.

Some of these men followed me with their eyes when I passed them on the way to class. Their stares were full of timid longing mixed with resignation. I imagined that they saw me as some-body young, vibrant, and light, an elusive object of desire, and it made me feel vibrant and light and elusive.

Solomon looked at me too, in a different way though. When I came to the office for my afternoon classes, I often found him smoking on the porch, leaning over the railing, his jacket clinging listlessly to his back. Sometimes he would look up at me, and the desire I saw in his eyes was certain and urgent and anything but timid. This frightened and excited me at the same time.

"There is this witch," I'd tell my mother and Len. "She works with Orthodox icons and black candles. Uses both God and the devil!" I talked about the nannies, and their vile employers, and how much they loved my lessons, and how their eyes filled with tears when they watched *Pretty Woman*. My mother asked me for more details, and I'd talk and talk and inevitably end up talking about Solomon, Solomon's office, and Solomon's movie post-ers, and Solomon's plastic penises, and Solomon's patients. I no-ticed that Len was getting tense. I was aware of his disapproving smirks, but I couldn't stop talking.

"This Solomon," Len said once. "He doesn't have a medical license, does he? He's kind of a crook, isn't he?"

"He helps people," I snapped. "What do you do all day?"

I didn't understand Solomon's work, though I had certainly heard of alternative medicine before. Making fun of the holistic medicine ads in *Our Brooklyn* was one of the few remaining plea-sures that united me with Len. There were three full pages of such ads. If only half of the healers were for real, the air over Brooklyn would have been crackling from the concentration of psychic en-ergy. But Solomon—I believed that he was for real.

I asked Evelina if Solomon had been a doctor in Russia. "No, no," she said. "He used to be a journalist. When they first came here, he tried to apply for jobs at all the big magazines, but they all laughed at him." Evelina knew this from Solomon's wife, who sometimes came to the office after work and lingered in the waiting room. She was a tall woman with rough skin and large bloodshot eyes. She never answered when I said hello to her. Evelina told me that she was a managing director at Morgan Stanley, and that Solomon was fully dependent on her. She'd even bail him out here at the office when he couldn't make rent. Apparently, the business wasn't doing very well.

Two weeks later Marina from my class found a job with an American family. She came to thank me with a small bouquet of carnations. My lessons had given her enough vocabulary to pretend she knew English. "They are giving me my own room," Marina told the other nannies, "and guess what else? My own bathroom. I've never had my own private bathroom in my life!" The nannies laughed and chatted, and soon became so loud that Solomon looked in to ask what the commotion was. "This is a great success, girls," he said. "A real victory. We have to run an article in *Our Brooklyn*." He brought a Polaroid from his office and asked Marina and me to pose next to a VCR stand. "Katya, step forward and raise your flowers to your chest . . . a little higher," he said. "Marina, you're a big girl, stoop a little. Yeah, like that. Perfect!" He took the photo out and squinted at it, as if willing the image to develop sooner. "You look lovely, Katya," he said. I blushed.

When the article came out, in the fresh Sunday issue of *Our Brooklyn*, I was beside myself with excitement. The author praised my teaching methods, and after reading the piece, I couldn't help but admire them too. He described how I'd come up with the idea of showing videos at my very first lesson and how I'd managed to develop this into a gracefully coherent system. He ended the piece by stressing how incredible this was: that at only twenty-two I had accomplished something that had escaped all other language teachers; I had created a method that made learning effortless and fun. And I had done all that as a recent immigrant myself. For me, that article was an even bigger victory than my publication in the *Reading World*. This was a great, great success and definitely the first of many even greater achievements. I finally had something to write to Sasha and Yulia. I made a Xerox of the article for them, and wrote how I planned to expand my method to teach immigrants from other countries too. I didn't want to limit it to teaching Russians; I would have students from all over the US. I would publish a book, or perhaps even a series of books, based on my method. I would create educational videos. I would be making more money than Len.

Sasha didn't reply at all. And Yulia wrote to me something later to say that she and Sasha weren't together anymore, and that if I knew what kind of a person he was I would never speak to him again. I tried to call her, but she wouldn't pick up.

My mother bought the issue of *Our Brooklyn* to show the article to Elijah. I asked if she wanted me to translate it into English, but she said that she could manage herself. She waited until Len left—to shop for cheap electronics for his parents—then spread the copy of *Our Brooklyn* over our kitchen table, pulled a few sheets of paper from the printer, took out the Russian-English dictionary, and set to work. When Len came back, loaded with

Crazy Eddie bags, she had successfully made it through the first three paragraphs and was attacking the fourth. She looked like she did when she was working on her textbooks, her back very straight, her dark eyebrows furrowed. The sight of her working so hard on my article made Len groan.

"This is a paid advertisement, Nina," Len said. "Paid advertisement! In *Our Brooklyn!*"

I screamed that I hated him, but my mother didn't raise her eyes; she continued to work with her usual diligence. She wanted to show it to Elijah first thing on Monday.

What none of us knew at that time was that she would never see Elijah again. He had died on Saturday night a few hours after my mother left, but she didn't get the call until Monday morning, minutes before she was supposed to leave for work. The supervisor called to say that my mother's appointment was canceled, because the client was deceased. She wouldn't provide any details. My mother wasn't a relative after all. She had to call everybody she knew at the agency, call after frantic call, until she was able to reconstruct what had happened from bits and pieces of information. Elijah had a stroke on Saturday night. His night nurse called 911. By the time he made it to the hospital, he had gone into cardiac arrest, and since he had strict DNR orders, they let him die. Elijah's niece was flying in from Chicago to claim the body.

I asked my mother if I should cancel my morning class and stay home with her. She said no. She refused to call Uncle Grisha either. She sat down at the kitchen table and remained sitting there. She couldn't stop talking about the DNR papers. She and Elijah had discussed it. This was exactly how he had wanted to die, when the time came. "When the time came," my mother kept saying again and again. "Do you know what that means?" she asked at some point. "It means never! He wasn't ready. I know that he wasn't!"

I was afraid that my mother would take to her bed, the way it happened after my father died, but instead she became restless. There was no work for her for a while, but she would leave every morning and spend her day walking around the streets, walking and walking and walking, sitting on park benches to take a break, going inside stores to warm herself, but other than that just walking.

One day, when I came home from work, I found her lying on the couch with a pack of frozen spinach on her face. The right side of her face was bruised and swollen and there was a small gash over her right cheekbone partly covered by a Band-Aid. I asked if she had fallen, but she chuckled and said: "No, I got into a fight. I was trying to find the Times Square and I asked this woman for directions and she wouldn't answer me."

"Why wouldn't she?" I asked.

"She kept saying, 'What?' and 'What?' and 'Excuse me, I can't understand you.' So I just came up very close to her and said: 'You're such a stupid fucking American!' and I laughed in her face."

Now it was my turn to ask: "What???"

"Yes, that's what I said."

"And then what?"

"She punched me in the face."

I had to sit down, but my mother started to laugh.

"I think I needed that," she said. "Don't worry, it won't happen again and anyway, they found me another client, so I'm resuming work tomorrow."

My mother was fired from the new job within two weeks, because she talked back to a client. She was fired from her next job as well, because she talked back again. But since most of the agency's elderly clients were racist at least to a degree, and white home attendants were in such short supply, my mother kept getting assignments, until the final incident.

Apparently, an elderly client said that she couldn't stand blacks and Jews equally, but at least she wasn't scared of the Jews. My mother growled at her. She said that she wanted to show her that Jews could be scary too.

Only then did my mother get fired for good.

But sometimes too
much talk about
money can distract
children from
abstract mathematical
concepts.

ELEVEN

My work meanwhile was going well. Following the article in *Our Brooklyn*, the number of my students tripled. The nannies now crowded in the waiting room vying for seats with Solomon's and Evelina's patients. Solomon's patients were the most timid of the lot, so they would end up giving up their seats and standing by the wall.

"Katya?" one of them said, when I walked into the office one morning. He was leaning against the window, so that his right shoulder touched the wilted-daisy poster. A thin man with longish hair and sad downturned eyes, he looked vaguely familiar, especially when he smiled, but I couldn't place him.

"It is you, isn't it?" he asked.

I peered closer and gasped.

"Boris Markovich?" I said.

B. nodded. He said that he had noticed me a few days ago, but wasn't sure it was me.

He looked different, very different from what I remembered. The beard. He had shaved his beard. His face without a beard appeared to be both puffy and exposed.

I asked what he was doing here. He looked away and mumbled something about problems with his back.

I had to rush, because my class was about to start, but I kept thinking about B. while pretending to listen to my students. Back problems! I thought. I imagined B. lying in Solomon's chair, with Solomon looming over him, moving his large hands over his body, chanting: "Your penis becomes big and hard and stays that way. Stays that way. Stays that way . . ."

When my class ended, B. was waiting for me in the waiting room. He offered to walk me to the subway and I agreed. He said that he had read my story in the *Reading World*. Sasha had sent him a copy. He'd thought it was quite moving. He'd felt strangely proud, even if he knew that he didn't have anything to do with it. His praise annoyed rather than flattered me. Then B. asked if I liked teaching. I said that I loved it. Solomon was amazing. He let me develop my own teaching method and it was working wonders. Then I told him that I had been married for two years. Len was amazing. I stumbled, because I realized that I'd just said this about Solomon, but B. didn't seem to notice.

He said that he worked as a temp in a Russian law firm. They paid next to nothing, but he didn't need much anyway. He lived alone. His wife had gone back to Russia and taken their son, Mark, with her.

"What about Max?" I asked.

He seemed surprised and touched that I remembered the name of his dog.

"Max died," he said.

B. walked me all the way to the subway entrance and headed back. I climbed the stairs leading to the elevated platform and looked down onto the street to try to spot B. in the crowd. There he was making his way through the Brighton Beach crowd, slouchy, hands in his pockets, as if he were trying to take up as little space as possible. It was hard to believe that I had been crazy in love with this man a mere five years ago.

He would be in the waiting room every Tuesday and Thursday night, staring at me with such intense longing that even Solomon noticed it. "He's my former teacher," I told him.

"Don't you toy with him," Solomon said. "The poor schmuck doesn't need another disappointment." I caught jealous notes in his voice, which made me very happy.

One night, as I was getting ready to leave after class, Solomon walked into my room. He pulled up a chair next to mine, sat down, and pressed the play button on the VCR. We watched the ending of *Pretty Woman* in silence. Evelina, my students, and all the patients had already left, and it was strangely quiet in the office, and strangely cold. I tried to keep myself from shivering as I listened to Solomon's tense breathing over the soundtrack of the movie. When the credits started to roll, Solomon asked if I liked the movie. I said that I liked it very much, only I couldn't understand one thing.

"What thing?" he asked.

"The fact that the guy *has* to be so rich. Isn't it good enough for them to find love? Why does the guy need to be a millionaire?"

"A billionaire. The guy's a billionaire."

Solomon turned the VCR off and took my hands in his. His hands were cold, like mine. He asked me when I had come to the US. I said, "A few months ago." He asked me if I liked it here. I told him how much I'd loved it at first. I told him about our trips to Manhattan when we first arrived. He smiled and squeezed my fingers. My hands were slowly getting warmer. I told him why I had stopped going to Manhattan, how I had feared that people on the streets would laugh at me. Then I felt a lump in my throat and stopped talking.

"Uh-huh," he said, "so you feel that Manhattan is closed to you?" I nodded.

"You're right," he said. "It is closed. But you know what would open it?"

The expression on his face hardened and I worried that our brittle new intimacy was already gone. I waited for him to start spinning optimistic lies about how confidence and pride could open the world for you. But he reached into his pocket instead, and pulled out a wad of twenty-dollar bills.

"This," he said. "This is what would open it." He shuffled the bills in his hand and put them back in his pocket.

He rose from his chair. I got up too. He walked up to me, put his arms around me. His lips brushed against my hair. He inhaled and moaned, "You smell like pickled apples."

Then he pulled me closer. We stood like this for a very long time, until I felt as if each millimeter of my body were being enveloped by his. I could feel the exact shape and size of his cock pressing hard into my stomach. This frightened me and I freed myself and moved away.

Solomon sighed. "You're right, Katya. You're a good girl. Now go. Go home."

I picked up my bag and moved unsteadily toward the door.

Outside, my legs were weak. I lowered myself onto the stone steps of the porch and sat there, hugging my knees. I was shaken, scared, grateful, disappointed, relieved, but mostly happy, insanely happy. The whole way back on the subway, I was chuckling and muttering random silly lines from *Pretty Woman*: "You people work on commission, right? Big mistake. Big. Huge. I have to go shopping now."

That night I burrowed under the blanket and made myself come, ignoring the lack of air and obnoxious *Tetris* beeps.

I still saw B. in the office every Tuesday and Thursday, but I didn't pay him any attention—not on purpose, no, but because my attention was sucked up by Solomon. We hadn't spoken since the night we'd watched *Pretty Woman* together, and I wondered if he thought about it as much as I did, and if he made himself come thinking about me.

"Tonight is my last session," B. told me one Tuesday.

"That's good, isn't it?" I said.

"Yes," he said. "Anyway, I found a job in Boston, so I'll be moving there."

Then he asked if I was in a rush to go home. It was already past eight, but Len didn't care when I came home. I could always say that I had an extra class.

"Let's go to the beach," B. said. We crossed Brighton Beach Avenue and headed toward the boardwalk.

It was an especially windy night. The gusts of wind kept pummeling us without mercy, pushing us to walk faster, messing our hair and clothes, smacking us across the face, so we had to keep our heads down and couldn't look at the ocean. It was dark anyway; the most we could see was the wave breaks in the feeble moonlight. The sound was spectacular though. All that whooshing and crashing, and the resigned grumble of the retreating surf.

All of a sudden B. stopped, took my hands in his, and started to recite a poem. I had to turn to B. and look right into his face, right into his mouth, and still all I could hear were separate words and disjointed lines.

My dear . . .

Tonight . . .

A breath of fresh air . . .

The ocean . . .

A lifetime ago . . .

The distance . . . the distances . . .

Between you and me . . .

I'm smoking in the dark . . .

Breathing in the rot of the ocean.

I didn't know that poem, but I grasped the general meaning. Love. Past love. Lost love. B. was reciting a poem about love to me.

"Brodsky," B. said when he finished.

I was excited, but also scared, confused, and a little embarrassed, even though I hardly understood what the source of that embarrassment was. I wouldn't be able to put it into words until fourteen years later, when B. and I were discussing love poetry. I said that I found it unsavory when a man used somebody else's love poetry in order to win over a woman, either to stir her heart or to get her into bed. In my view, it cheapened poetry. B. said that I was terribly terribly wrong. He said that the purpose of love poetry wasn't to make people fall in love, but to make them recognize the feelings they already had.

But back then, on Brighton Beach boardwalk, I felt overwhelmed. I didn't know what to say to B., except that it was getting late and they were waiting for me at home.

They weren't waiting. My mother was asleep. And Len was lying in bed with a fresh issue of the *Economist* that he could take from his office for free. "Late class?" he asked, and I nodded and went to brush my teeth. I couldn't fall asleep for a long time. I lay next to the snoring Len (he snored so very lightly that I found it touching), thinking about Len, and Solomon and B., and life in general. I came up with what seemed like a brilliant idea for a story. I got up and typed the first sentence. "Two men are in love with me, one with a broken dick, another with a broken soul." Nothing else came to mind and I abandoned the story and went back to bed. I was dying to tell everything to my mother, but I had to wait until morning.

"Do you think Elijah had a chance to send my story to the *Magazine*?" I asked her the next morning.

She said that she wasn't sure, but she hoped that he did. Then I said something else, surprising myself with the sudden clarity.

"I don't want to be married to Len anymore."

My mother looked at me in shock. This was not the reaction I expected. I thought she'd understand right away. But apparently

I had to spell it out. Len and I had nothing in common. Len and I didn't love each other anymore. I was only twenty-two. I didn't see the point of us staying together.

My mother started to scream. I was an idiot, she said. I was a child. I saw the world as a child. I acted like a child. I had a child's fantasies. It was her fault. She didn't know what she had done wrong, but she saw clearly that she had failed to raise a fully functional adult. I was stuck in my childhood. I didn't understand how life worked. I was too naive. Everybody told her that. Bella told her that. Even Uncle Grisha told her that, Uncle Grisha who was hardly better than a child himself. She couldn't help me anymore, and I wouldn't survive on my own. Definitely not here, not in the US. And Len, Len was the real deal. He wasn't very exciting, but he was devoted to me, to our marriage. I could always count on him. I had to hold on to him and hold on hard.

"But what about love?" I asked.

The great love that she and my father had. Wasn't it unfair that I would be denied that?

"Love!" she screamed. "You don't know what it means."

Love was awful! Love was like cancer! The affection that grew too large, its cells multiplying with amazing speed, forming growths that kept getting larger and larger, taking up the space reserved for the good working organs, pressing on them, squeezing them out, not letting them work. And the pain! I couldn't possibly imagine the pain! The last thing I should want was love.

I ran out of the apartment shaking. I didn't expect this at all. I didn't know what upset me more, my mother's view of love or the way she saw me, as a spoiled, obnoxious child. My mother couldn't have meant what she said, could she? Of course she couldn't. She was so proud of my success. I must have upset her by mentioning Elijah. I shouldn't have asked about him.

I managed to calm myself by the time I got to the office, but one look at my framed article on the waiting room wall filled me with disgust.

Len was right. It was a paid advertisement. A paid advertisement hanging on the wall between a photograph of the authentic witch from the woods of western Ukraine and a flyer for the miraculous new tea that Solomon had recently started selling.

The company distributing the tea sent us a new batch of posters and Solomon spent the better part of one morning hanging them up. Eventually, he decided that two would go on the left and right walls of the waiting room—one above Evelina's desk, and the rest on one wall of each of the rooms. He summoned me to help. I was holding a poster up, my palms against its shiny surface, while Solomon happily pushed cheap brittle tacks in. The tea business was going well, and I noticed that lately Solomon didn't look as glum as he used to. "One thing the cardboard walls are good for is sticking tacks into them," he said and winked at me from under the curling-down edge of the poster. We stood side by side, so close to each other that the folds of his jacket brushed against my hip. I marveled how little his proximity excited me. When I thought back to our movie night now, it was the image of his money that appeared in my mind. Everything else—the pressure of his hands on my back, the feel of his lips brushing against my hair—faded away, while that wad of crumpled, frayed, sweaty bills stayed clear in my mind.

"It's a beauty," Solomon said, stepping away from the poster. "I'll use it for a two-page ad in *Our Brooklyn* next week."

The new poster showed a steaming teacup with the word "cancer" dissolving in the bluish-white plume of vapor.

"Cancer?" Evelina asked after she peeked into her room.

"You don't understand, Evelina," Solomon said. "We're selling hope, not the cure. Hope is priceless."

"If it's priceless, why do we charge for it?" she asked.

The poster claimed that the tea cleansed the body of every harmful chemical substance it had ingested and promised relief within days. Boxes of the tea lay everywhere in the office, in Solomon's room, on Evelina's counter, on Evelina's desk next to her crystal ball, on the chairs in the waiting room, on the windowsills, and on the VCR stand in my room. The office worked as a team. Solomon always asked his patients if they wanted to learn better English, Evelina the witch always directed her ailing clients to Solomon, I was expected to praise Evelina, and everybody was expected to sell the tea. I didn't push the tea, but I didn't try to dissuade my students from buying it either. I didn't say anything even after I heard that more and more patients were complaining that the tea had brought them nothing but diarrhea. "How else did you expect to be cleansed?" Evelina retorted.

I wasn't making as much money as I'd expected either.

The advertisement in *Our Brooklyn* had managed to attract a few new people, but with several of my old students leaving, the total soon dwindled to even fewer than I'd had before. A couple of students left because they didn't like my thick Russian accent. Others left because they weren't satisfied with my knowledge of English grammar. Two women complained that I charged too much. Every time Evelina counted the profits from my classes, she let out a very audible sigh.

On Monday mornings, Len and I still walked to the train together, and Len still waved to me from the opposite platform, but I could barely make myself wave back. I noticed something that I hadn't noticed before. In the morning hours, there were one or two people waiting on my side of the platform. Almost all of the commuters stood on the other side with Len. They were going into the city, to work real jobs. I was going even farther away, to sell the Cinderella dream and a laxative hyped as a magic potion. More than once, I saw something like pity in Len's expression. I think it was his pity that I truly couldn't stand. But also his kindness. And especially the genuine joy in his eyes when he ran upstairs with an envelope from the *Magazine*.

"Look, they did write to you after all!"

I had thought that I wasn't really hoping that my story would be published in the *Magazine*, but once I saw that envelope, my heart started to thump like crazy and I couldn't deceive myself any longer. I had to admit to myself that I had been desperately hoping for acceptance. What was more—I had been completely unprepared for rejection.

"It's not that big a deal," Len said to me as I lay on the bed sobbing. But he did try to console me anyway. "They seemed to like the story, didn't they? See here? The woman says she was very impressed. And at the end, she asks you to send them other stories."

"You don't understand!" I mumbled through the mucus and snot. "They're just being polite! Probably because Elijah asked them to."

"Yes, Elijah did come through on this," my mother said. She took the letter from me and hid it among her things as a sort of memento.

Strangely enough, the rejection didn't diminish my resolve to leave Len; it was only getting stronger day after day after day. I kept thinking of my half of the money my mother and I had made by selling the Moscow apartment as "my freedom money." I could leave Len and sustain myself with that money, until I found a better job. All I needed was a push.

I was itching to do something bad, something vile that would be sure to destroy my marriage.

One night I stayed behind, after my evening class. I waited for the last of Solomon's patients to leave; then I went and knocked on his door.

"Katya, is that you?" he asked.

I walked into Solomon's semidark red-and-blue office. He was sitting at his desk, looming over rows of plastic penises.

"What?" Solomon asked.

The telephone rang in the waiting room, but neither of us looked in its direction.

"How does your method work?" I finally asked.

Solomon looked up at me with a quizzical expression, as if he couldn't believe that I'd ask something silly like that, when we both knew perfectly well why I was here in his office. He threw a quick glance at his mobile phone—a bulky Nokia with chunky white buttons—and asked me if I wanted cognac. I shook my head. He poured himself cognac in a paper cup and told me to sit down.

There was nowhere to sit, except for the narrow lounge chair. I sat down and leaned back, letting my hair fall over the edge of the chair. The enormous Irène Jacob was staring at me from the right, her mouth half-open, the word "Masterpiece!" hovering over her head like a halo. Juliette Binoche, on the left, looked away from me, branded by the words "sexy . . . mysterious" on her forehead.

The telephone rang again. Then again. "Somebody is having a dick emergency!" I quipped.

"Shh!" Solomon said. He finished his cognac and rose from his chair, pushing it away so hard that it knocked against the wall. I felt my entire body turn into this liquid dripping mess, which had never happened to me before. He came up close, swung his leg over me, and pushed his hands against the back of the chair. He was straddling me but standing up. His crotch was right in my face, the entire thing, living and breathing and straining the thin material of his scrubs held together by a worn-out white string.

"I've wanted this for such a long time," he said. His voice was so hoarse that he almost croaked out the last word.

I'd wanted this too. I'd wanted this ever since I sat down in this chair for the first time, a few months ago. In fact, I'd wanted this a mere few minutes ago.

All I needed to do was to pull on that white string, but I couldn't bring myself to do it. My mouth went dry and I was suddenly paralyzed with an awful premonition.

I have to do it, I was willing myself. I have to!

The phone rang again. This time the sound was sharper, louder, closer. It was Solomon's Nokia that kept jerking with each ring, knocking against the glass surface of the desk.

"Shit, it's my wife," Solomon said and rushed to answer. "Yes, I'm working," he said.

I sat up, marveling at how quickly Solomon went limp.

"No, Katya's not here. She left. Yes, I'm sure that she left. Wait! What do you mean? Who called you? Who is Len? Wait! What? Oh, shit! Wait! Maybe I can still catch her outside."

He hung up and looked at me. I could tell that something horrible did happen, even though I didn't pull on that string.

"Your mother is in the ER," he said. "New York-Presbyterian on Avenue U."

We ran toward Brighton Beach Avenue, where Solomon hailed me a cab. It didn't occur to me to ask if Solomon knew what was wrong with her, until the cab arrived and I climbed in. "Heart attack, they think, she collapsed on the street," Solomon said and shut the door for me.

For the ensuing forty minutes or so I was absolutely sure that my mother would die. I was especially sure of it as I was running around in the blinding light of the New York-Presbyterian halls, having followed directions to the wrong wing, then to the wrong floor, opening one wrong door after another, peeking behind wrong partitions and catching glimpses of people strapped to cots, bound in gauze, entangled in tubes, some moaning, some drooling, some unconscious, some of them probably dying right at that moment, right as I was looking at them.

When I finally found my mother, she had dozed off. She was half sitting in bed, her head hanging to the right. Her eyes were closed, but she looked alive, more alive than other patients I'd seen. Len was sitting in the small armchair by her side. He was leafing through a magazine in his lap, and holding my mother's hand in his free hand. He looked at me, and for the first time in a long long time I saw the old Len in him, exposed, tender, trying so hard to be brave.

"No heart attack!" he whispered. "Her blood pressure is very high though, so they wanted to keep her for a little while longer."

I rushed to him, kneeled by his chair, buried my face in his lap, and started to sob.

I quit my job the very next day, and a few weeks after that enrolled in a technical translation class so I could have a grown-up profession. A few months later, I got pregnant and we started looking for a house in the suburbs. We found the perfect house on Staten Island. A narrow three-story semidetached, it stood in a tight community of identical narrow houses, like a worn hardcover in a crowded bookcase. The design was called a mother/daughter house, because it had a tiny separate apartment off the side of the house for a hypothetical mother, or a real one as in our case.

I used my freedom money as a down payment.

Use Escher's drawings to explain the concepts of topology, special paradoxes and impossible combinations

TWELVE

How do you sustain x days of a loveless marriage?

That's easy—you compartmentalize.

When I was six, my mother introduced spatial paradoxes to me. She used the drawings of Maurits Cornelis Escher. We had a stack of Escher's prints tucked behind the glass doors of our bookcase. One of the prints was called *Relativity* and showed a house that looked neat and solid at first glance but attacked you with its craziness if you held your gaze.

"I hate it!" I said. "It's scary!"

"Show me what makes it scary," my mother said.

I pointed to a man casually walking on the underside of a staircase, perpendicular to the rest of the house.

"Okay," my mother said, "now rotate the drawing all the way to the right."

I did.

Now that particular man was doing okay, but the previously normal parts of the house suddenly turned crazy. I said that I especially hated the upside-down dinner table on the bottom.

I kept turning and turning the print, watching how craziness migrated from one spot to another.

"Do you see what's going on here?" my mother asked. "Each part of the drawing is working perfectly well, they just don't work as a whole."

Our house on Staten Island was an Escher house. This type of architecture turned out to be essential to sustaining my marriage for so many years. The secret was that I could conduct the different parts of my life in the different parts of the house and ignore the fact that they didn't work as a whole.

The ground floor was divided into two parts, my mother's apartment and the heated garage.

My mother's apartment was a tiny studio with its tiny alcove of a bedroom and its own kitchen that also served as my mother's living room, her study, and even a makeshift math school for local kids.

The garage served as Len's home office, where Len did work for his own software company, SoftUniverrse. (The extra *r* was a necessity caused by the fact that there was another company called SoftUniverse. I liked to roll the extra *r* the Spanish way, as in the word *perro*.) Len would come home from work, have his dinner, and disappear into the garage, making it to the bedroom long after I was asleep. On weekends he would go to the garage right after breakfast and stay there for most of the day. This schedule was extremely helpful for reducing our opportunities to fight with each other. There was one problem though. The garage didn't have a door connecting it to the rest of the house, so every time Len needed to use the bathroom he would have to exit through the aluminum garage door and enter the house through the front door, which he often found locked. Since it was impossible to make our doorbell work, Len would have to knock, then bang, then kick the door, yelling and frightening the neighbors. "Sorry! I must have forgotten that you were home, Len," my mother would explain. My mother and Len had had a single affectionate moment at the hospital, but since we'd left Brooklyn, their relationship had been slowly progressing to a steady cold war.

The second floor had the large living/play room that was crowded with not-yet-discarded toys and also housed a TV set and shelves with our "good" books (meaning books we had brought from Moscow). I kept all our books in English in the upstairs bedroom under and around my bed, where I did most of the reading. There was also a kitchen, spacious and bright, designed for lengthy family dinners, which we had only once or twice. Actually, the largest gathering of people our kitchen would see was my mother's funeral, when I threw one of our heavy chairs at B. and made an ugly dent in the wall. The best feature of our house was that the kitchen's narrow glass door opened onto the patio. The patio overlooked the small park between the rows of houses, where the kids, even when they were really young, could play unsupervised. If I woke up very early, I liked to drink my coffee on the patio, alone, in blissful silence. I wouldn't go near it at other times, because it was only inches away from the patios of our neighbors. The neighbors on the right were relentless barbecuers; they would grill their food all day, every day—they even grilled bananas for breakfast. The neighbors on the left had a mean dog who wouldn't stop barking. Ever. The dog is significant, because it caused one of the biggest fights I would ever have with Len. My mother and I were wondering if the dog was male or female. Len said: "She's vicious and cowardly; of course it's a female!"

The second floor also served for housing extra people. When Len's parents came to visit, they would sleep on the couch and take up the entire kitchen to chop vegetables for a never-ending succession of salads and soups. I would hide out in the bedroom, which was what Len did when Sasha came to visit. Len and Sasha couldn't stand each other, because each of them believed that the other was a pretentious fool. Yulia seemed to be avoiding me, but Sasha and I had reconnected two years after we had left Brooklyn. He lived in Germany now and made his living as a documentary filmmaker. He would visit New York about once a year, alone or with one of his boyfriends.

Note to an astute reader. If Sasha ever was in love with me, it was probably because I wore boys' clothes and looked like a boy. I blame my Soviet upbringing for the fact that I didn't pick up on this sooner.

Len wasn't very fond of my new friend Anya either. She was a nurse who worked at a cancer center in New Jersey but lived a few minutes away from me on Staten Island. We met through our daughters, who attended preschool together. Anya had established a routine of "no bra" visits. That meant that if one of us felt really shitty, she could throw a winter coat over her pajamas, pull snow boots over bare feet, and drive straight to the other's house, where she could sob in peace, unconcerned about uncombed hair

or bobbing breasts. This became essential to me during the unhappy phase of my affair with B.

Anya was also the only person with whom I could talk about
sex. I remember discussing "whether size matters" on my patio.

Anya said that for her it was more about sensual intelligence.
But I advocated for size. "See," I said, "it has to be able to reach
all my secret nooks."

And Anya slapped me on the back and said that I was a real
poet.

Still, the most important parts of my life were conducted on
the third floor of my Escher house. There were three bedrooms,
the small one for Len and me, the smaller one for Dan, and the
smallest one for Nathalie.

Most of the space in our small bedroom was taken up by our
queen-size bed, and that was where I worked. Len managed to
fit a tiny desk between the bed and the window overlooking the
neighbors' barbecue, but it was hard to fit a chair between the
desk and the bed, and even harder to fit my body between the
chair and the desk. I preferred to write on top of the bed. Cross-
legged, barefoot, the laptop where it was supposed to be by definition—in my lap. "Always keep your laptop on a hard surface,"
Len would tell me again and again. And I would nod, but secretly
think: "Why is it called a laptop, then?" I loved it in my lap. A
warm being. With all those complicated sounds, whirring, beeps,
buzzing. Like something alive. Like an extension of my body. A
necessary organ that was keeping me alive. I bought our quilted
bedspread from a garage sale (most of our household items came
from there as well). It was old, with threads come undone here
and there. Sometimes my bare toes would get caught in the loops

of loose threads, which resulted in cuts. Exquisitely thin cuts as if drawn on my skin by the finest of pencils. The density of the cuts depended on my concentration. The more challenging the story, the deeper the cuts. My workspace was hardly adequate, but it would have never occurred to me to complain, because my writing career was such a miracle that I half expected it to be taken away at any moment.

About three years after we moved to Staten Island, I got a letter from the editor at the *Magazine*, the same editor who had rejected me years ago. She had addressed it to my old Brooklyn address, and it had taken more than several months for the post office to forward it to Staten Island. The editor wrote that she had been promoted to a more senior position and had more freedom to publish less established authors. She said that my story had made quite an impression on her and she was eager to see more of my work. She included her phone number and email address. I read the letter on our patio and when I finished I started to scream so loudly that the neighbor's dog stopped barking for the first time in her life and retreated to the far corner. Then I ran downstairs to tell my mother. Or rather I waddled downstairs, because I was eight months pregnant. Downstairs, my mother and three-year-old Dan were doing math together, counting candy like I did at his age. When I told my mother about the letter, she started jumping up and down. Dan climbed off his chair, scattering candy all over the floor, and started to jump up and down too. I couldn't help but join in, which in my condition meant gentle squats rather than jumps. Len was the only skeptical one. He said: "Don't count your chickens before they hatch!" He had recently bought a book of American idioms (Barnes & Noble 50 percent off sale), and was using them all the time. "Do you even have anything to show her?" he asked.

I had to admit that I didn't. The only writing I had done in the three years since we left Brooklyn was freelance technical translation, with original work limited to the philosophy statement and some user manuals for SoftUniverrse. "That's all right," my mother said. "Writing is like riding a bike—you can't unlearn it." I doubt if that's true, but that time I trusted my mother. I shut myself in the bedroom and devoted myself to a new story, while my mother relieved me of all household duties and took care of Dan. The only problem was that my mind was thoroughly blank. I didn't have any ideas. I went to look through my old files, hoping to find something there. I found a few unfinished sketches in Russian that I had started back when we lived in Saint Petersburg, none of them were sufficiently inspiring. I was about to despair when I found a file with the name "The Perfect Dilemma." I had no idea what that meant. I pressed "open" and saw the following sentence: "Two men are in love with me, one with a broken dick, another with a broken soul." That turned out to be enough to get me going. I finished the story in a week and emailed it to the editor.

Don't count your chickens before they hatch, Len told me again. But this time the chickens hatched! Three months later, my story appeared in the *Magazine*. The editor called me herself to tell me the news. "We have five hundred thousand subscribers. On Monday, you will wake up famous."

That Monday morning, after Len had left for work, my mother and I put Dan and the newborn Nathalie into the family minivan and drove to the local Barnes & Noble. There it was, the issue with my story, right on the magazine rack. We decided to celebrate right there in the Barnes & Noble café with three slices of chocolate cheesecake, two cups of decaf cappuccino, and one hot chocolate. Nothing for Nathalie, but then she was asleep anyway, in the detachable car seat that we placed on top of the table. This was early morning, so the café was mostly empty save for two elderly women at the adjacent table. "Have you seen the new issue of the *Magazine?*" one asked. "I peeked," the other said. "The Russian story is awful. There is the word 'dick' in practically every sentence." And the first woman sighed: "It looks like the *Magazine* is lowering its standards year after year."

My mother and I exchanged looks. "Now that's real fame!" she whispered, and we both started to laugh.

The *Magazine* publication led to a book deal, the published book led to a slew of teaching jobs, tons of freelance assignments followed, with my mother eager to take on child-rearing duties every step of the way. A little too eager? I'd ask myself, but wouldn't wonder for too long.

Back when we still lived in Brooklyn, it was the news of my pregnancy that lifted my mother's depression. She became active, resourceful and alert in a way that she hadn't been since Elijah had died. She would go and study all these pregnancy books, and spend half a day exploring Brooklyn groceries, hunting for the best fruit and vegetables we could afford. She would come back loaded with bags, her cheeks flushed, her eyes sparkling, gushing about all the things that she'd seen on the street. She was the one with the pregnancy glow, while I was losing weight, experiencing all sorts of ailments, and suffering from depression that morphed into apathy once Dan was born. I loved him so much—I loved everything about him, from his smell, to his weight in my arms, to the intensity of his stare, but the mere thought of having to get up and put on my clothes to take him for a walk would be enough to plunge me into despair. "I'll take him," my mother would offer, and I'd start weeping with gratitude.

And this was how it happened that my mother gradually supplanted me in all the traditional motherly duties. She was the one to wake them up before school, to feed them breakfast, to pack their CheapLot backpacks, to meet them after school at the bus stop, to supervise their homework, to teach them math and Russian. She would get very upset if I tried to "meddle" in any of that. She was a renowned educator—this was her thing! I often found that I didn't have enough energy to fight her, but also, having the hardest and the most boring parts of the job of motherhood taken care of was too irresistible. She did all the dirty work, and I didn't even have to be grateful.

The rest of the important parental duties were performed by Len. He provided most of our income, and supervised the kids' hygiene. "Time to brush your teeth!" "Time to buy new sneakers!" "What are you doing wearing that shirt three days in a row?" "Is it my imagination or do you stink like a skunk?" He was also good for emergencies—always ready to take care of a sick kid in the middle of the night, especially when it was something serious, when we had to jump into the car and rush to the hospital.

So, what was my role? Oh, I was a cool parent, the kind that lets the kids stay up late, takes them to grown-up events, and encourages them to watch *Pulp Fiction* and *Fargo*. "What are you watching? *Barney*? Are you kidding me? Let's watch something cool!"

Warning note to cool parents. Being a cool parent usually means that you are not parent enough.

I was also the one to handle the important philosophical issues, such as good and evil, right and wrong, and life and death. My favorite thing to do was to take the kids on long walks and talk to them about science, and the earth, and art, and the intricacies of love, and the meaning of life. Dan and I liked to explore the "secret places" of Staten Island: salt marshes, remote beaches, shipwrecks, and mysterious paths that led into wilderness, where you could encounter anything at all, like the cat shantytown we found in the middle of a forest. Nathalie and I liked to walk to Historic Richmond Town a few blocks away from home, and stroll among the pretty houses, climbing ruins, peeking into windows and hidden alleys, trying to uncover fascinating facts about the past. Two of the most fascinating facts were that the outhouse had a square hole in the seat, not a round one, and that the old inn had a rule of "no more than five people in one bed."

I told the kids about the visits to the Kremlin shortly after my mother died. We established a routine of taking long beach walks about an hour before sundown. More often than not, we would end up talking about my mother, sharing memories and anecdotes. Once, when Nathalie was fourteen and Dan seventeen, I told them how I had vomited whipped cream all over my shoes during the performance of *Swan Lake*.

"Eww!" Nathalie muttered. And Dan laughed.

"What I don't understand," I said, "is why your grandma wouldn't stop me from eating all that shit."

Both kids looked at me incredulously.

"*You* never stopped *us*," Dan said.

"Yes, you *never* did," Nathalie confirmed.

I had no idea what they were talking about.

"Remember how you used to take us to BAM to see all those foreign plays?" Dan said. "Nathalie was only seven or eight, and I was ten? We would always stop by that tiny Italian place. We would all get penne alla vodka and I would throw up when we got home. Every single time. And yet you never objected when I ordered it."

This was true. I didn't object. I was so happy to get out of the house, away from Len, and from my mother too, to spend time with the kids on my own, to take them someplace that I enjoyed, that I would honestly forget about the consequences. Or rather I wouldn't let myself think about them, because I didn't want to spoil the fun.

"But why did you order it again and again?" I asked Dan.

"Because the pasta was good!" he said. "And I was excited. I loved going to the theater. The plays were awful—all those sad people speaking foreign languages—but I liked going there, taking the express bus from Staten Island, going over the Verrazzano Bridge, looking at the ocean from there, then driving into the Battery Tunnel and emerging from there in a completely different place, with crowded streets and huge buildings and cars."

"Yes!" Nathalie said. "I loved that too, and I loved being the youngest one in the theater."

Dan hated the attention, but Nathalie loved it. People would smile at her and ask: "Theater lover, aren't you?" And she would beam. And I would beam too, never questioning the wisdom of taking a seven-year-old to see Beckett or Wedekind.

"There is sand in my eyes," I said. "Let's go back."

Note to parents of children. Please, think about this before you start judging your parents.

The kids knew that the three adults in the family had different functions, never confusing them. So it was always like this:

"Grandma, I'm hungry!"

"Dad, I need a new bike,"

and "Mommy, I'm scared of death."

Sometime after we moved to Staten Island, a huge CheapLot store opened a few blocks from our house. They sold everything from furniture to toys to expired snacks. The variety of offerings reminded me of Cult Goods, the Moscow store that I'd loved as a child. My mother would go there every other week to stock up on items that would be irresistible to the kids, like toy cars, and tiny dolls, and animal slippers, and Play-Doh, and off-brand candy, and old cookies that tasted like Play-Doh. She would store all that on countless shelves in her little apartment, turning it into a Hansel and Gretel house, where she could lure the kids to trap them and teach them math. Lots and lots of math.

I would come home after work and see my kids through the open door of my mother's apartment, sitting at her table with their math books, enacting yet another math problem with their toy cars and tiny dolls, the floor littered with candy and cookie wrappers, which would make me feel simultaneously:

1. Angry—with my mother for feeding my kids crap.
2. Jealous—of my mother for replacing me and spending time with my kids.
3. Jealous—of my kids for replacing me and spending time with my mother.
4. Grateful—because I could sneak past them and go write in peace.
5. Guilty—for feeling all of the above.

So that was how our Escher house functioned. Wait, I almost forgot. There was one more space. A small backyard, muddy, overgrown with weeds, and isolated from the rest of the house. There used to be a wooden staircase leading there from the patio, but it got destroyed in one of those fall hurricanes that tend to batter Staten Island worse than other boroughs. The contractors said that they couldn't fix it unless they replaced the entire patio, and quoted a price that was so insane that we decided to forget about the staircase.

Without the staircase, the only way to get to our backyard was through the back door of my mother's apartment and down the narrow path dividing our house from the neighbors' territory. The path was flooded most of the time; you had to wear rubber boots to get to our backyard, and nobody considered it worth the trouble, except for my mother and me. She planted a puny apple tree in the corner, which didn't bear any fruit but still reminded us of our Moscow gardens. We would bring a pair of folding chairs out there and some tea in a small thermos, and we would sit under the apple tree together and talk about our life in Sevastopol, and Moscow, and Brooklyn, or make fun of Len's parents and sometimes even Len himself.

Did this happen often? No, not really. I couldn't help but feel resentful of my mother for stopping me from leaving Len while I still could.

Negative numbers

There is nothing more baffling or intimidating, unless you learn to apply that to real life.

1.) money debit/credit balancing sheets for kids?

2.) Temperature

3.) Diving ⇒ depth under sea level

THIRTEEN

I don't remember being baffled or intimidated by negative numbers. My mother taught me about them when I was eight or nine, and I grasped the concept right away. But while it wasn't baffling to me, it was terrifying. My mother used a large pot and a wooden ruler to explain the concept to me. She half filled the pot with water, then put the ruler in. She made a mark on the ruler where it touched the surface of the water. That would be zero, she said. Above zero there were your regular numbers. Below zero was your negative space; that was where your negative numbers lived. I could barely see the ruler underwater; it looked distorted and scary. I thought of negative space as some sort of dark underworld, and it was right here in the middle of the kitchen, on the table where we ate, in the pot that we used for making soup.

"Let's do some sums now," my mother said. And that was probably the scariest thing about the negative numbers, that you could add them up and even multiply them, making their negative value even more negative, which brought you deeper into the underworld.

I had avoided having anything to do with negative numbers for most of my adult life, until Yulia suddenly reappeared in my life with her own take on the concept. This happened in 2006, right after I published the piece about my wedding dress in the *Important Fashion Magazine*. Yulia said that she read the magazine religiously and it was quite a shock for her to see me there. The last person you'd expect to see in a fashion magazine! Yulia worked as a main media liaison for an international media conglomerate. She used her connections to find my new address, and here she was sitting across from me in a sleek downtown restaurant with a copy of the magazine in her lap, shifting her eyes from me to the photo of me in the magazine and laughing. "Now I understand the magic of retouching!" she said at one point.

Yulia herself looked well, thinner than ever and dressed in an expensive ensemble in different hues of green, including enormous shades in green frames.

Yulia was on her third husband and couldn't believe that I was still married to Len. No, she didn't have any kids. No way! Thank God!

She refused to talk about Sasha, but was more than happy to talk about her career. She had gotten a degree in psychology, and worked as a family therapist for a few years, but then she got sick of it all and moved to London. Her current job was amazing. They had already launched a glamorous print magazine and even more glamorous social media club, and a radio broadcast and a TV channel were in the works The entire thing was called the Résistance—spelled the French way.

The name made me laugh.

"Laugh all you want," Yulia said, "but we are going to topple Putin one day."

The Résistance was funded by exiled billionaire Nikolay Kotov and had the goal of connecting super-rich and super-successful Russians living all over Europe. The idea was that armed with so much money and brainpower, the opposition would finally have a chance, and Kotov would be the one to head it. Or at least this was how the project was being sold to Kotov. I remembered that Sasha had mentioned the Résistance once. He said that all the talk about forming the opposition was pure bullshit, and a more apt name for the magazine would be *Asshole Monthly*.

I had to admit that the issue that Yulia gave me as a gift confirmed Sasha's assessment. I opened it on the bus back to Staten Island and saw nothing but the usual glamorous fluff.

The first piece that caught my eye had the headline "Marusya Keeps Stumbling." The piece detailed the myriad problems experienced by owners of fashionable teacup pigs. The main problem was that Moscow winters were too harsh for these animals, and it was impossible to find warm pet clothes that would fit a teacup pig, and so people were denied the biggest pleasure of teacup pig ownership—the ability to walk them down Moscow streets on a tiny leash. The photo featured the most adorable teacup pig, her minuscule legs clad in human baby booties. I doubted that Marusya could topple Putin, especially if she kept stumbling.

The rest of the pieces were hardly better, so I skimmed through them, until I found a long interview with Yulia herself, entitled "Doctor Divorce."

Once again, there was nothing about politics. The interviewer talked about Yulia's "subversively flirty" clothes before focusing on her past work as a couples therapist.

Q: Yulia Nikolaevna, you were notorious for being very blunt with your patients, even urging them to get a divorce rather than continue therapy. Is that true?

A: Absolutely! In my professional opinion, there is no point in prolonging the agony of a dying marriage.

Q: But how can you tell for sure if a marriage is salvageable or not?

A: I gave my patients a very simple exercise. I called it "A Balance Sheet of a Marriage." They had to list all the important aspects of marriage, like personality and sex and finances. Then they identified both positive and negative aspects of each element, and assigned value points to each one, because it was very unlikely that any single element of a marriage would be entirely positive or entirely negative. Then they had to tally up the points and see whether the total was positive or negative. If it's negative—you know what you have to do.

Q: Thank you so much, Yulia Nikolaevna! I'm sure our readers will be tempted to try it!

A: They better!

I don't know about other readers, but I was certainly tempted. In fact, I couldn't even wait until I got home. I found a pen in my bag and started tallying points right in the margins of the *Résistance*.

Good	Bad
Kids:	
Len is an incredibly reliable father. If there is an emergency, he will drop everything and be there for the kids. He is great at remembering dentist appointments and buying new sneakers on time. We're mostly on the same page about the kids' upbringing. Except that Len wants them to have less contact with my mother, but he understands that's impossible since we live together.	He doesn't know how to listen or talk to them, and he doesn't seem to enjoy spending time with them. He thinks that it's wrong that I enjoy spending time with the kids. He also thinks that I'm an exceptionally bad parent, and sometimes in the heat of an argument, he will even say that the kids would be better off without me, like if I died or something. To be fair, he doesn't say that often.
50	-50

My mother:	
He lets her live with us.	He can't stand her.
50	-100

Personality and intelligence:	
He is a decent, honest man. Thorough, reserved. Intelligent.	He is not that kind. His mind isn't flexible enough. He is not open to new ideas. He can't ever see the world from somebody else's perspective.
50	-50

Good	Bad
Sex:	
We have more than enough for a married couple, and it's never uncomfortable or deeply unwanted. We know what each of us finds unpleasant and never venture there. And when our married friends or more importantly TV characters mention the frequency of their sex, we find ourselves in the top 20 percent, which is very uplifting.	But it's so, so boring! I had always imagined sex to be this crazy force. Am I never going to experience the single best thing granted to a human being? Okay, but what if that amazing sex simply doesn't exist? What if all the people who say that they have had amazing sex are lying? A lot of people I know believe that amazing sex is the stuff of fiction. Why can't I accept that? Because I know in my heart that this is not true!
50	-100

His job:	
Len has always had a steady job as a computer programmer and made good money. In addition to that, he founded his own start-up, which isn't earning any money but isn't losing any money either.	Len doesn't have any time for the family.
100	-100

Good	Bad

My job:

He's proud of the fact that his wife is a published author.

He rarely complains that I'm not making enough money.

He has never read anything I've written. Not even a magazine piece.

Once a year, when we file our joint return, he will say with a laugh that my combined income from two teaching jobs and countless publications doesn't make a third of his salary. (It makes more than a third!)

50	-50

Interests:

There are several things that we both like.

Four films: *Pulp Fiction*, *Fargo*, *Seven Samurai*, and the cult Soviet romantic comedy *Irony of Fate*.

Two novels: *War and Peace* (only Len skipped most of the peace) and *The Master and Margarita* (but Len loves it and I merely like it).

Easy hikes (but he never has time for that).

He hasn't read a book in fifteen years or so.

I hate computer programming, and fail to understand how his start-up devoted to database security and architecture is exciting.

We ruin those beautiful breakfasts by having one or another explosive argument.

Good	Bad
Interests: *(continued)* Sunday breakfasts—baguette with butter and jam, fruit, berries, coffee in a French press, all luminous in the morning sun.	
50	-50

Affection:

There are times when I feel so much affection toward Len that it makes my heart hurt. Sometimes, I will enter the garage to get something, and see Len sitting at his computer with his back to me. I will see his shoulder blades under a checkered shirt, and the thinning hair on his crown, and his long fingers frozen midflight over the keyboard, and I will rush to hug him from behind and kiss him on the back of his head. And he will lean back to linger in the warmth of my arms and call me *solnyshko*, which is like "sunshine" in English, but warmer.	But what if this is just habitual affection? Not one caused by genuine love?
100	-1

Good	Bad
Future:	
I know that Len would never leave me.	The thought of being with Len for the rest of my life fills me with such horror.
100	-300

By the time the bus crept up the Verrazzano Bridge, I'd tallied up the numbers.

The result was -201, which meant that I needed to divorce Len immediately.

The thought of divorce made me sick with panic. But I tried to be rational about it. I thought that maybe I should make a separate balance sheet for the divorce. I would assign negative value to the awful aspects of the divorce, and positive value to the ones that had the potential to make my life better. I started with the effect the divorce would have on the kids—the scariest aspect of all.

Negative	Positive
Kids:	
Will be horribly damaged.	Will eventually be okay.
-1,000,000	10

My mother:	
We would have to sell the house. Where would she live???	I could probably find a cheap enough apartment with a separate bedroom for her. She would love being with us all the time.
-1,000	0

Negative	Positive
Basic survival:	
I can't survive without Len. He said so himself many times. He said that I lack vital survival skills, like the ability to drive on a highway, understand mortgage payments, and remember to schedule teeth cleanings.	Oh, come on! That's shameful and ridiculous! I am a healthy, fairly privileged adult living in one of the most affluent countries in the world. Of course I can survive.
-100	100

My job:	
There is a possibility that nobody would ever publish anything that I write ever again. My name would be completely forgotten and nobody would offer me another teaching job.	It's certainly possible, but very unlikely.
-1,000	100

Sex:	
Even if I find a suitable partner, I'm such a "delicate flower" (quoting Len) that it might take years to figure out what it is I want. Nobody has the patience for that. I might never have good sex again.	I will have the freedom to look for new exciting partners. I will understand myself better and know what I want.
-100	100

Negative	Positive
Love:	
What love? Love is bullshit. Love doesn't exist.	I might find real love.
-100	1,000

This time I didn't even have to tally up the points to see that the negative numbers screamed against the divorce. Divorce wasn't possible. But I didn't want to stay in a marriage that was decidedly not working either.

The only solution was to go back to my marriage balance table and fix the results there.

This wasn't something that my mother taught me. She taught me that the very idea of math was that it was strict, precise, and firmly grounded in reality. She would be shocked and disgusted if she knew that her own daughter was essentially fucking with math. But hadn't I rejected math in favor of fiction-writing years ago? What if this was something to do with who I was? What if I couldn't deal with reality unless I could fix it?

I fixed the numbers in my job row first. Why would I decide that the fact that Len didn't read my novels or stories was a negative thing? Didn't it give me more creative freedom? I could write whatever I wanted without worrying that it would offend or anger Len. I went ahead and changed the minus sign to a plus sign.

Then I fixed the numbers in my mother row. Wasn't the fact that Len let her live with us more important than his feelings toward her? Wouldn't it be worse if he loved her but refused to live with her? I went ahead and eagerly changed the values there too.

I also fixed the numbers in my interests row, because I remembered one more thing Len and I liked to do together—watch *SNL*, even though Len preferred the political jokes and I the fart-and-shit ones.

It was the sex row that made me struggle the longest. Wasn't boring sex in a marriage perfectly normal? Wasn't the boredom what made it so comfortable?

I was about to up the number in the positive column, but then I remembered two recent episodes.

One episode happened on a camping trip. Neither Len nor I was particularly fond of camping, but camping was considered such a wholesome family activity that we couldn't possibly consider ourselves a wholesome family unless we did it. The only problem was that we couldn't figure out how to have fun as a family, or as a group. According to the Escher house rules, it would've been easier for Len to do something with the kids without me, and the same went for me. For me, the best part of the trip was when Len said that he had to work for a little bit. He had plugged his laptop into an outlet attached to the bathroom facility and sat down at a nearby picnic table, and remained there for hours, while I took the kids for a walk. We tasted some blueberries and lingonberries and wild sorrel. We saw a raccoon, a hawk, and something that looked like a wild pig. The pig inspired us to invent a game called "guess the oink." One of us had to oink in a certain way, and the others had to guess whether the pig was happy, angry, disappointed, paranoid, jealous, or desperately sad. We all laughed so hard that we lost our way a couple of times. By the time we came back, the campground was full, other tents were set up and other fires were lit, and there was different music playing. We made a fire too, and roasted thick slices of kielbasa and made some tea. Then Len and I engaged in one of our fights. I said that if the kids wanted to pee at night, they could crawl out and pee right by the tent. But Len pronounced that disgusting and said that one of us could take them to the bathroom. I said that the bathroom was filthy, and you could slip on somebody's shit in the dark and drag that shit into the tent. And Len said that all the shit was in my head. But then we remembered that this was a quality-time family camping trip and stopped yelling at each other. Len agreed that the bathrooms were filthy, and I agreed that we should go there anyway.

I was the one who woke up wanting to pee. I zipped up my jacket, groped around to find the opening, and crawled out of the tent. It was so much colder outside the tent that I almost crawled right back in. I considered peeing right by the tent, but I was afraid that the sound of my peeing would wake Len up. Thankfully it wasn't completely dark. I could see the path leading to the toilet pretty well. What I hadn't realized was that I wouldn't know how to tell which tent was ours on the way back. I couldn't even remember which color it was. The cars were parked elsewhere, and all the tents and all the firepits looked more or less the same. On one of the middle tents the right flap was slightly open—I must have left it open when I crawled out. I walked there, dropped on my knees in front of the tent so I could crawl in, and opened the flap wider. There I saw two people engaged in the act of oral sex in the soft glow of an iPhone lying in the corner. I was so stunned that I didn't retreat right away. The woman was lying on her back diagonally to the entrance with her head pressed against the far-right corner of the tent. She was covered by a blanket, except for her left knee and foot, her shoe and sock were still on, as were her pants, lowered to her ankles. She had to open her knees far apart, since her ankles were bound by her pants. Her left knee was round and fat. The man was under the blanket—a lumpy moving mound, with his feet (no shoes, just socks) pressing against the near-left corner of the tent. They were barely making any sounds, just panting a little. I shut the flaps closed and moved away, hoping that they hadn't seen me. I recognized them as a husband and wife, members of a group that had sat at the firepit right next to ours. All large and heavy people. They had been making s'mores and they'd offered some to Dan and Nathalie. I was confident now that our tent was to the left of theirs, so I crawled there and lay down next to Len. I couldn't be mistaken, could I? Was that man going down on his wife? In the cold, not-very-clean tent? Yes, he was. I could hear their panting from my tent and see the slight movements of the wall of their tent. I imagined that once the woman reached her orgasm, she would go down on the man and would be as tender and generous with him. And they were what? In their late fifties. At least that old. And they wanted each other so much that they had to do it right there and then. And they loved each other so much that they chose the most tender, complex, and time-consuming of all sexual acts. I couldn't even imagine Len and me doing that. I suddenly felt so bad that I had to quietly utter that desperately sad oink.

The second episode took place a couple of weeks later and was probably inspired by what I had seen on the camping trip. One Saturday night, around ten o'clock, I went to the garage and asked Len to drive us to the beach. "Let's look at the moon," I said.

We left the car in the deserted parking lot and walked to the beach, but it was cold and overcast and we couldn't see the moon, just the yellow patches of light breaking through the layers of clouds. I was the first to return to our car, and I climbed into the middle seat instead and asked Len to come join me. "It's warm in here. You'd be surprised!"

Within minutes a police car pulled up. Two cops were blinding us with their flashlights, speaking through a loudspeaker. Saying the same thing over and over again as we fumbled with our clothes. "Are you okay, ma'am? Ma'am, you have to answer. Sir, we need to see her face. We need to see your face, ma'am. Ma'am!" Eventually, they wrote us a ticket for indecent behavior in a public place and let us go. But it was such a nightmare. I was shaking from shame the entire drive back. Len was squeezing the steering wheel in silent rage. He acted as if it were my fault. And it was my fault. I was the one desperate to prove that we too could have exciting outdoor sex. "One day we will laugh about this," I said when he pulled up our driveway.

That day never came.

But sitting there on the bus with the issue of the *Résistance* in my lap, I went ahead and added +50 points to the entry for sex. As the kids' PE teacher always said: "It's not the result that counts, it's the effort!"

By the time the bus made it to the last stop, I had enough positive points to stay married to Len.

Note to an inquisitive reader. I wonder how many other people are doing that, putting so much effort into faking the math so that their marriages appear tolerable at best. I'd love to see some statistics on that.

You can cautiously introduce doing sums with negative numbers.

FOURTEEN

When I was eighteen, Irina, my mother's favorite student, killed herself by swallowing crushed glass. I couldn't imagine a more horrible death. My mother cried for days. And I felt incredibly guilty, because I had been insanely jealous of Irina. My mother used to go on and on about her. "Irochka is wonderful!" "Irochka is the smartest!" "She's doing very important work with negative numbers." I used to hate her, and now she was dead. I would see her in my nightmares all the time. She would be sitting in the university's lecture hall, eating shards of glass from a paper bag in her lap as if they were potato chips, making these protracted chewing motions with her lower jaw like cows do. There was a little bit of blood dripping from the sides of her mouth, and she looked terrifyingly sad. People said that she killed herself because of unhappy love, but I secretly believed that she glimpsed the true darkness of the negative numbers and couldn't handle it.

For me, these glimpses into darkness happened every time I finished writing a book. While I was working on a book, my mind was fully engaged, grounded in that highly structured space, but once I stopped it became untethered, wild, prone to wandering into dangerous places.

My agent told me that it was perfectly normal to feel like this. That this was a sort of postpartum depression for writers. "Didn't you experience postpartum depression when you gave birth to your kids?" she asked me. I had, but it felt like something completely different. After childbirth, I felt emptied, apathetic, my mind so lazy and clouded, as if it were wrapped in layers and layers of cotton wool. When I finished a book, I suffered from the opposite menace—a heightened clarity.

I knew that my marital math was bullshit, I knew what it was that I wanted—to leave Len—just as I knew that I didn't have the guts to do it.

The only thing that made me feel slightly better was reading long emails from my readers, people who wrote to say that something in my fiction clicked with their own experiences and created the unexpected feeling of connection, making them feel less lonely. I kept the letters in a special Gmail folder, and when I felt especially bad, I would shut myself in my Escher house bedroom and get into bed with the laptop and a box of tissues. There weren't that many letters, so I would read the same ones again and again, weeping over moving moments.

Note to my best readers. Postmodernism, the fourth wall— what bullshit! I started writing fiction out of loneliness and desperation, as an attempt to connect to other people. Remember that woman at the Russian store who sold me

caviar? Remember how she and I had a fleeting moment of
true connection? I depend on my readers to connect with
me in this way. And when I feel that I succeeded, I'm moved
to the point of tears.

Most of the emails were from strangers. But there were a few
from people I knew. One was from my mother's friend Rita, who
had read one of my stories in Russian translation and was impressed by the way I captured our Moscow neighborhood; one
was from one of Dan's teachers, who felt proud because I wrote
about the profession of teacher with such respect; and there were
two emails from B. One was a short note I received right after my
debut publication in the *Magazine*. He recognized himself in the
man with a broken dick, and while he tried very hard to remain
impartial and praise the literary merits of the story, I could see
how hurt he was. I left that note unanswered. He sent me the
second email about two years ago, and that one was very different from the first. It was a long, thoughtful, and genuinely moving analysis of my two novels and collection of short stories. He
seemed to have read every single thing that I'd written, and while
he provided some specific criticism, he focused on my growth as
a writer, on the subtler changes that propelled me forward from
one book to another. He wrote about his life a little. He had
earned his PhD in film studies at Harvard and had been lucky
to find a teaching position in New York. He concluded the email
by saying how proud he felt of my career, even if he knew that it
was ridiculous, because he couldn't have possibly influenced me.
I wanted to answer him this time; I kept composing the email in

my head, juggling half-finished sentences, none of which were satisfactory. Then I put B.'s email aside. Then I forgot about it. Then I remembered it, but so much time had passed that I decided not to bother. I never did answer it. But I read it again and again, dabbing my eyes every time.

I found that my postpartum depression would get worse with each new book, and when I finished my third novel, exactly a year before my marriage collapsed, it hit me especially hard. That time the depression coincided with a heat wave, which I coped with by lying on the floor of my bedroom next to the AC vent. After a week of this, my mother became worried and began looking for something to make me feel better. She came up with a brilliant plan. We would stay at Uncle Grisha's dacha for a week, which would be good for everybody. Uncle Grisha's "dacha" was actually a stationary trailer in Eagle Lake, a trailer park in the Poconos. And so what that the trailer was ugly—it stood right on the lake. And so what if it had a leaky roof—it hardly ever rained! And so what if the toilet didn't always work—we were in the woods!

Len was the only one who hated the place, but he didn't have to stay there, just drive us there and back, and as a reward he got to spend the whole week in the empty house, which he loved more than anything.

The trouble didn't start until the way back.

Len was driving in silence. I sat on the right side of the middle row of our minivan, and I could see the right side of his droopy nose, his shiny, furrowed forehead, and his tightly squeezed mouth, all of which were meant to express how much he resented having to drive us to and from the place that he hated so much. I found him so unlovely and so unloved at that moment that I was overcome by some sort of squeamish guilt toward him. Which did nothing to alleviate my anger. I was getting madder and madder at him. I was tired and uncomfortable, because there were all these shopping bags, next to me, by my feet, in my lap. We always stopped at the supermarket in the Poconos on the way back, because everything there was so much cheaper than in New York.

Among other things, there were twenty glass jars of Thai peanut sauce, several packages of Eggo frozen cinnamon-toast waffles, a whole pack of V8 cans, and six two-liter bottles of Coca-Cola meant for Dan's upcoming birthday (all of those items were on a huge sale). I had been so excited about the bargain prices, but now I was doubting the wisdom of our purchases.

The kids didn't look very happy either. They were in the back seat, engaged in their usual low-key squabbling. Nathalie was annoyed with the sounds Dan's Nintendo DS made, and Dan was annoyed with Nathalie's elbow being too close to his side. My mother was in the front passenger seat, half sleeping, half battling motion sickness, nodding off until her chin bumped against her chest—that would rouse her and she would inquire if the kids wanted a snack. This annoyed me too. There weren't any snacks left. They had eaten their carrots and apples a long time ago, and they weren't supposed to eat anything else until we got home. They were twelve and fourteen! They didn't have to be eating all the time! But as we were passing the pink stone walls of some New Jersey town, meant to protect the neighboring developments from the noise of the highway, my mother found a piece of old chocolate in her bag and tried to throw it to Dan over my head. It landed on the floor between the seats.

"Great, now it's going to stain the car!" Len said. Then he asked for some water.

The bottle in my lap was empty. My mother never drank anything on car trips so that she wouldn't need to go to the bathroom. I asked the kids. Dan reached for his bottle but dropped it to the floor and it rolled under the seat. "Sorry, Daddy!" Nathalie said, but immediately ruined her attempt at sympathy by giggling.

I said that we had warm Coca-Cola and warm V8 in the shopping bags.

"Cola, please," Len said.

I took a bottle out of the bag and unscrewed the top, mindful of the foam. Not that I cared about stains, but I cared about peace in the car. I did a very good job of unscrewing—not a drop of foam came out. Then I put the lid in my lap, picked up the bottle by the middle, and thrust my hand out.

"Here," I said.

Len's eyes were on the road, his left hand on the steering wheel. He reached with his right hand, which he bent toward me over his shoulder. I moved the bottle closer. He picked it up by the neck. Why would he pick it up by the neck? I thought. The next instant he flipped the bottle over and the dark liquid gushed all over his arm, his right knee, pooling in a puddle on the car floor. Len's reactions have always been very quick, so he restored the bottle to the upright position almost right away, and the car didn't so much as swerve. But the damage was done. Once the puddle dried, it would leave the stain of all stains.

"What the fuck did you do?" Len screamed.

"What did *I* do?" I screamed back.

"Why did you open it?"

"Why did you flip it?"

The kids started to giggle.

"Shut up!" Len screamed. "You think this is funny, huh? You think this doesn't concern you? You know why? Because you think that you're passengers in this car and I'm your chauffeur. This is your attitude, right? This is your attitude to life as well. Once a passenger, always a passenger. Just like your mom. Taking it easy. Not giving a shit. Right? Passengers. That's what you are."

Thankfully he delivered this lecture without turning back.

"I'm sorry, Daddy," Nathalie said. "We'll help you clean it."

"What a suck-up," Dan mumbled, annoyed that she always seemed to come up with the right thing to say.

I turned back to admonish him and saw that Nathalie was covering her face, struggling to contain more giggles. Her entire body was shaking, and her hands were squeezing her cheeks, making her look like a hamster. I'd had barely any time to admire her effort when I felt the unstoppable wave of laughter rising up from the depths of my own body. Now this would be a disaster.

Len and I had been married for sixteen years by that time, and all those years I tried to explain to him that I can't do anything at all to control my laughter, and he still didn't get it.

"Why don't you think about something sad?" Len would ask. I tried that. It didn't help. Nothing helped. Not even thinking about my grandmother's death, or my grandfather's death, or my father's death.

"Okay, how about this," I said to Len once. "Sometimes I laugh so hard that I pee in my pants. If I could control it, I would!"

He shook his head.

There was this one time when Nathalie fell off the bed twice in a row. She was barely three and an awfully fussy sleeper. When she fell for the first time, I ran up to her and picked her up and comforted her. But an hour later she fell off the bed for the second time. She said: "Not again!" That "not again" just killed me. This was my kid and I pitied her with all my heart, and yet I couldn't contain my laughter. I was sitting on the floor, stroking the crying Nathalie on her back, shaking with laughter, when Len walked in on us.

"You're a psychopath," he told me.

That time in the car, I tried to hold it in, as hard as I could. Then, when it became clear that I couldn't, I pushed the bags to the floor and moved to the left so Len wouldn't see me. I tried to laugh into the bag with frozen waffles to muffle the sound. It helped, but only for a second or two. Soon my laughter grew so potent it was completely futile to try to conceal it. The bag with peanut sauce jars fell off my lap, and the jars started rolling around the car floor, which only intensified my laughter. My eyes were clouded with tears, but I could see how Len was getting tenser and tenser, readying to blow up.

"God, please, let it pass. Let me stop," I thought. Then I realized that I was actually praying to stop laughing and it struck me as unbearably funny.

Soon the kids joined in and it seemed as if the whole car was shaking with laughter. Thank God, my mother was too carsick to laugh. Oh, no, shit no! She was laughing too!

I expected Len to start screaming, but he didn't. He kept driving. Eyes on the road. Perfectly composed.

I was starting to calm down. There was less pressure on my chest. I knew from experience that in a few moments the laughter would die down, and once I stopped, everybody would stop too.

But the next moment Len turned to me with a raised fist and a mad expression. He swung and the blow was so great that the entire car started to shake. He couldn't have hit me with such force, I thought. And then I realized that he hadn't. He hadn't hit me! Another car had crashed into our minivan, and the minivan was spinning on a busy highway, out of control. It was a matter of seconds before another car would crash into ours, then another, and we would all die. I prayed, and I prayed, and I prayed. God, Something, please spare us! Spare us! Please!

And God spared us. The minivan swerved to the right and crashed into a guardrail, which stopped the spinning. I was afraid that the gas tank would blow up the way it always happens in movies, so I grabbed the kids and pushed them out of the car, and then opened the door for my mother and dragged her out too. Len came out of the car from his side. We all seemed to be okay. "Well, nobody died," Len said. He was shaking.

We sat in the grass for quite a while. The police came. Roadside assistance came and took away the car. Then we walked about a mile to the nearest exit with a rest area and a McDonald's. Len bought us three Happy Meals to share and we sat down in a large booth by the window to wait for a cab home. My mother kept going to the bathroom and back. Nathalie's face was tear-streaked, and Dan kept hiccupping. "Well, that was an adventure!" Len said.

I couldn't bear to look at him, because I'd discovered something definitive about our marriage. Not only did we not love each other, but we hated each other so much that we had come close to dying because of it.

I remembered how when Len and I got married, our love was so strong that it felt like a presence. Something amorphous but dense, something you could touch if you moved your hand through the air. I thought that the lack of love wasn't only empty space. It had a physical presence too. Negative presence. And like negative numbers, it had the ability to multiply and grow. You couldn't stop it.

I can't tell why—I don't think this was something rational at all—but the next day I went and found B.'s email in my fan folder and wrote him a short note asking him if he wanted to meet.

High dimensional
Spaces occur in
the sciences.

FIFTEEN

Eight months before my mother died, I came close to dying myself. What happened was that Len grabbed my neck and proceeded to squeeze it until I started to choke.

I had just told Len that I was leaving him for Victor, my rich Russian lover. He took the news reasonably well. I think he was even relieved. Our life together had become so unbearable that any option seemed brighter than staying together. We went to a small deserted park a few minutes away from our house so we could discuss the future in peace. In peace, yes: the park was achingly peaceful. We got out of the car and sat down on top of a nearby picnic table with our feet on the bench. There was a large oak tree towering over the table, and the ground was covered with last year's brown leaves and occasional acorns. We'd even brought hot tea in a thermos, and we were taking turns drinking it out of the thermos's plastic top. We were courteous and even affectionate to each other. Len asked me all kinds of questions about Victor, and my answers seemed to reassure rather than anger him.

The fact that Victor was both committed and rich made the logistics of the impending divorce appear manageable.

Then Len asked me about B. I tensed even though I wasn't surprised. I'd always thought that Len had known about B. for a long time. I admitted that I had been in love with B., but it was over. It turned out that Len *both knew and didn't know.* Or rather he knew but wouldn't admit to himself that he knew. My confession forced him to fully know. And he couldn't take it. He dropped the thermos top to the ground and pressed his hands to his face. His knuckles went very white, and his breathing was so hard that he seemed to be moaning.

I wanted to touch Len's shoulder, but I was afraid that he'd hate that. I said: "Len." He didn't react.

The next instant Len reached for my neck and squeezed it as hard as he could. I don't remember if I fought him, I must have fought him, but I don't remember it at all. At first I wasn't even scared; I thought he'd let me go in a second. But he didn't. And then I got scared. Very scared. And it was as if the world came closing in on me, constricting me in a tighter and tighter space. I remember willing myself to get smaller, to get really tiny so that I could, if not escape, then at least fit inside that grip. Then I didn't have any thoughts anymore, and everything became murky and viscous. I don't know how much time passed before he let me go. Obviously not too much, or I wouldn't be alive.

He helped me to sit up afterward, and pressed his face to my legs and stayed like that, sobbing.

Before that moment, I truly hadn't realized (or wouldn't let myself realize) that by pursuing my love for B., I was doing something horrible to Len. I'd always thought that I was doing something horrible to myself.

One of the results of the compartmentalization was my grossly mistaken belief that what I did in one of my lives couldn't possibly affect people in the others.

Note to disconcerted readers. Yes, I realize how strange and shocking it sounds, that right after Len's violent assault, I was only thinking about how **I wronged him**. I never blamed him afterwards either. You're free to analyze me any way you want, but this was my reaction, and it would be dishonest to pretend otherwise.

When I wrote to B. after the car accident, I wasn't sure if he would answer me at all, or if he still had the same email address. He wrote me back within an hour. Yes, of course he wanted to see me.

I didn't know where to meet him. Anya suggested the Goat's Hoof in Chelsea, which she described as an unremarkable little bar.

I saw that the Goat's Hoof was a mistake as soon as I walked in. The dimmed lighting. The predominance of red in the decor. The paintings of various goats, all looking human and horny. The deep benches. The glimmering cocktails. The couples holding hands over tables, while their knees touched under the tables. I sat down at an empty table thinking this place set the tone and sent the message better than any conversation could. And this was the wrong message. It had to be the wrong message. I didn't want to have an affair with B.

But if I didn't want to have an affair with B., what was it that I wanted? Why had I asked him to see me? I needed some time to figure that out. I had an urge to run away from that bar, but it was too late. I saw B. at the entrance, removing a leather jacket, scanning the place with an anxious and hopeful expression.

I waved at him, thinking that perhaps everything would be okay if I managed to maintain my cool, to remain cautious and firm. He was shorter than I'd remembered, but also much better-looking. He had grown his beard back, and his dark, downturned eyes sparkled with excitement.

I smiled. He shook his head. Neither of us seemed to know what to say.

"My heart is beating really hard," B. said and reached for the little card listing the signature cocktails. I ordered a vodka martini, and he ordered something tropical and sweet. His phone rang. He put it on ignore.

He reached into his shoulder bag and pulled out a copy of my third novel.

He started leafing through it, then put it down.

"I wanted to ask you for an autograph, but now it seems silly and wrong," he said.

I agreed with him that it was silly.

A waitress put our drinks down. His glass was filled to the brim and loaded with slices of fruit. B. lifted it up, and some of his drink splashed over the cover of my novel. A puddle of orange liquid gathered around my name. I was afraid that I'd start laughing and wouldn't be able to stop and whatever brittle connection we had would be destroyed, but for some reason I didn't feel like laughing. B. was so nervous that it relaxed me.

"So, how long has it been?" I said. "More than ten years?"

"What? Since my broken dick? Fourteen," he said, dabbing at the book with the napkin. "That was the lowest point in my life, but once I left for Boston everything started to fall into place."

"That Dr. Solomon must have been a wizard!" I said.

B. shook his head.

"I've always thought it was you who cured me. You were my shock therapy. The look on your face when I recited Brodsky! Nobody's ever despised me that much."

I said: "I didn't despise you! Not even a little!"

"I deserved it. Of course I did. I had such a crush on you back then! You can't imagine. I think I managed to pull myself together to prove to you that I could."

But he never contacted me, I thought, except years later to congratulate me on the story. It was possible that he was scared of rejection, but a more likely scenario was that as his life kept improving, he didn't care as much. I could see that he was creating this romantic narrative even as we spoke. But I could also see that he was being sincere, he wasn't doing it for my sake, to flatter or manipulate me; he was trying to make sense of things for himself. I was impressed with my own maturity. I wasn't seventeen or twenty-two anymore. I was thirty-six, I was an adult, I was a married woman with two kids, I was a writer with a well-developed professional ability to put myself into other people's shoes and understand their motivations. I was immune to the craziness of love. All I wanted was to get to know a bit more about B.

We sat and talked for a long time, about this and that, movies and books, and our lives and feelings and thoughts. I realized that I had never talked to B. as an equal before, and that I hadn't really known him. I used to see him as a blank screen for my romantic projections, without trying to understand him as a person. Perhaps this was how he used to see me too. In Moscow, he was a young idealistic teacher, and I was a teen madly in love with him. In Brooklyn, he was a thoroughly lost recent immigrant, and I was an elusive object of desire born out of nostalgia more than anything else. But now, now we were a man and a woman, opening up to each other for the first time in our lives.

B. said that the luckiest thing in his life was that his ex-wife, Oksana, decided that she couldn't handle being a single mother and shipped Mark back to B. He might not have been the perfect father, but Mark was the closest person to him.

I said that my kids were that for me.

"What about your husband?" B. asked.

I said: "He's not."

B. stared at me intently.

His phone buzzed; he checked the screen and said that it was Nadya, his wife of two years. She was a wonderful woman and she had been very good, even healing, to him. But she didn't trust him.

"Do you love her?" I asked.

"No," B. said.

He walked me to the Staten Island bus stop, and while we were waiting for the bus, I asked him if he still remembered which Brodsky poem he recited to me on Brighton Beach. He said: "Of course I do." I asked him to recite it for me again. B. looked around and chuckled in embarrassment. We were not alone at that bus stop; there was a small queue of people behind us, and a fidgety man in front of us who kept running into the road to see if the bus was approaching. I dared B. to recite it anyway. He leaned in and half said, half whispered the first lines:

"My dear, late at night today, I went outside

to get a breath of fresh air."

This sounded so intimate that I had to look away. I listened to the rest of the poem while staring at B.'s chest, at the frayed edge of his leather jacket, the round leather buttons, at some sort of silver chain stuck in the opening of his shirt. This was the first time that I ever got a Brodsky poem. And this was the first time I was deeply moved by any poem at all. When I suggested that B. recite the poem, I thought of it more as a joke. Now I was embarrassed by my reaction. I couldn't look at B. even after he finished reciting. I pointed to his silver chain and asked him what it was. He said that this was his cross.

"But I thought you were Jewish," I said.

He said that he had converted to Christianity while studying at Harvard.

I asked if I could see his cross.

He pulled the chain out of his shirt, untangling it from his graying chest hair. It was a small silver cross engraved with words in Church Slavonic. I said that I had studied Church Slavonic in college and asked if I could read the engraving. He leaned still closer. I took the cross in my hand—and peered into the letters. They still held the warmth of his body. My heart was beating so hard that I was afraid B. would hear it. I thought I could hear his heart too.

"When did you know?" I asked B. a month later, after he told me that he loved me for the first time.

"When you were holding my cross," he said.

And that was how a whole new room was added to my Escher-house life. The room so vast that it seemed to open up into another dimension. Or rather a high-dimensional space was created, like the one in my mother's flash card.

Sometimes I think that I turned to math the way B. turned to Orthodox Christianity, to fill a spiritual void that became acutely unbearable after my mother died.

If you think about it, math is as good a religion as any. It's both endlessly abstract and irresistibly precise. You can grasp the entire world with the help of math and make it seem less cha- otic, unpredictable, and scary. Isn't this why my mother started to work on her last book to begin with? She must have felt that something was wrong; she must have glimpsed into the chaos of death, and so she turned to math—her safe, perfectly structured space.

One way to describe love according to the gospel of math is as a condition that causes a dimensional shift. The emerging new world that contains love becomes so vast that it opens into an entire new dimension, dwarfing all the worlds that existed in your life before you fell in love.

B. and I couldn't spend that much time together. We would go to a motel about once a month, and we would see each other in the park by the river twice a week. The rest of the time we kept in touch through email, and we wrote to each other so much and so often, hundreds of emails a day—some long, others containing just a couple of words—that it seemed as if we never parted at all.

In those emails we covered everything: the minutiae of the day, childhood memories, philosophy and religion, favorite movies and books, people in our lives, work problems, sex and love. I emailed him from my personal account, so I would usually delete the email thread at the end of the day, but B., who had been writing to me from his work email, didn't have to do that. At one point, the university decided to change servers, and he had to convert all of our emails into a text file so they wouldn't disappear. Most of the letters got lost or truncated in the process, merging together so sometimes it wasn't possible to tell where one letter ended and the next started, and at other times it wasn't even clear which one of us wrote what.

I kept thinking about you the entire time, remembering all these insane details.

Like what?

Like the fact that the three birthmarks on your face form a triangle.

I took the wrong exit last night, kept driving down the same roads someplace in southern New Jersey, to get back on the turnpike, but, you know, the crazy thing about it was that it was all somehow about you. I don't know how to explain it, but it was like all the gas stations, and overpasses, and the factory smoke, and these planes flying right over the highway, it was all filled with you.

I watched *Mulholland Drive* with the kids tonight. I didn't get it.

Oh, no! Please, try watching it again. It takes patience and a certain freedom of imagination. Think of the second part as Betty's hallucination before she dies.

You were so close today, I still feel your breath on my neck.

I kiss you in my mind, in all the places where I kissed you today, and all the other places where I couldn't reach.

Your smell drives me crazy.

Do you want me right now?

Yes! Like crazy!

Right now? Right this minute?

Yes!

Have you ever read Brodsky's *Watermark*?

No.

It's an essay about Venice. Here, this is my favorite passage: "I simply think that water is the image of time, and every New Year's Eve, in somewhat pagan fashion, I try to find myself near water, preferably near a sea or an ocean, to watch the emergence of a new helping, a new cupful of time from it."

Cupful of time! So beautiful!

One day we'll go to Venice together.

Promise?

Promise!

You know, the more I see you, the more I miss you, and the less I see you, the more I miss you.

This is some sort of stupid math, isn't it?

In the first happy period of our love, which lasted for nine months or so, B. and I must have written thousands of emails to each other. Thousands—I am not exaggerating! But that doesn't mean that the other areas of my life suffered. This is the mathematical miracle of happy love: it can expand one part of your life to a crazy degree without diminishing the others. I was writing and teaching better than ever; I had more energy for my kids, more patience for Len, and more warmth for my mother. When I look at it now, I don't understand how I could have been so naive. Everybody knows that there is no such thing as having a happy or peaceful love while being married to someone else. It's a time bomb. It will blow up. It absolutely will. There is no way around it. The only question is how much destruction that blow will bring.

But perhaps I wasn't that naive. Perhaps I chose to ignore the timer, the way people do about death. Or perhaps I ascribed too much significance to the fact that my life had been highly compartmentalized.

There was one time when Len caught B.'s name in the long chain of emails in my inbox and asked who it was. I said he was my colleague and we were working on a project together. Len seemed satisfied with my answer, and I dismissed the incident altogether.

In my mind, my affair with B. didn't concern Len at all. It wasn't Len's wife who was in love with another man; it was an entirely different version of me, the version Len didn't know, want, or understand. Len's wife, who walked around the house in sweatpants, leaving a trail of used tissues and apple cores, and later cuddled with Len in bed, had nothing in common with the woman who rushed to meet her lover in a clingy dress and stiletto heels, or sat hunched over her laptop composing love letters to him.

It was as if I were an actress playing several different parts at the same time. Say the same actress has a lead in three different shows. She is Lady Macbeth in one, Elizabeth Bennet in another, and a US presidential candidate in the last one. The fact that her character in *Macbeth* arranges to murder her rivals cannot hurt the chances of her other characters to secure the presidency or win over Mr. Darcy.

I even shared this sentiment with B. in one of our longer emails, and he wrote that he felt exactly the same way.

The first person to break into my new world from the outside was my mother. One day she reached into my purse and found my balled-up panties there. She hadn't meant to pry, she said. Dan needed money for his school trip, and she didn't have enough cash.

I suggested we go to the backyard. We put on our rubber boots and went over there, carrying the chairs and tea, careful not to splash in the puddles. As we walked, I was feeling excited rather than apprehensive. I was sure that this time my mother would understand.

We unfolded our chairs under the apple tree and poured out the tea. I didn't tell her that the man was B., because I didn't think that was important, and because I thought it would make my mother mistake my feelings for B. for yet another bout of childish obsession.

I was in love, I said. I met a man, and what we had together was real love. He was married, but it didn't matter, because he didn't love his wife, just the way I hadn't loved Len in a long time. This was love, real love. I'd never felt like this about anyone.

My mother listened to me in silence, nodding from time to time. I was so relieved and so grateful to her that I felt like dropping to my knees and sobbing into her lap, as I used to do when I was a child.

Then she asked: "Are you having an affair with him?"
I said: "Affair? No! This is not an affair! I love him! What we
have together is exactly what you and my father had."
My mother sighed and said: "When are you ever going to
grow up?"
I couldn't take it. I jumped up, picked up my chair, and
stormed toward the house.

I stopped speaking to her after that. It wasn't conspicuous
or dramatic; I just avoided speaking to her as much as I could.
I would answer her questions, and I would occasionally tell her
some everyday unimportant things, but I wouldn't engage her in
conversation and I would find ways to escape if she did.

Often when I needed to ask her something, or when I needed
to share some important news, I would delegate the task to either
Dan or Nathalie. "Mom is rushing off to work, but she wanted
me to tell you that she's having a new story published in the
Magazine soon." Or: "Mom is busy working on her book upstairs, but she wanted me to ask if everything went all right with
your doctor's visit."

Nobody questioned me about this, but if they had, I would
have had to admit to myself that I wasn't speaking to my mother
because I found it oppressive. The fact that she knew what my life
was really like, the fact that she judged me, and the fact that she
was disappointed in me.

When I finally told Anya and Sasha about my love for B., they
weren't exactly supportive either. Anya sounded both jealous and
skeptical, and Sasha started to laugh: "Not B.! Not again!" But
their reactions didn't offend me at all, probably because I didn't care
about their opinions nearly as much as I cared about my mother's.

Once my mother bumped into me in the kitchen. I was standing by the counter eating. When she walked in, I turned away, hoping to stave off any attempt at a conversation. She started opening and closing drawers, pretending that she was looking for something. Then she said something under her breath, and I had to ask: "What?"

"Why do you act like that?" she asked.

"Like what?"

"As if you couldn't stand me." Her voice broke and she hurried to leave, before I could protest.

But she was right. That was exactly how I felt about her for the entire duration of my affair with B. I couldn't stand her. I especially couldn't stand her when the troubles started.

Cancer is a
geometric
progression

SIXTEEN

This was one of the first notes my mother made after her diagnosis. I can't tell for sure where she was going with this, but the obvious suggestion would be that she wanted to explain how cancer worked through the concept of exponential growth.

Or rather to explain exponential growth using the example of cancer. Cancer is all about cell division, right? Cancerous cells multiply too fast, making the tumors grow with dangerous speed, which saps strength from the rest of the body.

I will never forget how my mother likened love to cancer when I was twenty-two and told her that I wanted to leave Len and look for real love. How she screamed that love was awful and dangerous, and it had the power to destroy you from within.

Fifteen years later, I saw that she might have been right. Love does have that power. Unhappy love, that is.

Nine months into our affair, Nadya, B.'s wife, opened one of his emails to me.

"It's hell," B. said after he broke the news to me. "I'm living in hell. But I can't leave her."

We were sitting on a bench in the park crowded with all these pointless people and their pointless children and dogs.

"Why?" I asked. "Why can't you leave her?"

"I can't stand the thought of causing her pain."

This expression sounded strangely familiar. Then I remembered. This was what Sergey told my mother about his wife. Right before he left her.

"What did you say to Nadya?"

"I promised that I'd stop seeing you."

I started to shiver from the cold, anger, and fear. B. made a motion to hug me, but I moved away.

"Will you stop seeing me?" I asked.

"I can't stop. I love you."

This was the conversation B. and I would have every day, sometimes twice a day. We would inevitably start it every time we saw each other and continue in the endless chain of emails. The same shit over and over again. All the exciting subjects, like sex, childhood memories, movies and books, philosophy and religion, were gone. All we did to each other was hurt, cry, beg, forgive, and hurt again.

I feel awful, but I can't see you tomorrow.

But it's my birthday! [But it's our anniversary.] [But it's the only time I can see you.] [But we haven't seen each other in such a long time.]

Nadya's sick again.

What's wrong?

Some sort of cold, she's had it on and off ever since she found out.

That sucks.

Are you being sarcastic?

Go to hell!

Look, I want nothing more than to be with you all the time! You know that. You must know that. But I don't have the heart to leave Nadya. I can't do to her what Oksana did to me.

If you're not going to leave Nadya, you have to give me up! You can't torture us both like this!

I can't give you up. I love you.

You're a coward!

I know.

Don't give me up!

I won't. I love you.

I love you too.

I don't want to keep living like this!

Are you going to leave Len?

I want to, but I'm scared.

Why? Because of the kids?

Because of the kids, yes, and because of math, because of negative numbers.

I just can't hurt Nadya like that.

But you're hurting me!

Yes, I am. But I don't feel as bad when I'm hurting you.

Why???

Because I love you.

You're a piece of shit!

. . .

Forgive me.

We'll figure it out.

How?

Perhaps we shouldn't see each other so often. We should cherish what we have, and not be greedy.

Is this some sort of your Christian bullshit?

You're an idiot.

. . .

Are you there?

Please answer.

Please forgive me.

I am here.

Please forgive me.

No, you forgive me.

I love you so much.

I love you too.

I can't take this anymore. I'm afraid that I'll start hating you soon.

Are you trying to hurt me?

No. Yes!

It's amazing how fast your life deteriorates when you're in the middle of an unhappy love. I couldn't stand my mother at all, I couldn't stand our house, and I could barely stand Len.

I stopped writing within a month. My mind was blank. I would force some heavy wrong words into convoluted sentences, but the result would be so bad that I'd start sobbing in frustration. In two months I stopped reading—I couldn't focus. Soon even talking to the kids became hard. Dan told me that every time he tried to talk to me, I would space out within a minute or two. Once he decided to test if I was listening. He said: "Mom, they're building this new trailer park right on Mars. Let's go there this summer. They don't have enough air to breathe, but they give out free hot dogs to make up for it." I failed the test by nodding and saying: "Sure, let's ask Dad to drive us there. Hot dogs, how great!"

I can only hope that my students didn't attempt to test me like this as well.

There were days that I spent in bed, doing nothing except for pondering the expression "consumed with love." I found it to be incredibly accurate. I shared it with Anya during the next "no bra" visit. She poured me some Sheridan's that was so sweet it made my teeth ache. I was taking tiny sips and washing it down with coffee.

"You talk about love the same way my patients talk about cancer," Anya said.

She was right. I was disgusted with myself.

"You need to stop seeing him right away!"

Sasha said the same thing.

"You need to run!"

What annoyed me about their advice was that they kept using the word "just."

"Just get ahold of yourself."

"Just pull yourself together."

"Just deal with it."

Unless the word "just" had an added meaning of "with the help of magical powers," urging me to "just do" something sounded like telling a person consumed by anxiety to "just calm down" or a clinically depressed person to "just lighten up!"

Strangely enough, Yulia turned out to be the only one of my friends to take me seriously. She came to New York on business and got in touch with me. We met at the same restaurant where we'd met the last time, and the first thing she asked me was: "Are you sick?"

I said no.

Yulia shook her head. She said that she'd thought that I looked like shit the last time she saw me, but now I looked like double shit or something.

I started to laugh; then I started to cry. Yulia looked frightened. She said she was joking; she asked me to forgive her. She grabbed my hands and squeezed them so hard that I felt her heavy rings cut into my flesh. I felt like I had to tell her about B., and once I started I found myself unable to stop.

"So you love him that much?" she asked with genuine warmth.

I said yes. Then I added that this was nothing like the stupid obsession I felt for B. when I was seventeen. Back then I didn't know what he was and didn't know what I wanted. Now, I was certain that I wanted him, just the way he was.

I said: "He's my person. Do you know what I mean?"

And then it was Yulia's turn to cry, which embarrassed her to no end. She pressed herself into the corner of the banquette and placed her elbow on the table to cover her face with her hand.

She said that she knew exactly what I meant. She felt like that about her second husband, the one she married after she found out that Sasha was gay.

"What happened?" I asked.

"I got pregnant. He made me have an abortion. Then he left me for another woman."

I tried to hug her, but she jerked away from me.

"Stop! People are looking!"

I had never cared about decorum myself, but it moved me that it meant so much for Yulia. And to think that I had bought her tough talk about making balance sheets for her marriages. "What I need is an exorcism," I said. "Nothing short of that would help."

"Actually, no," Yulia said. "I can offer you something better."

And like that she was back in business mode. She told me that the reason she had come to New York was that the Résistance was expanding to North America, where she planned to establish the elite club. They would create the special community open to all subscribers, but only the small elite group would have visibly different privileges, like having a larger photo on the community's social media site. And of course, only the elite members would be invited to the elite parties— think *The Great Gatsby*—also very visible events, because half of the Résistance content would be focused on covering those parties.

"The beauty of my idea," Yulia said, "is that the regular member would be watching elite members as if from behind a fence. Their desperation to get in would be bound to create enormous buzz for the project."

"So are you going to make me an elite member?" I said.

Yulia snickered into her drink. Her confident mask was back on; it was hard to believe that she had been crying over unhappy love a few minutes ago.

"Making you an elite member would be a stretch, don't you think?" she said. "You're not really a Blavatnik-type person, are you? I can make you a regular member for free and sneak you into some of our elite parties."

I said, "Okay, so I'll meet a handsome freedom-fighting billionaire who will fall madly in love with me and will want to marry me? Perfect! B. will be insanely jealous!"

Yulia shook her head. "That's not very likely, is it? And anyway, if anybody's marrying a billionaire, it would be me."

We started to laugh, then we started to drink, then we spent a couple of hours together laughing and drinking. I felt better than I'd felt in months.

When I got home, everybody was asleep, except for Len, who was still working in the garage. I went straight into the bedroom, plopped onto the bed, and opened my laptop. There was one new email from B. I knew what was there without opening it: "Are you there? Lo. B." He had started spelling "love" as "lo." in the past few weeks, as if to suggest that what we had was truncated and incomplete. I braced myself for that "lo." and opened his email. It was much longer than usual, five paragraphs at least. I took the length as a good sign at first, then as a disturbing sign, then as a sure sign of disaster. My hands were shaking and I couldn't bring myself to read those five paragraphs for a long time, and when I finally started reading them, I would stop every few sentences and go back to the beginning, afraid to read further, dreading to read the last line, refusing to comprehend its meaning, because once I did, it would be all over. But I couldn't put it off forever. Eventually I read to the end. And it was over. And B. was the one who ended it.

"You were right," he wrote. "We can't go on like this, and I'm the one who has to make a decision."

I got dizzy and nauseous, and for a second I got scared that I'd throw up all over my old bedspread. I stood up with great effort, my legs were barely functioning, and walked toward the bathroom.

Once I finished in the bathroom, I had the urge to check my email again, because this couldn't possibly be true. But it was. Of course it was. Nothing had changed. He ended the letter with a plea to keep in touch with him. Even though we wouldn't be seeing each other anymore, he needed to hear from me now and then. He wrote, "I want you to know that I will always care about you."

His "care about you" made me so angry that I felt like doing something violent, but I was too tired to move. I took two Ativans, got into bed, and fell asleep.

When I woke up the next morning, I was afraid to open my eyes. I was in the room that used to be inhabited by my love for B. So what now, I thought. Now that the love was destroyed, the room couldn't possibly stay the same. It must be scorched, covered with debris like a site of nuclear disaster. But no, it looked exactly the same. A boring suburban room, not very neat or welcoming, but perfectly livable.

As did all the other rooms of my Escher house. I was amazed by the signs of how smoothly life in the house had gone on in my absence. Nobody else experienced it as an Escher house. What seemed like a crazy disjointed structure to me was a wholesome home for the other inhabitants. Which brought me to an inevitable conclusion: that our house was fine, that I was the upside-down person.

What are
the odds?

SEVENTEEN

What are the odds of meeting a handsome billionaire within a month of having the love of your life break it off?

Pretty slim.

And what are the odds of that billionaire offering to marry you? I would say zero, or even less than zero. If I tried to solve this problem with the help of my childhood calculator, it would certainly beep and scream "ERROR" at me, as it did when I attempted to divide numbers by zero.

And yet this is exactly what happened. I met Victor and he asked me to marry him. The only explanation I have is that the extreme upside-downness of my life at that moment matched the extreme upside-downness of Victor's, and this was what produced the extremely unlikely result.

Nikolay Kotov, the money behind the Résistance (or the money behind *Asshole Monthly*, depending on how you looked at it), was visiting New York City. Yulia thought that it was time to introduce him to the NYC segment of the opposition and saw no better way to do it than to throw a party. In addition to the obvious movers and shakers and celebrities, she also invited a token number of starving artists (exactly one for each discipline—one fiction writer, one poet, one visual artist, one composer, and one choreographer). I got to be the token starving writer.

The party wasn't quite up to *Great Gatsby* standards, but it was lavish enough, with hired models, a Balkan jazz orchestra, Dom Pérignon, foie gras, and slabs of raw salmon. If this was supposed to be a political gathering, nothing in the atmosphere of the party suggested it. In fact, the only remotely political conversation tidbit I overheard was about real estate. A heavyset young man in very expensive eyeglasses was asking a heavyset older man in very expensive shoes if he thought that sanctions against Russia would affect property prices. The shoes man kneaded his meaty chin and said that he didn't think so. People circulated in two large rooms and a huge terrace overlooking the Hudson; there was also another smaller terrace in the back. Nobody appeared to be happy or relaxed. The token artists mostly clung to the walls. Glamorous women looked tortured by their clothes; moneyed men carried an expression of chronic constipation.

Yulia herself was flying around the room, flattering women, flirting with men, and managing the myriad of little problems. She was wearing a long silvery dress and enormous shades in green frames. Her spaghetti straps kept sliding off her shoulders, and her eyeglasses kept sliding down her nose, and she kept fixing one or the other while tipping the champagne glass in her free hand. Needless to say, she didn't have any time to talk to me, and since I didn't know anybody else, I was making silent circles around the room while keeping my eye on the caterers with their irresistible trays, so I could lunge forward and get a piece of salmon or foie gras before other people got to them. I imagined that my movements resembled those of a heron fishing by the edges of a lake. I was wearing a light dress with a years-old wine stain across my chest. This was my only suitable dress, and I decided that the stain was okay, because people would assume that it was a fresh stain. All I needed to do to maintain the impression of the stain's freshness was to keep it moistened and carry a glass of red wine with me at all times. I probably didn't have to do that, because nobody looked in my direction anyway.

In the middle of the evening, Kotov himself deigned to honor the guests with his presence. At six foot eight, he towered over everybody else in the room. I remembered a recent piece in the *Résistance* that claimed that Kotov was the tallest of the world's richest people and the richest of the world's tallest. A mob of people wishing to get close to Kotov formed within seconds and gradually drove him into a corner. Some guests were content with mere proximity to Kotov's body as their friends snapped pictures of them and the great man together. But others were more imaginative in their quest; the token poet presented Kotov with his book, a translation of Pushkin's verses into English, and the token visual artist handed him a painting, an abstract rendering of Russia's political future. Kotov kept staring above their heads, seemingly lost. There was something quixotic about his appearance. He looked as if he didn't understand Russian or didn't understand what he was doing at that party.

I didn't understand what I was doing there either. Plus, I was getting queasy from all the champagne and foie gras. I had a brief flashback of vomiting in the marble and gold splendor of the

Kremlin Palace, so I grabbed my jacket and rushed to the back terrace for some air.

And that was where I met Victor. When I entered, Victor was standing in the dark corner of the terrace, looking out at the dark part of the city, ignoring the river and the lights. He turned to me, and I saw that he was short, slender, and exceptionally graceful. His face was half-obscured by the dark, but when he moved into a spot of light I saw the tense, tired expression of somebody who had recently experienced a loss. I recognized it because I saw the same expression in the mirror every day.

"I have an extra ticket to the opera," was the first thing that Victor said to me. "Tomorrow at eight. Do you want to come with me?"

I said yes, before he had a chance to tell me which opera.

I didn't even have to lie at home. I said that somebody at the Résistance party offered me a free ticket to the opera, and it would be a pity not to use it. My mother sighed. Len couldn't care less. The kids were relieved that I wasn't taking them.

The next day, right before I had to leave for the opera, an email from B. came. There was just my name. "Katya . . ." I took it for a pathetic attempt to pull on the string attached to my heart. The attempt was successful—my heart reacted with pain.

"Go to hell!" I screamed at my laptop and didn't reply.

Victor and I met an hour before the performance, in a bar near Lincoln Center. In better lighting, he looked older—both his beard and his wavy light brown hair had some gray in them. I figured that he was about ten years older than me. Wide cheekbones and slanted green eyes made him appear catlike, wary, slightly threatening. As did his chiseled nose, constructed of sharp lines and bold curves. He was impeccably dressed. Victor suggested that we have some champagne, but I was still queasy from last night's party, and asked for hot tea. He ordered for us. I was surprised by the superb quality of his English. I wrote books in English, but my spoken language wasn't nearly that good. Victor spoke a classic old-school British, but with forceful Russian undertones, which made simple sentences sound like military commands.

I thought of a TV program my mother and I once saw in Russia. The host was telling how Georgy Chicherin, one of the first Soviet diplomats, came to deliver a speech at some international convention. All the British diplomats were snickering, expecting a dumb Russian hick to speak some mangled English, but when Chicherin opened his mouth, they fell silent, because what they heard "was not just good English, but brilliant English, the best English they had ever heard, Chicherin's English!" I remember how my mother and I laughed at these words. This was Soviet propaganda at its comical extreme. Soviet people were meant to be superior in everything, even in their spoken English. We even started using the expression "Chicherin's English" as an inside joke. But now, listening to Victor's "Chicherin's English," I understood something about New Russia that had escaped me before. The country was emerging from a series of humiliating shocks. The Cold War had been lost. The Soviet Union had collapsed. Its status as a world superpower was seriously diminished. The new capitalist autocracy was both pathetically criminal and dangerously unstable. The first batch of Russian elite became a laughingstock for the supposedly more civilized Western world. What with the Russian nouveaux riches sporting garish dresses, garish sports cars, and garish gold watches. What with the parties boasting live camels and live flamingos, where their wives, daughters, and hired prostitutes were dressed the same and were indistinguishable from each other.

Victor belonged to a different, later generation of Russian elite. They had to work very hard at distinguishing themselves from their predecessors. Out went garish clothes and garish tombstones; in came culture and superior education. Fluent English wasn't enough anymore; it needed to be standout English. And if you had to err on the side of too much perfection, so be it. This was why the idea behind the Résistance media project made at least some sense: it appealed to people who cherished their superiority.

Victor said that he had looked me up online. I feigned surprise even though I had looked him up too. I knew that he had a PhD in physics but had decided to abandon science in the nineties to build his own business. I knew that he was massively rich. And I knew that he could read and write in six languages, but speak with fluency in four: Russian, English, Spanish, and Italian.

Victor was impressed that I was a writer. He found one of my old stories on the *Magazine*'s website and read it in one sitting. He didn't like it at the beginning, but by the end he was choking back tears. He sounded sincere, and I was moved. He said that he had recently sold his business, because it wasn't safe for him to remain in Russia. He had two children from his first marriage, who still lived in Moscow. He used to read them bedtime stories on Skype, but now his daughter had outgrown them, and his son hadn't been that interested to begin with.

I said that I had two children too. He said he knew that. He'd read it in an interview. He also knew that I was married.

"Unhappily, I take it?" I nodded. Then he checked the time and asked if I wanted to hear the story behind that extra ticket. I nodded. "Okay," Victor said, "I'll give you the short version." For the last few years he had been living in Italy. He came to New York to propose to Alexandra, his girlfriend of two years, but it was only here that he found out that she'd been cheating on him for the entirety of the past year. A cruel grimace distorted his features, and for a second he looked like an enraged lynx. That moved me too, the fact that he was capable of love rage. I felt like I owed him a straight story too. I told him exactly what was going on in my life, about the Escher house, about Len and B. and how much I longed to find a way out. I was afraid that Victor would judge me, but he seemed moved by my honesty.

On the steps leading to the Met, Victor asked me if I believed in signs. "Astrological?" I asked. "No," he said, "religious ones." He was an Orthodox Christian. Like B.! Like B.! Like B.! I thought. Why, why, why couldn't I stop thinking about B.?

Victor said he liked to read ancient religious texts. There, characters would always receive signs from God. Like a dove flying right over their heads, signifying a turn for the better, or sudden lightning in the dry sky, warning about imminent disaster. Most of the characters either missed or disregarded the signs, but the wise ones took them seriously. There was one time when Victor wanted to take Alexandra to church to pray for his dead brother. Victor was still living in Moscow then, and Alexandra had come for a visit. There was one church he particularly liked. It was always open and there would always be somebody in there. Praying, lighting a candle, or sitting quietly in the pews. But that time, when he brought Alexandra, the church was locked. Bolted shut!

"So you believe that was a sign that your relationship would end badly?" I asked.

"I don't know," Victor said. "I'm fascinated by signs, but I don't know if I believe in them."

We walked into the building, and only there, while moving toward the ticket check along with the crowd, did I remember that I still didn't know which opera we were about to see. "I thought you'd never ask," Victor said. "*Lucia di Lammermoor.*"

I never liked *Lucia di Lammermoor,* and also I could never enjoy listening to opera in the opera house. There were too many distractions. The grandeur of the building, lavish decorations, tons of extras, but especially live animals. In this performance, the scene of the hunt boasted two live greyhounds. Our seats were in the front orchestra, but I leaned in even closer to see the dogs better. The larger one looked languid; she moved slowly in a peaceful and superior manner. The smaller one didn't look as confident; she lagged behind. I wondered if the animals were given some sort of mild tranquilizer before the show.

"Not an opera lover, are you?" Victor whispered. I was embarrassed. I closed my eyes and forced myself to listen. The music swelled; the voice of Lucia went up and down and then up again, where it stayed for a breathtaking (in the literal sense) never-ending vibration. I was holding my breath along with the singer when I heard a strange commotion a few rows behind us. I turned back, but I couldn't see anything. Somebody in the back gasped, then yelped. An old patrician-looking couple in front of me both turned back and said, "Shh!" the man stretching the sound, but the woman in a sharp tone. The commotion didn't stop. If anything it was getting worse. Somebody started to scream; then another voice yelled for help. A group of ushers rushed there, and I half rose in my seat to see what was going on. I saw an old man slumped in his seat asleep, and a younger man next to him fanning his program over the old man's face. Other people tried to make it past them to the exit. I looked at Victor; he took my hand and squeezed it tight. Soon the security guards and the paramedics arrived. The singing was still going on; then it stopped abruptly, and the curtain went down. There was a loudspeaker apology for the brief interruption. One of the patrons had gotten sick. They were asking other patrons to remain in their seats until the sick person was removed. Then they would continue the performance. The paramedics secured the old man on a stretcher and wheeled him down the aisle to the exit. My seat was the closest to the aisle, and one of the paramedics, a plump, bearded young man, bumped into my shoulder. I got a glimpse of the old man's face, white, immobile, his eyes open and white, the irises of his eyes rolled all the way to the back. The fat paramedic caught me staring and covered the old man's face with the edge of the blanket, then changed his mind and uncovered it. There were gasps and groans all over the place. The young man sitting next to Victor said: "Oh my fucking God!" I turned to Victor and asked what he thought happened. He said: "The old man died." There was not a note of shock or hesitation in his voice. It occurred to me that he must have seen many people die. Then he told me to get up. I said that nobody was allowed to leave yet, but he insisted that we do. We both got up and walked into the aisle; there he took my hand and led me to the exit. Victor walked so fast that I had to run to keep up with him. We didn't stop until we'd gone out of the building and reached the fountain in the middle of the plaza. It took me a while to catch my breath.

The first thing that I said was this: "A man actually dying on us—now that is an obvious sign!"

"A sign of what?" Victor asked.

"That our relationship is doomed!"

This seemed to startle Victor. He looked into my eyes with a quizzical expression. I realized that I had said something stupid. What relationship? Victor had offered me an extra ticket; he hadn't even asked me on a date yet. I was afraid that he was busy forming these exact words in his head—What relationship? I haven't even asked you on a date yet. I tried to come up with something that would make my words seem like a witty joke. But the next moment Victor stepped up and pulled me close, his arms circling me, his hands pressing into my shoulders and back. He kissed me with such force that I couldn't even tell if I enjoyed it or not. I mean I enjoyed the fact of the kiss immensely, of course I did; I just couldn't tell if I enjoyed the sensation.

Victor ordered a car to take me back to Staten Island, and as soon as the car drove away, I checked my messages. There were seven new ones from B.

"Katya . . ."

"Are you there?"

"I miss you."

"Katya . . ."

"I need to know that you're okay. I'm not going to pester you."

"Please, say something."

248

"Katya . . ."

I felt my pain on reading them wasn't as acute as before. Meeting Victor must have toughened my heart.

When I got back, the house was dark, except for the feeble light coming from the garage, which meant that Len was still working. He must have heard the car, but he didn't come out to greet me. I heard some rustling in my mother's room followed by her calling for me, but I decided to ignore her and rush right upstairs.

She caught up with me as I was about to enter the bathroom. "How was the opera?" she asked in a voice carefully modulated to express her pain, worry, loathing, and disgust. She managed to look gaunt and deathly pale too.

"Really good," I said, pretending not to notice her expression. "Great production, they even had live dogs." (They also had dead audience members, but I didn't mention that.)

At these words, she clutched her stomach and doubled up as if in pain. This looked so fake that I didn't even get angry. I went into the bathroom and closed the door behind me.

Once in bed, I turned onto my stomach, buried my face in the pillow, and tried to distract myself by thinking about Victor. I hadn't felt aroused during the actual kiss, but now as I imagined the pressure of his hands on my back (his hands were surprisingly large and strong for his compact frame), his face mashed against mine, his tongue forcefully opening my lips to get inside, I wondered what his dick looked like.

My phone beeped. I thought it would be another pleading message from B. and got angry and annoyed, but when I saw that it wasn't I couldn't help but feel disappointed.

The message was from Victor. "I know that you're thinking about the dead man right now. Try to see it in a positive light. Dying in the middle of your favorite aria is an excellent way to go!"

I wanted to reply that I was actually thinking about his dick, but I thought better of it and wrote: "Thank you. I needed to hear that."

Victor and I spent the following two weeks as if living out a mellow romantic comedy. I told him that I couldn't engage in another affair while I was still with Len, and he said that he understood, that he wouldn't pressure me into anything. Both of us enacted more palatable versions of ourselves. It wasn't like we put on masks—we remained ourselves; it was that we intuited which version of ourselves would be more palatable to the other and instinctively assumed it, while keeping all the other (less palatable) versions in check.

Victor would come to meet me after class and we would go on long walks, visit museums, have meals together, and simply talk, while exchanging occasional kisses like furtive thirteen-year-olds.

Sometimes (perhaps too often) we talked about Alexandra and B. I complained about B.'s indecisiveness, and his inability to let go, and especially about his insistence that it was easier for him to hurt people he loved because it made him feel less guilty. Usually, Victor listened with patient understanding, but one time he couldn't resist and said: "He sounds like a whiny asshole!"

Victor never complained about Alexandra, but he kept comparing me to her, greedily hunting for every little thing that made me "better." For example, he was delighted to know that I was an early riser. "That means you are eager to meet the day!" he said, adding that Alexandra used to sleep until twelve and linger in bed until two or three.

This bothered me, because I felt that Victor was using me to kill his love for Alexandra. He was also trying very hard to interpret our meeting each other as this absolute right meant to correct all the wrong, this absolute good to make up for all the bad.

But then wasn't I doing the same?

Even sex that I had with Victor felt like atonement for all our problems.

It was exemplary.

My love life hasn't been that rich when it comes to variety or the number of partners, but I have experienced the six major variations of sex in terms of quality.

Exploratory (Len)

Tender (Len)

Routine (Len)

Mind-blowing (B.)

Painfully sad (B.)

Exemplary (Victor)

If the meaning of the term "exemplary" is not clear, here is how I explain it. Both Victor and I tried hard to prove to ourselves and each other that we could have wonderful sex, and there were moments when it was wonderful, but at other times we tried a bit too hard and it was exemplary rather than good. Kind of like Chicherin's exemplary English.

Two weeks after we met, Victor took me to dinner at the Most Elegant Restaurant in NYC. The atmosphere reminded me of the Grand Wedding Palace where Len and I got married. The memory made me intensely anxious. As did the gleam of the caviar in a tiny silver dish in the middle of the table. As did the quiet hiss of the champagne in our flutes. Victor was saying something to me, but I kept staring into my flute, counting bubbles coming up to the surface in an attempt to calm down. Then Victor covered my hand with his, and its heft and warmth grounded me, made me come back and focus on his words.

He was saying that he knew how crazy this sounded, but he felt like he knew me. And he also felt that we matched incredibly well. In fact, he thought that I was exactly the type of woman he'd always hoped to meet. In other words, he was almost sure that he wanted to spend the rest of his life with me. Every time he would make a point, he would squeeze my hand a little. I looked at his hand over mine and once again marveled at how large it was. Then I noticed a square white Tiffany box in the middle of the table right next to the dish with caviar. He let go of my hand, prodding me to open it. Inside the white box, there was a blue leather box, and inside the blue leather box, there was a tiny black velvet box with rounded corners.

"Go on, open it!" Victor said.

I thought of the Russian folktale where Koschei the Immortal gets killed. There is an iron chest, and inside the iron chest there is a hare, and inside the hare there is a duck, and inside the duck there is an egg, and inside the egg there is a needle, and if you break that needle Koschei the Immortal will die.

Victor took the little box from me and opened it himself. There was a sparkly engagement ring sitting in a silk cushion. I was still in love with B.; I was still married to Len. In fact there was my old wedding ring embedded in the flesh of my finger. I was sure it would take a lot of effort to remove it. Looking at the new ring made me sick.

Victor saw my reaction, but interpreted it in a different way. "Do you think I bought it for Alexandra? No! Of course not! It's a new one. I bought it yesterday."

It hadn't occurred to me that this was the ring Victor had bought for Alexandra, but later I thought that even if it was a different one, it still wasn't meant for me. I don't think Victor realized that himself, but he had come to New York to propose, and he needed to go back to Moscow engaged, even if to a different woman. Otherwise, he would've felt too much like a failure.

I could see how eager he was to make that leap, to do something explosive and huge, the sheer enormity of which had to drown out his pain. Yet he couldn't help but see that I was resisting going along with his plan.

He squinted at me and said, "Let's try to be rational about this."

I saw that rationality was sort of a second religion for him, a more reliable one than Christianity. He believed that if only he managed to stay rational, he could withstand the tumult of the world. I used to believe in rationality too, but I relinquished my faith about the same time that I relinquished my faith in math.

Victor started by asking me a series of questions.

Every time he asked one, he would fling a finger in the air in that showy, superconfident gesture that I learned to love, then learned to hate. But back then it seemed to hypnotize me.

"Are you sure you want to divorce Len?"

Index finger in the air.

"Yes!"

"Are you sure you want to stop obsessing over B.?"

"Yes! Oh, yes!"

Index and middle fingers in the air together.

"Do you think we have a chance as a couple?"

Softer yes.

"Is there any benefit in doing this later rather than sooner?"

I didn't say anything, because I couldn't come up with an answer.

"Good," Victor said, closing his hand into a fist. "The ultimate decision is made. Now let's discuss how we do it."

What followed was a very detailed plan of action that Victor had drawn up a few days before, after consulting his lawyer and his accountant. (I later found it very funny that Victor's accountant knew about his plans to marry me before I did.) Victor started with long-term plans. He would prefer if we lived in Europe together. His home was in Italy, but London was possible too. I would lose my teaching job, but I would have all the time in the world to write my books. He would find a nice place for my mother right next to ours, and he would arrange for my kids to attend an excellent school.

I squirmed, and Victor interpreted that as my unwillingness to move to Europe. He assured me that it would be perfectly fine if I decided to stay in New York. I probably wanted my kids to finish their education in New York, and to be near their father until they went to college. He could certainly understand. He was willing to buy an apartment in New York for us all. He would have to spend some time supervising his businesses in Europe, but that was manageable. For this summer, he was proposing a trip to the Alps and then Sardinia? Or he was open to suggestions. He wanted to take all four kids with us (mine and his). He said that while he was sure that his kids would love to be in the company of mine, he was a little worried that my kids would be bored. But he promised to look for some fun activities suitable for their age.

Victor's short-term plan was more frightening. He was leaving New York in a week. He had some urgent business in Milan, but after that he would be free. He wanted me to spend at least two weeks with him, in his villa on Lake Garda. It was very important for him to see me in his home, on his turf, before we got married.

But, of course, I would have to tell Len first. I would have to be completely honest with him. Then Len and I would tell the kids together. It was better for the kids like that. He had asked a child psychologist specializing in divorce. Then, after we told the kids, we had to start divorce proceedings right away: the faster it was done, the less painful it was. He would pay for a lawyer. He would still pay for a lawyer even if it didn't work out between us.

The only thing that made me happy about Victor's speech was the fact that he considered the possibility of us not working as a couple, because that meant that he wasn't completely insane.

"Have some caviar!" Victor said after he finished. "I'd hate for it to go to waste."

He took one of the little blinis from the plate, spread some caviar on it, and handed it to me.

I chewed and swallowed without registering the taste.

Katya used to love
hyperbolic geometry.
Straight space.
Straight line.
Straight story.
But what if space
is not straight.
What then?

EIGHTEEN

I cried and cried and cried over this note. Because it was clear that my mother was losing her mind when she wrote it, but still knew who I was and remembered that I had loved hyperbolic geometry. She was right. I used to be crazy about hyperbolic geometry when I was a child. I'm still crazy about it.

I always thought that Lobachevsky came up with the concept of hyperbolic geometry, because he refused to believe that reality was as straightforward and as limited as implied by conventional science. For example, he objected to this postulate (offered by Euclid around AD 450).

For each straight line and a point not on it, there can be just one line parallel to the first that goes through that point.

This sounds so right, and it's so easy to check on a simple piece of paper.

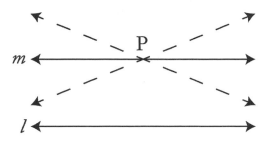

But Lobachevsky refused to confine his mind to a stupid piece of paper. He imagined a space that was enormous and curved. And in that space there could be many parallel lines drawn from the same point.

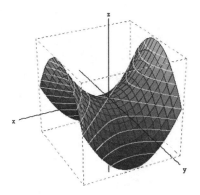

When Lobachevsky first presented his theory, other mathematicians pronounced him crazy, but he kept insisting that he was right.

"He was like Giordano Bruno," my mother told me. "Giordano Bruno who was burned at the stake for insisting that the earth revolved around the sun."

He discovered that reality was actually wilder and more crooked than people thought it was, or rather, than people *wanted to think* it was. He proved that there were things beyond our concept of the possible. Lobachevsky's theory gave me strange solace. It made me feel that my crooked life was in sync with the general crookedness of the universe.

Soon after that caviar dinner, I told Anya, then Yulia, that I was over B. and falling in love with another man. He was handsome, intelligent, and incredibly rich. We were getting married!

"No, you're not!" Anya said. "Are you fucking crazy?"

But Yulia only shook her head and said that she had underestimated me. Then she asked, "Did you tell Len?" I said I was going to tell him soon.

I couldn't reach Sasha, so I sent him a text message. I described Victor as a Russian Gatsby.

Sasha called me from Berlin at 2:00 AM and started to yell. I had to get out of the bed and tiptoe downstairs so I could talk to him.

"His money is blood money!" Sasha screamed at me. "His business is built on corpses! Don't you understand how Russia works? You can't become an oligarch by being a nice, loving man!"

"He doesn't have enough money to be considered an oligarch. He's not Kotov!"

"How much money does he have?"

I had to admit that I had no idea. "I'm sure it's under a billion," I said, hoping that the word "under" would placate Sasha.

"Under a billion, huh?" he said. "Poor fucker can't seem to ascend to the Forbes list. So how exactly did he build his business?"

"He used to go on lots of business trips prior to the Soviet Union collapse," I said. "It helped him to establish all these connections abroad after perestroika."

At this piece of information, Sasha's tirade turned into unintelligible screaming. I heard somebody speaking angry German in the background, most likely asking him to shut up.

I said that it was 2:00 AM, and I was going back to bed.

"Listen," Sasha said in a softer tone. "I'm sorry that I screamed at you, but please, don't marry the guy. Promise me that you won't."

I said goodbye and hung up.

Upstairs, I found Len awake and staring at me from the bed through the semidarkness—we never found blinds that would completely block the light from the neighbors' security lamp.

My heart fell.

"So," he said, his voice quivering with hatred, "a call at 2:00 AM?"

"That was Sasha from Berlin—he must have confused the time."

"Your imaginary gay friend—how convenient!"

That was so stupid that I almost laughed. Len had met Sasha many times. Sasha was at our wedding. Sasha had stayed with us on several occasions. Len certainly knew that he wasn't imaginary.

I said, "Let's go to sleep," got into the bed, and turned away from him. The sharp creak of the bedsprings told me that he had turned away from me as well.

I woke up at six. Len wasn't there. I got up and went to check on the kids. They weren't there either. I had a fleeting paranoid thought that Len had kidnapped them; then I remembered that my uncle Grisha had picked them up last night to take them to the Poconos for the weekend.

I went downstairs and saw Len in the kitchen, sitting at the table with my phone in his hands. He didn't attempt to hide it from me.

"Aren't you going to work?" I asked.

"No," he said, not taking his eyes off the phone screen.

Len was trembling a little, as if he were rocking on waves of anger and hurt. I also saw his resolve to "behave like a man no matter what," which for him probably meant calm as opposed to hysterical, when everything inside screamed that hysterics were just what he needed, were what would make his pain a little less. I wondered how men even knew what the appropriate mode of male behavior was. From their fathers, their friends, movies, books?

"So, Victor Suvorov. A new lover, I presume?" he asked, tapping on the surface of my phone. That "I presume" broke my heart. Or rather Len's attempt to sound cool and unperturbed broke my heart. He wanted to mask his fear, his desire for this to go away, his need for what was about to happen not to happen. It was as if he were silently begging me to lie.

I wasn't going to lie this time.

I said, "We need to get a divorce."

We both fell silent and stayed like that until we heard my mother coming up the stairs. I had completely forgotten that she was home!

She was slowly making her way up the staircase, groaning, making the stairs creak and groan with her. She stopped in the middle when she saw Len and me together. She spoke to us from there, from the darkness of the staircase into the light of the kitchen, her feet planted on the middle step, both her hands grabbing on to the railing.

"Good morning!" she said.

We said "good morning" back.

"It's Friday. Aren't you going to work?" she asked Len.

"Not today."

Then she said that her colonoscopy appointment was later that day.

"Do you need anything?" Len asked.

She said no. She had everything. She was going to use an enema and then poop nonstop to clean her bowels. She wanted to make sure that we wouldn't barge in at an unfortunate moment.

Len winced at the word "poop," as he always did. I was sure my mother had used the word on purpose.

I said that we wouldn't barge in.

Then my mother started her descent in the same slow and creaky manner. She had almost made it to her door when we heard a long, loud, reverberating fart, after which she hurried into her room and shut the door behind her.

I couldn't help but laugh, and Len gave me a reproachful look, but then started to laugh himself. We couldn't stop laughing for a long time. We would stop for a second, but then look at each other and continue to laugh.

"Let's go somewhere where we can talk in peace," he said.

I made some tea, poured it into the thermos, and we drove to the park. There we sat at the picnic table and had a calm, grown-up conversation. Everything was peaceful until Len pinned me down and tried to strangle me.

Afterward, Len asked if I wanted him to take me to the hospital. I said no, I felt fine, I just needed to get away. I asked him to drive me home so I could get my purse and go to Manhattan.

I was more worried about him. I said that he shouldn't be alone today. He should go to a friend's. Len chose his skiing buddy, nicknamed the Snow Baron, who had recently lost his job, so he was bound to be home. He dropped me off at the bus stop and drove to the Baron's place in Hoboken, New Jersey.

I went to Victor's, where I spent several hours sobbing and talking about Len and how worried I was about him.

"Worried about *him?*" Victor said. "Look at your neck! We should go and file a police report!"

I screamed: "No!" I screamed that I absolutely wasn't doing anything to hurt Len! I screamed that Victor didn't get it.

Victor went very still, his eyes narrowed into tiny threatening slits, and said in a quiet and calm voice that I should never ever raise my voice at him again.

My phone rang. It was Len. I grabbed the phone and ran up onto the freezing roof deck so I could talk to Len in private. He said that he would sue for full custody, and considering what a whore and a monster I was, he would get it. He sounded drunk. I don't think he had ever been drunk before. His voice became high-pitched, whiny, and revoltingly mean. There were other drunk voices in the background, and I figured that the Snow Baron must have called his other jobless friends, and now they were drinking together, swapping stories of their awful wives and giving Len various contradictory advice on what to do with his.

Len held me on the phone for a long time. I was barefoot on a snow-covered roof deck, and I had to run from one snow-free patch to another while listening to Len's insults.

Finally, Len got tired of berating me and got off the phone.

I sat down on a little stoop so I could have my peace before I had to go down and face Victor. After everything that had happened, I wasn't sure if I had enough resolve to go through with the divorce and be with Victor. I was wondering if I should go back to Len and beg him to forgive me. At that moment it was hard to imagine that I would ever want something like an affair again, so I was ready to promise everything.

It was then that my mother called me with the happy news about her colonoscopy results. And it was then that I screamed at her that her symptoms weren't real.

I was about to go down when I heard Victor's steps on the stairs, light, but resolute. He skipped the ladder and pulled himself up out onto the roof. He found me hunched on the stoop and sat down next to me.

He asked me for my phone; I gave it to him without thinking. He dialed Len's number.

I was terrified; I expected Victor to threaten Len or worse—to humiliate him—but he said: "Trust me, I know what I am doing." He spoke to Len in a very calm voice. He said that he had been through a divorce, and he certainly knew what Len was going through, and that the best, and in fact the only thing to do right now was to sleep it off. There was a stunned silence on the other end, then Len said, "Thank you," and hung up.

Victor led me downstairs, gave me his warm sweater, and made me some tea.

I was struck by the disparity in how we looked. Victor was dressed in a crisp, light green shirt and impeccably groomed. I had the same sweatpants on that I'd worn to the park; there were pine needles and dirt stuck to the back. My hair was disheveled, my neck bruised, my face blotchy and wet, my eyes so puffy that I could barely see.

Victor asked me if I was sure that I wanted to divorce Len and be with him. I thought that if I answered no, Victor would be relieved. I was about to answer "no" when Victor moved closer, put his arms around my shoulders, and hugged me very tight.

"I think I figured out something about you," he said. "You act like a child, and I usually hate people who do that. But with you it's different. You act like a child because you're a child in a way. You never did manage to grow up, did you?"

I gasped at his words. This was the first moment when Victor managed to get through the more palatable version of myself that I had created back on our first date to please him and get a tiny glimpse into my true self. He grasped something very important about me, and he seemed to accept it.

Note to a reader. Would you give up a man like that? Blood money or no blood money? Really? Well, I couldn't.

"I'm sure that I want to be with you," I said. He asked if I was coming to his place in Italy. I said that Len was planning to take the kids to Mexico for the winter break, so I would come then.

"I will miss you," Victor said and then added, "I still can't believe that I met you. It's a miracle!"

And that was exactly what it was—a miracle, something that is possible only in the realm of the curved space.

Lobachevsky didn't receive due recognition in his lifetime. Back when he first published his findings, other mathematicians ridiculed him. "Is he trying to suggest that parallel lines cross? Seriously? Crazy!"

There was another mathematician who had an inkling of a similar idea at about the same time. But he was more cautious than Lobachevsky. He never developed his theory, because he knew that his peers would see it as crazy. As a result, few people outside math circles remember his name. Which was Carl Friedrich Gauss. That same Gauss who was so much smarter than me as a child, who came up with the brilliant solution to his teacher's problem when he was only nine.

Who is the big fat loser now, Carl Friedrich Gauss?

Operations in a
curved space?

NINETEEN

The kids took the news better than I expected. I decided not to tell them about Victor until I was positive that we'd stay together. All I said was that I was going to Italy to write. But I told them that Len and I were separating. They had clearly been waiting for something like this to happen. Each of them had a best friend whose parents were divorced—Masha and Zac. Both of them were fine, there was no reason to think that our family wouldn't be fine too. The kids asked some practical questions concerning their daily lives, such as "Will Grandma still live with us?" and "We won't need to switch schools, will we?" and when they received satisfactory answers, they seemed to accept the fact of the divorce.

What I dreaded was telling my mother. I asked both Len and the kids not to say anything to her, because I needed to wait for the right moment. But that right moment wouldn't come, and one day when I came home from work, a sobbing Nathalie rushed to hug me. She kept saying that she was sorry, so sorry, so very sorry, but she couldn't help it—she told Grandma. She told her on the way home from school. Grandma asked her why she was so sad, and she started to cry, and then Grandma asked her why she was crying, and she told her. But it wasn't that bad, it was all better now, Grandma was better, she had almost stopped crying.

And that was how my thirteen-year-old daughter did the hardest part of the job for me. I wonder now if I subconsciously manipulated her into doing that for me. I couldn't handle telling my mother, I was afraid of her wrath, her pain, her open disappointment in me, and so I pushed it onto her other daughter, her better daughter.

We decided that Len would stay in the house until he and the kids left for vacation and that he would move out right after they returned. The Snow Baron had plenty of empty rooms at his house, and was willing to rent them to Len.

Now that Len and I knew that we wouldn't have to stay together for the rest of our lives, it felt as if the burden was lifted off. We both found untapped resources of affection for each other. We were better to each other than we had been in years. It wasn't that we rediscovered our lost love—we knew that the people we used to be seventeen years ago were gone—but we were trying to get to know the people we had become. We slept in the same bed, where we would press our bodies against each other, seeking comfort in the familiar and still unknown. The sex wasn't premeditated, or vengeful or passionate. It felt like the most natural thing to do. So natural that I didn't once feel like I was doing something wrong. I definitely didn't feel like I was deceiving Victor, for example. If he asked me, I would've told him the truth, but frankly I felt it was none of his business. Victor was far away, and even though we exchanged phone calls and emails, he didn't seem real anymore. My upcoming trip to Italy didn't seem real either, even though the date was getting closer and closer.

I had a ticket to Milan for December 22.

On December 20 Len and the kids left for Mexico.

As soon as they left, I went down to my mother's place after avoiding her for such a long time. She was bent over her desk cutting up sheets of lined yellow paper. This was a sign familiar from childhood. This was what she always did before starting a new book. I had a series of instant flashbacks of her sitting like this, cutting up paper, from twenty, twenty-five, thirty years ago.

I was struck by how much she had aged. Not in twenty years but in a couple of months. She looked haggard and ashen, her back was bent more than usual; it seemed like she had lost a lot of weight. For the first time in a long time, I was actually concerned about her health. But I reminded myself that I didn't have to worry—her colonoscopy had been fine; her doctor had been so happy with the results that he'd cried!

I sat down across the table from my mother and asked if these were notes for a new book. She took off her glasses, so now they dangled on her chest on a thin chain she had bought at CheapLot. Yes, she said, she had come up with an idea for a new book. She cleared her throat and snickered in an almost embarrassed way.

"You might find it crazy," she said, "but this time I want to write a math textbook for adults. Not for mathematicians but for regular people, who haven't thought of math in ages, whose knowledge of math is dusty and tattered like their old school backpacks."

"People like me?" I asked.

My mother wiped her glasses with a tissue (You don't wipe them with a paper tissue! I thought) and put them back on. She was trying to gauge whether I was making fun of her or not.

"Yes," she said. "People like you. I want to show how math can be relevant to your everyday life."

"Oh, so a math self-help book, then?"

"You could say that," she said, and went back to cutting. She was hurt by my sarcastic tone, but not too much, because she hadn't expected me to be encouraging.

"I have a ticket to Milan on Friday," I said.

She removed her glasses again and looked straight into my eyes. I was relieved to see that her expression was finally free from either reproach or resentment.

"You can't order the heart around," she said. This was a Russian saying. It was more resolute than "the heart wants what the heart wants" because it also implied that you had to obey the heart's orders. My mother had never spoken in sayings before. It took me aback and puzzled me.

I continued to think about what she'd said after I went back upstairs. Was this a positive message? If you couldn't order your heart around, did that mean that you had to follow its orders? Did that make it okay to leave your husband and be with the man you loved? But I didn't love Victor. I was hoping to grow to love him, but I certainly didn't love him now. At the rare moments when I let my heart's guard down, I knew that I still loved B. Was that what the saying meant? That I shouldn't go to Italy because I didn't love Victor?

I opened my inbox full of emails from B. where he begged me to let him know how I was. I had promised myself that I would never answer them. I was so angry at myself for breaking that promise that I was especially curt. I wrote that Len and I had separated, and that I had met somebody else, and that I was flying to Italy tomorrow. He replied within thirty seconds, begging me to see him before I went. I wrote that I could see him today at six, at the Goat's Hoof.

I didn't know what I expected to happen.

I knew what I hoped for. That same old thing—that B. would say he was finally ready to leave Nadya, that he wanted us to be together, all the time, forever and ever. I also knew that this was not going to happen, because if it could happen, B. would've written me about it.

So I guess what I expected was to cause B. maximum pain. To sting, to scald, to strike, to stab him. To make him see that he was truly losing me. To make him realize how much he still loved me. To make him understand how miserable he was going to be without me.

And so I opened my closet to pick clothes to see B. in, trembling with anger. This will show you! I thought, putting on one of my new expensive T-shirts that Victor had bought for me and I had kept hidden from Len in the back of my closet. This will make you wriggle in pain! This will make you want to die!

Note to women going to see the love of their life for the last time. Why, why, why do we think that what we wear matters?

LARA VAPNYAR

I entered that bar poised to keep my cool, my head high and my gait languid. But then I saw B. sitting at a dimly lit corner table, tired and sad, his wrinkles deeper than I remembered, the circles under his eyes darker. He looked like an adult who had to plow through his painfully responsible adult life, and I looked like a silly, vengeful child.

He asked me questions about the divorce, about my mother and my kids and how they were taking it. I said that the divorce was hard, but easier than I'd expected. He said that reality was rarely as bad as our fears. Then he sighed and started kneading his face with his hands for what seemed like a long time. When he asked me his next question, his eyes were half-hidden behind his whitened knuckles. "Is it serious with that new guy?"

I said, "Yes." He moaned, but his pain didn't bring any relief to me.

I said that we were getting married. I told him whatever I could about Victor, trying to downplay his wealth so B. wouldn't talk about "blood money" like Sasha.

"He sounds like he might be good for you," B. said. "But then what else can I say, right? This is nobody's fault but mine."

He finished his beer and poured himself half of what was left in my glass. That was what we always did in restaurants. I saw that he did this without thinking.

"I tried to leave Nadya a month ago," he said. "She got into a car, went onto the highway, and swerved into oncoming traffic. She says it was an accident, that it was raining and the roads were slippery."

"Is she all right?" I asked, making an enormous effort to sound kind.

"Yes, yes, she's fine, just scared. She doesn't have anybody except for me."

And I had so much and so many. Except for him. I could feel a surge of anger rising, but I managed to keep it down.

"I thought you needed to know that."

"No, I didn't," I said, standing up.

He put two twenties onto the table and rushed out of the bar after me. He walked me to the bus stop and we stood there waiting for my bus in silence. When we saw the bus approaching, B. grabbed me and squeezed me so tight that I was afraid he would crush my ribs. "I love you," he said, "I love you. I can't promise you anything, but know that I love you."

I was crying so hard all the way to Staten Island that a man who sat next to me drinking orange Gatorade offered me a travel pack of Kleenex, and ten minutes later his remaining Gatorade.

The next day I flew to Milan.

Victor was waiting for me at the airport, impatient, nervous, pressing a modest bouquet of roses to his chest. I was relieved to realize that I really liked him. I must have forgotten how much I liked him in the tumult of the past month.

I yelled: "Victor!" and waved at him.

He seemed to be relieved as well.

He had a car waiting for us at the airport and two hours later we arrived at Victor's villa on Lake Garda.

The first thing I noticed about the villa was how cold it was. Chilling to the bone. Victor had asked his housekeeper to run the heat three days before our arrival, but she must have confused the dates and didn't turn it on until that morning. Victor offered to book a room at a hotel, but I said that I would prefer to stay. I wanted to feel what his home was like. "It will be fun," I said. "We will be like a pair of vagabonds breaking into somebody's house, burning furniture for heat." Victor liked the idea, except for the burning furniture part. He asked the housekeeper to bring tons of firewood. We spent most of the day sitting by the fire, drinking wine, eating prosciutto stored in Victor's cellar, telling each other funny stories about our Russian childhoods, all the while dressed in two sweaters each. I refused to take off the sweaters even for sex, which we had on the sofa by the fire. I took off my jeans and my panties, but not the sweaters and not my thick woolen socks, so the sex was less exemplary, and in my view much better.

After that first very cold day, the heat managed to seep into every corner of the house, making it simultaneously toasty and bright, bright because we could finally open the shutters. Yet I could feel that some of the chilliness was hidden inside, which made me resistant to the beauty and also less emotional than I'd expected myself to be.

A couple of times, when Victor left for a business meeting, I went on long walks around the town. The view of the lake framed by the mountains was truly magnificent, but for some reason it too left me cold. I preferred to walk in the opposite direction from the embankment. Most of the streets led up into the mountains, so if you walked away from the lake for forty minutes or so, you would leave the town behind and find yourself on one of the trails leading into the wilderness, and if you walked long enough, if you walked for days, you would find yourself either dead or at the very top of the Alps. That thought inevitably made me turn back down, so I spent the rest of the day walking down the promenade, stopping in the little cafés to drink espresso among the festive old ladies and forlorn old men leisurely drinking their wine.

I thought about B. a lot, but I didn't miss him. He was absent no matter where we were geographically.

I didn't miss Len either.

I missed my kids, badly. I did worry about them, but I longed for them more than I worried for them. I thought how much fun it would be if they were here with me right now, walking the paths all the way to the Alps and sampling delicious pastries afterward. I sent them emails, and they sent emails back to me mostly gushing about all the fun things they did in Mexico. Nothing in those emails suggested that they missed me. I didn't want to call them. Len was the only one whose phone was working in Mexico, and he'd promised to call if something happened to the kids, but he'd made it clear that he didn't want to hear from me. I could certainly understand. He didn't want to hear my voice, knowing that I'd just fucked another man and would do it again and again.

What surprised me was that I missed my mother. I kept thinking about our last conversation, how she sat there wiping her glasses with a paper tissue, looking so frail, and I wanted to hug her. Not for her, for me. I wanted to feel her physical warmth, something I hadn't wanted in years. Once, while walking down the cold empty street sloping toward the lake, I even said "Mama" out loud, startling an old lady standing by the gates of her villa. She must have thought that I was calling her and looked at me expectantly. I shook my head. I didn't want any mama; I wanted mine.

When Victor was home, he liked us to cook together, or do other domestic stuff like shop for groceries, or pick furniture from a catalog, or discuss whether we wanted the gardener to plant more roses in the spring. His eagerness to talk about the future frightened me, because it often felt as if he were trying to entrap me in his life rather than to involve me, so I wouldn't be able to escape.

One evening, Victor introduced me to his mother. Via Skype, because his mother lived in Russia. Victor's mother was a tiny woman dressed in drab Soviet-style clothes. She didn't look like Victor at all, except for some barely distinguishable mannerisms that they had in common, like raising and lowering their shoulders when they spoke. She didn't smile or even look at the camera; she sat with her hands folded in her lap and her back very straight, staring straight ahead. Her eyes never met mine. I was both disturbed and relieved by it. I said that her son was a wonderful man, but I wasn't sure if she heard me. She congratulated me on the engagement and wished me all the best, reciting a long list of specific wishes (that I have excellent health, peace, happiness, professional success, that I preserve my youth for a long time). Then she said goodbye and started to cry. She fumbled with something on the keyboard, then moved closer to the screen and looked straight into the camera for the first time. "Vitya," she said, "how do you turn it off? Vitya, turn it off! Please, turn it off!" Victor turned it off and sighed. "She is not the same since my brother died," he said.

I met Victor's kids in the same way, via Skype. The girl was nine and the boy was four. The kids looked exactly like Victor and exactly like each other. They had the same slanted eyes and small chiseled noses, but whatever made Victor look catlike and slightly menacing made the kids look kittenish and sly. They were sitting on a floor pillow, their eyes fixed on an iPad placed on the rug between them. There was also a Yorkshire terrier jumping around. At one point he landed right in front of the iPad and I saw his wet beard fill the entire screen. Both kids were exquisitely polite to me, up to the point when Victor told them that I had two children too. Victor's son turned away from the screen and started playing with his toy cars, and the girl visibly tensed. Wanting to reassure her, I said that my kids were both in their teens, that they were basically adults, and my son even had a small beard. "Like my daddy?" she asked. "No," I said, "more like your dog." Then she finally dropped her mask of exquisite politeness and started to laugh.

I could see Victor hovering as I talked to his kids, watching me, and watching them, trying to gauge our reactions. When the call was over he squeezed me in a hug. "They loved you!" he said. "They did. I can tell!"

Then he buried his face in my hair and whispered: "I think we're going to make it. Don't you?"

I said that I did. I honestly did.

Limit definition

$$\lim_{n \to c} f(n) = L$$

topological net

TWENTY

Topological net? Seriously? I know nothing about topological nets. I don't even understand what it means. You probably need a PhD in mathematics to understand what it means. And yet I can't let it go. I feel that I must understand it. This is what I've been doing obsessively ever since my mother died. Looking for ways to use my mother's notes to sort out the mess I made of my life. Looking for nonexistent connections between complex mathematical concepts and the events of my life. Delving so deep into advanced mathematics that I often lose my way. Really stretching it when I think that one or another theory almost fits. I have to be honest here—I fail to understand what "limit of the function" means in mathematical terms.

But if I stretch it, I might make it out to mean that every function has a limit.

Eight weeks before my mother died, Victor sent me four emails with our photos, because all the photos wouldn't fit into one email. The subjects were: "Photos 1," "Photos 2," "Photos 3," and "Photos 4."

I was sitting at my mother's desk, grateful for the opportunity to check my email in peace, while my mother was a few feet away from me, dozing in her bed in an opiatic haze. The first photograph of Victor and me standing on the Lake Garda embankment blinded me with its colors. The deep blue of the sky, the softer rosy blue of the water, the gleaming orange balls hanging on the orange trees, looking more like Christmas tree decorations than real fruit, my brand-new navy blue woolen coat and my hot-pink cashmere scarf. It was a soft scarf. I had given it to my mother to wear to her chemotherapy appointments, because all our other scarves irritated her skin. At some point she had vomited all over it and I'd had to throw it away. But here it was in the photo, clean, cheerfully pink, flapping in the wind almost parallel to the shore.

I paused before opening the rest of the photos. These were photos of me taken a month before, yet they seemed to be from another world, another life, another reality.

My whole life now was devoted to seeing my mother on that last journey, being her guardian, her nurse, her intimate companion, but also her Charon in a way. This was a reality filled with sights, sounds, and smells of the process of dying, smells of the body and smells of extraneous objects (the most surprising smell being of rubber and plastic, because people accumulate so many rubber and plastic things when they're about to die). Even the language we used in the family became different; what used to be a homey mix of Russian and English had to make space for a lot of hostile Greek roots. Metastasis, ascites, dysphagia.

I thought that if I opened the rest of the photographs, that other bright reality would come rushing into the room and clash with the present one. I imagined the oranges from the trees on the Lake Garda embankment springing from the computer screen into my mother's tiny apartment, smashing into the countless vials with pills, bouncing off her desk, rolling under her bed.

But when I finally looked at them, I noticed that the photos, arranged in chronological order, were a perfect example of a line graph. The same line graph I had used to determine when Len's and my love died.

The last photo where Victor and I looked happy together was dated December 28. It was taken by a waiter at some fish restaurant on Lake Garda. There is a huge plate of grilled fish between us on the table, and an old oil painting of fishermen sorting their bounty right above it. One fisherman is in the process of overturning a basket of fish, so it looks as if the fish—some of them still alive—are about to pour all over our heads and join the fish on our plates. Victor's arm is over my shoulder; we are both looking up and giggling at the ridiculousness of the painting.

And here is another restaurant photo snapped by a waiter. This one is from Venice. Victor and I are sitting in the Terrazza Danieli, indoors. We're wearing matching sweaters, bought a day before in a Transit Par-Such store. "*Morbido! Morbido!*" the saleswoman kept cooing, and I knew that the word must have meant something else in Italian, but it made me feel morbid. I'm looking into the camera, trying so hard to smile that my lips end up being squeezed in a thin ugly line. Victor is looking at me. He's both wary and worried. The budding anger makes his features appear sharper, his eyes even more catlike.

The date on the bottom is December 31.

I can't say that our love died between December 28 and December 31, because we didn't love each other. What died in between those dates was the hope that someday we would. But on the morning of December 30, Victor and I were still okay. We were having breakfast together. Suddenly, Victor pushed his plate away and said: "When do you have to go back to New York? January 5? Let's take a short trip to Venice. I want us to do something memorable before you go."

I was beside myself with happiness. Not only had I always wanted to see Venice in winter, but I also dreaded that first New Year's Eve after my family's collapse.

We packed in no time, Victor called his driver, and an hour later we were already in the car, on the way to Venice.

As we drove I spotted the word "Salò" on one of the road signs. The name pricked me in a vague, uncomfortable way, but I couldn't understand why. Victor snickered seeing my reaction. "Yes, yes, it's that Salò," he said, "the seat of Mussolini's republic. It used to give me the creeps, but I'm used to it now."

Despite its history, Salò looked quaint. The promenade merging with the lake of iridescent blue, the mountains in the background lacking the grandeur you expect of the Alps, neat, well-cared-for villas painted soft pastel colors, the gentle fog making everything look like a drawing smudged with impatient fingers. There was not a soul in the streets. I thought the lack of tourists would give the place a more real feel, but since there were no locals either, it looked more like an abandoned movie set than an actual town. It was the image of the movie set that finally made me recognize the cause of my discomfort. *Salò*, that revolting Pasolini film that I saw with Sasha and Yulia on B.'s recommendation. The memory made me angry. B. was following me everywhere, even to this modest little town with immodest Nazi history.

It didn't help that Victor decided to read Brodsky's *Watermark* in the car. Not that, I thought, please, no! But it was only logical to read one of the most lyrical descriptions of Venice on the way to Venice.

Victor read surprisingly well. His manner was subdued, almost self-effacing. He let the text shine. B. didn't. He always put too much feeling into his recitations, making the poems or the passages more about him than anything else. I had to stop thinking about B.! I slipped my right hand inside my left sleeve and pinched myself on the delicate flesh right above my left hand. Again and again, harder each time.

"A 'cupful of time,'" Victor said. "Isn't that an amazing image?"

Shut the fuck up! I thought.

Sometimes I think that if the weather in Venice had been better, things could have turned out differently. It wasn't bad, just gray, and sad, and cold. Actually, the temperature in Venice was five degrees higher than on Lake Garda, but it seemed much worse. In Venice, the cold felt like something liquid that dripped into every crevice between the layers of our clothes.

The first thing we had to do was buy some warm clothes.

I thought shopping in expensive boutiques would be fun, kind of like that scene from *Pretty Woman* I'd showed to my English students, but I found it oppressive. In the small space, the attention the salespeople lavished on me was too intense. Every time we entered a store, I had the desire to dash for the exit as soon as possible, so I would agree to every item they pushed on me, and say that no, I didn't need to try it on. I ended up with a pile of ugly, ill-fitting, ridiculously expensive winter clothes, which looked bad both in reality and in photos.

In one photo, I'm standing on some nondescript street corner, wearing a short, belted, puffy coat with two collars—one stiff and frilly, pushing into my chin, and the other furry and soft, draped over my shoulders. Under the coat you can see dark blue corduroy pants tucked into mossy-green winter boots. The best feature, however, is my hat, a huge Russian-style fur hat with flaps tied together under my chin, so it looks like I have some sort of furry beard.

Okay, I can't resist. But I'm making it really small and barely legible to preserve the fictional status of this book.

I loved our hotel suite though. The living room had four framed Canaletto prints on the walls. All four were of Piazza San Marco and looked more or less the same, if you didn't peer too closely, but I peered too closely and I saw all these exciting subtle differences, which reminded me of the exercises my mother pushed on me when I was little. I wanted nothing more than to sit in the armchair in the middle of the room and count things in the paintings to see which of them had more items of each category. Two children, three dogs, four umbrellas, five red hats, six brown hats, seven white stockings, eight baskets, nine clouds—no, wait, those were actually two clouds joined together, so ten clouds. But unfortunately, we couldn't stay in the hotel the entire time, because if we did that, it would've been a waste of Venice.

On December 31, the weather suddenly turned nice with the sun breaking through the gray layers of the sky and giving the city some color. We spent the entire morning aimlessly walking around, which is the best thing you can do in Venice. I wanted to get lost, but Venice, though seemingly twisted, turned out to be too compact for getting lost, and no matter which route we took, we would eventually end up facing Hotel Danieli.

"Let's take a boat to Torcello," Victor offered at some point. "That's our only chance to get away."

We sat on the deck, looking at the milky pale water, which was almost the same color as the sky, save for the shimmery pink line on the horizon. Everything was so quiet and still that I jolted when Victor started to speak.

"I met a girl at Danieli once. More than twenty years ago."

He was poor then; he had to work two jobs to save enough money for a trip to Venice, where he had always wanted to go. He stayed at a cheap pensione, sharing a room with a man who sang in his sleep, and he hardly ate anything but pasta with canned sardines, but he loved every second of his trip. Especially that feeling that anything at all could happen to him at any moment. Once as Victor was walking along the embankment, he was caught in a pouring rain. He looked around and saw that he was steps away from Danieli. He had passed it before and knew that there was a beautiful bar right in the lobby, so he decided to go there and order a cup of tea, because even in a place like Danieli, how much could they possibly charge you for tea? Once inside, he sat on the edge of an upholstered chair and ordered tea, trying to mask the intimidation behind his confident fluent Italian. Chicherin's Italian? I thought. His clothes were soaked through; he was cold and shivering in the room full of wealthy, smug people sitting in their dry clothes, sipping their expensive cocktails. And then he spotted a girl, sitting alone a few tables away from him, blowing into her tea to cool it. She was modestly dressed and clearly as uncomfortable as he was. She smiled at Victor as if to show that she didn't belong here either. She had such a simple, open face, not much makeup, just a bit of mascara smudged under her eyes. He wanted to talk to her, but he couldn't summon enough courage. They sat there at their separate tables, smiling at each other from time to time. Then the rain ended, and the girl picked up her heavy raincoat and headed for the door. He wanted to run after her, but he hadn't paid his bill yet, so he sat there like an idiot watching her walk away, with that stupid wet raincoat trailing the floor. He couldn't stop thinking about her for a very long time.

Apparently, he was still thinking about her, I thought with a mix of tenderness, fascination, and jealousy. And then I came up with a brilliant idea. I said: "Let's reenact the scene." I would go into the lobby and order tea. Victor would walk in some ten minutes later. We would sit away from each other, exchanging meaningful glances, only this time he would actually come up and talk to me!

I expected Victor to laugh at my suggestion, but he loved it. We were planning to have dinner at the Terrazza Danieli anyway, so we decided to reenact the scene in the lobby right before dinner.

The Danieli lobby looked exactly as Victor had described it, gleaming with marble and gold, filled with rich-looking people. I walked in there alone, in my belted coat and fur hat with flaps. One look at my reflection in one of the antique mirrors made me feel out of place, which was perfect for the role I was going to play. I sat down in a chair in the back, facing the door so I could see Victor as soon as he walked in. The waiter brought me tea in a thick white teapot. I poured some into my cup and blew on it, trying to channel that girl. She was in Venice on her own. I wondered what it was like to be in Venice on your own. Free and hopeful. That girl woke up every morning not knowing where the day would lead her. The possibilities were limitless. She was sitting there blowing on her tea, but at any moment a heavy door could open, letting in the man of her dreams. A man who would meet her eyes, and see her and want her, see *her*, want *her*, as nobody had ever seen or wanted her before.

I got myself so worked up that I started to tremble, the cup jingling against the saucer in my hands. And then Victor opened the door, and everything immediately felt wrong. He took a few steps and stopped in the middle of the room, searching for me. He looked nervous, the anxiety breaking through the haughty expression he always assumed in especially fancy places. Our eyes met for a second, but I looked away, because I wasn't supposed to see him yet according to the script. But then Victor didn't act according to the script either. He was supposed to pick a spot a few tables away from mine, but instead he walked up to my table and sat down across from me. He looked upset. I asked, "What's wrong?" and he shook his head and said, "Let's go."

A wiser person would've dropped it, but I wasn't a wiser person, so I kept pressing and pressing all through dinner, until Victor finally told me what was wrong.

"When I walked in, you looked at me with such disappointment!"

"I was playing a role!" I said.

"Okay, I know that, you were playing a role. But your disappointment was genuine!"

I guess my relationship with Victor could've ended there and then. But it didn't. We made up. We were honest with each other. We both admitted how hard it was to banish our recent loves from our hearts, and focus on the future, on each other. If anything, that incident brought us closer.

We watched the New Year's Eve fireworks from our balcony, drinking champagne straight from the bottle. When it turned midnight, we made a traditional Russian toast: "To the New Year! To new happiness!" which suddenly struck me as very strange. Was it meant to encourage people to discard their old happiness and look for a new one? Fortunately, I was too drunk to share that thought with Victor.

Right before we went to bed, Victor proposed something unorthodox. "Let's meet the New Year at sunrise."

"Let's!" I said.

We set the alarm clock for 6:15, but when it rang, we didn't feel that enthusiastic anymore. I got out of bed and walked toward the balcony, squinting and groaning. When I finally managed to pry the blinds apart, I saw a solid mass of heavy gray clouds hanging low over the rooftops.

"We won't see anything today," I said.

"Well," Victor mumbled and fell back asleep. I couldn't sleep. I lay there for a while, tossing and turning and making Victor groan, until I realized that this was my only opportunity to explore Venice on my own. I put on my blue corduroy pants, my green boots, my puffy two-collared coat, and my rabbit hat, put the room key in my pocket, and went out.

It was drizzling, with tiny beads of rain latching on to the fur of my collar and hat. The city contours seemed to be dissolving in the fog. I found my way to the embankment, following the wind and the sounds of the water sloshing against the borders. Soon I heard the dull rattle of the approaching vaporetto. The electronic tableau read: San Marco–Zattere–Cimitero di San Michele. I counted the stray money in the pockets of my puffy coat—I had enough for a return ticket—and ran toward the dock.

It was too cold to stay on the deck, so I dove inside and stayed there the entire time, as the vaporetto noisily made its way toward the cemetery. I absolutely didn't plan to do anything crazy; I wanted to visit Brodsky's grave, because this was something a cultured person was supposed to do. Honestly!

I was the only passenger to get off the vaporetto at the cemetery, and I was the only visitor there. In fact, the gates had just opened. There was no map, and I didn't want to ask the old man at the gates for directions, so I wandered around along the labyrinthine paths, hoping to stumble onto Brodsky's grave, until I saw this sign.

By that time I was so cold that that *uscita* option looked much more attractive, but I picked Brodsky.

The headstone was simple and white though darkened by the humidity. There were some rotting roses scattered on the ground around the grave, but I didn't notice them until I felt a sharp thorn piercing the flesh of my knee through my corduroy pants.

I don't know how it happened, I still can't believe that I'm capable of doing something like that, but I found myself on my knees, in the cold dirt of the cemetery path in front of Brodsky's grave, begging Brodsky to please please please do something so B. and I could be together.

I don't remember how I got off my knees, or how I walked back to the vaporetto stop, or whether I had to wait for the vaporetto for a long time. But I remember that as soon as I stepped onto that vaporetto, I was hit by the most intense embarrassment I had ever experienced in my life. I made a solemn promise to myself that nobody would ever know about this.

Note to a sharp reader. Yes, I know, I know. I just broke that promise.

When I got back, Victor was already up and having breakfast at the little table facing away from the balcony. The TV was on and turned to a Russian channel. The host was reciting the news in a rapid and arrogant manner.

"Did you go for a walk?" Victor asked.

I said that I'd ended up going to the cemetery.

"Oh, you did?" Victor said. "Have some breakfast."

I said that I wasn't hungry, and went to take a shower, and as I stood savoring the warmth, I made a decision. Actually, I'd made that decision on the ride back from the cemetery, but it had been too cold for the thought to take shape into something solid and coherent. I couldn't possibly stay with Victor after what had happened at Brodsky's grave. I knew what I wanted and I knew what I didn't want. I couldn't lie to Victor and especially to myself anymore. And not because I had become an honest or rational person all of a sudden, but because I physically couldn't. I had exhausted my ability to lie.

I came out of the bathroom, got dressed, and sat down at that little table across from Victor. He poured me some coffee.

I took a few sips and said that I wasn't going back to Lake Garda with him. I was going to New York. I would call the airline and ask if they could change my ticket, and if not, I would buy a new one.

It wasn't working between us. He must feel it too.

Victor turned away from me, pressed his fist to his forehead, and sat like that for a minute or two with his eyes closed. Then he turned and said: "Yes, I feel it too. Of course I do." I took off the ring (this one, unlike the one that Len gave me, slipped right off) and handed it to Victor. For some reason, I expected him to tell me to keep it, and I was prepared to insist on giving it back. But he took it from me right away and went to lock it up in his wallet.

"Tiffany has a generous return policy," he said with a bitter snicker. "They must know how these things turn out."

It occurred to me that this would be the second time in two months Victor was returning an engagement ring to Tiffany. I thought that despite his name and his quest for perfection, Victor was a bit of a loser, at least when it came to love. I felt such a rush of affection for him that it made me wonder if perhaps we did have a chance as a couple after all.

I got on a flight with a connection in Rome, and all the way to Rome, I kept thinking whether I should go back to Len. There was no sense in upending everybody's life now. I would beg Len to forgive me, and he would forgive me and take me back. I wouldn't be happy with Len, but I wouldn't be desperately unhappy either. Once my love for B. finally died (and it would die, wouldn't it? It had to die at some point!), I would be only moderately unhappy.

The layover in Fiumicino was only fifty minutes, and I used the time to get my last cup of real Italian espresso in the airport café. I sat down at the tiny marble table, unfastened my coat, and put my rabbit hat on the empty chair next to me. I was stirring my espresso, pondering if I should call my mother and tell her that I was coming home. I decided against it. I knew that she would ask me what happened and I didn't want to get into it over the phone. I was about to check my email when I realized that my cup was empty. The problem with espresso is that you can't possibly savor it. Can't drink it leisurely while checking your email. I had to order another espresso. There was so much junk among my emails that I almost missed one from B. I felt a familiar jolt of pain. I didn't want B. to know that my new relationship was already over. I was kicking myself for bragging to him about Victor. Assuming I was going to keep in touch with B. (and it seemed childish not to), I would have to tell him that it had ended. But he'd ask why, and I didn't want him to know that it had ended because of him. I was in the middle of spinning some plausible story about Victor when I finally opened the email from B.

There were only six words.

"I left Nadya. I love you."

No, I didn't drop my espresso cup to the floor—I managed to put the cup down in one piece—but I did have to grab on to the edge of the table to keep my balance.

I read his message again and again, but I couldn't believe it. I'd imagined receiving this message so many times—these exact words—that it couldn't possibly be true. I kept rereading it until I heard the boarding announcement for my flight. A few minutes later, as I was running down the moving walkway, I remembered that I'd left my rabbit hat in the café. And right after that I remembered about Brodsky. Brodsky! It was Brodsky. He'd come through for me. And only then did I let myself believe that this was happening.

B. was free. B. loved me. We would be together.

Time dilates

TWENTY-ONE

I'm pretty sure I had never heard about the concept of "time dilation" before. My mother had never discussed it with me when I was a child. I wonder why. Could it be that she hadn't found it useful before? Perhaps she understood its meaning only now, at sixty-seven, as she was rushing toward death with greater velocity than she had ever expected. Or perhaps she decided to include "time dilation" in her notes because she saw death as the ultimate gravitational field, pulling us all right to its center. Anyway, soon after I realized that my mother was dying, something changed in my perception of time as well. I didn't experience time as a smooth flow carrying me forward anymore, but as a series of sharp painful leaps.

Seven months before my mother died, I spent the happiest three days of my life.

I spent them with B., in a cheap Staten Island motel called Bella Luna, where he took me after meeting me at JFK.

No, the births of my children were not the happiest days of my life. Both times, I was physically torn apart, and heavily drugged. And when I held each of them in my arms for the first time, I felt heart-wrenching affection mixed with terror, rather than happiness.

The time I spent with B. on my return from Italy gave me pure happiness. It was a different happiness from the one we experienced at the beginning of our affair. Back then we felt drunk; this time we were happy and sober.

What I can describe is our fourth day together, which I happen to remember in the tiniest detail. We woke up very late, and had breakfast at my favorite McDonald's, decorated like a fifties drive-in restaurant, with those neon-colored booths made to look like cars. After breakfast we went for a walk on the beach. It must have snowed while I was in Italy, and there were patches of snow melting on the sand. The wind was attacking us in sharp gusts, and I kept saying that this was like some insane Arctic fairy tale and begging B. to wear a hat. B. refused to wear a hat, his hair was flying in all directions in the wind, he was smiling almost the whole time, and his dark eyes looked impossibly bright.

Then we went back to the motel, turned the heat all the way up, and jumped into the bed. Sex was not as intense as during the first three days, but it was somehow better, simpler, happier. Afterward we fell asleep, even though it was still light out.

We woke up to a phone call. My first thought was that it was Len, calling to say that something had happened to the kids, or that it was my mother and something had happened to her. I was afraid that B. and I were too happy, that happiness of such intensity couldn't go unpunished. Then I realized that it wasn't my phone ringing, it was B.'s.

He sat up in bed and looked at me in panic. "It's Nadya."

I sat up too and pulled the sheet up to my chin, because I couldn't bear to be bare-breasted while he talked to Nadya. I could hear that she was crying. Not wailing, but rather whimpering. B. got out of the bed and carried the whimpering Nadya into the bathroom. His butt was all creased from the motel's sheets. He closed the door behind him and fumbled with the lock for a long time because it wouldn't close all the way.

He was in there for ten minutes or so, mostly silent, mumbling something occasionally, and when he emerged, he was wrapped in a towel. Now he was the one who couldn't bear being naked.

Nadya was in bad shape. Really bad. He had to go.

He asked if he should give me a ride home. Home, I thought. Home. He wasn't coming back. I said no, I'd call a cab. I did my best to act supportive. I helped him pack, even though I wanted to scream and grab on to him and not let him go.

Then I went up to the window, pushed the blinds away, and watched him put his bag into his car, get into his car, turn the ignition, pull out from the parking lot, drive unsteadily down the hill toward the main road.

An hour later, I called a cab to take me home. I dragged my suitcase up the steps leading to the porch, opened the door with my key, and walked in, panting from the effort and misery.

My mother heard the noise and asked who it was from her apartment. I opened her door but didn't see her. She must have been reading in her bedroom alcove. All the better, I thought. I couldn't face her now.

I spoke to her from the threshold.

I said: "It's me, don't get up!"

Then I said that it was all over with the guy in Italy, and with the guy I loved it was over too. Then I added that the divorce was still happening. I was positive about that. I had been considering going back to Len the entire time I was in Italy with Victor, but the three days I had spent with B. made that impossible. I couldn't possibly go back to Len.

I walked out of my mother's apartment, but then I remembered to tell her something else, and came back.

I said that I needed some time on my own, before the kids came home. So I was asking her not to bother me, not to come upstairs or even talk to me. I would really really really appreciate that. She said, "Okay."

I went upstairs, plopped onto my bed, and dove into my grief. I had two full days to indulge in it. I would cry and scream and do whatever I wanted to do, so that by the time the kids came home, the acute stage of my grief would be over, and I would be able to pull myself together, and figure out how to handle this new stage of my life, and act as normal as I could. I guess what I imagined was some sort of Grief Express vacation. There were moments when my pain was so severe and all-encompassing that it could be mistaken for happiness. I felt like all my nerve endings were open and raw, which made me feel as if I were expanding, as if I were able to experience the world as fully and as acutely as anybody ever could. Everything I saw or touched or tasted had this tragic tang.

I didn't hear from my mother for the entirety of that first day at home, and I was grateful to her, but also a little disappointed. I had asked her not to bother me, but didn't she worry about me? Didn't she care how I felt?

The next morning I woke up feeling so bad that I had to abandon my perfect grieving plan. I jumped into the car and drove to my family doctor's office to beg her for antidepressants. The doctor was a sweet bug-eyed Romanian woman. She said that she was a family physician, not a psychiatrist, but in her opinion what I had was situational depression, which wasn't really depression at all. I dropped to my knees and grabbed the lapels of the doctor's white coat and said: "Please!" She must have decided that I wasn't as mentally healthy as she'd thought I was and gave me samples of Zen-pro, a new expensive antidepressant.

The first dose of Zen-pro made me violently nauseous. I had never experienced anything like that, because this nausea was overwhelming and didn't lead to vomiting and didn't have any end in sight. As I lay on the bathroom floor with my forehead pressed to the cold floor tiles (I found this position slightly less unbearable than all the others), I wondered how I would feel if B. appeared in front of me right now and said that he had changed his mind and realized that we must be together for the rest of our lives. I wouldn't have cared. Zen-pro made me too sick to care. I was relieved to discover that there was a force stronger than my love for B.

My mother knocked on the door just as I managed to pull myself up and was sitting with my back pressed to the toilet. She must've heard me retching and was worried.

"I'm fine, Mom," I said. "Please, go away."

Note to an angry reader. Yes, that's how selfish I was. But don't waste your breath. You can't possibly make me feel worse about that than I already do.

My mother didn't go away. She knocked again. She said that she needed me to take her to the hospital. Her voice was different, feeble and croaky.

Her voice scared me. I scrambled up and opened the bathroom door for her.

She was leaning against the wall. Trembling. She had to hold on to that wall to keep her balance. She was white and frighteningly gaunt. Her features were distorted by a grimace of pain. Then I saw her stomach. It looked like an enormous balloon, taut and heaving, about to blow up.

And like that my nausea was gone. I rushed out of the bathroom and grabbed my mother by the shoulders, just as she started sliding to the floor.

TWENTY-TWO

It usually takes days if not weeks to get a cancer diagnosis. All those countless tests, bloodwork, biopsies, MRIs.

My mother and I got it even before we made it to the hospital. From a medical technician in the ambulance. The guy took one look at my mother and asked me what kind of cancer it was. He was a burly guy who spoke with a strong Eastern European accent. I said that my mother didn't have cancer. She'd had a colonoscopy! It was clean! It was perfect! He turned away from me. What an idiot! I thought.

But then an admitting intern at the hospital took one look at her and immediately requested an oncologist.

The oncologist arrived at the same time as the first batch of test results. He was a cheerful middle-aged guy with fake teeth that must have been cheap, because they looked faker than fake teeth usually do.

Ovarian cancer, he said. Metastatic. Stage four. Lots of secondary tumors. He recommended the surgery right away. Because without the surgery my mother could be gone in days.

I looked at my mother. She wasn't reacting to his words; she appeared to be confused. She was smiling at him like an eager student trying to please the teacher. I wondered if this was the effect of painkillers or something worse.

Meanwhile, the doctor continued with his speech. It was a simple surgery. With a simple name. Debulking. All of her reproductive organs had to be taken out. But she didn't need them anyway, did she?

"You don't need that anymore, *mamacita?*" He smirked at my mother.

I don't think I ever hated anybody as I hated that doctor at the moment when he called my mother "mamacita."

mamacita (when addressed to a dying older woman who speaks English with a strong accent):

1. Somebody who is less than an American
2. Somebody who is less than a woman
3. Somebody who is less than a human being
4. Somebody whose impending death is an appropriate subject for your cool, lighthearted jokes

Example: "Hey *mamacita*, why don't I take your organs out?"

I told my mother that I was taking her home. We would find other doctors, better doctors; we definitely wouldn't agree to any treatment until we had a second opinion. We were incredibly lucky, I said, because my best friend, Anya, worked at a cancer hospital and personally knew the best oncologists in the country. My mother smiled with relief. The nurses had drained the liquid from her abdomen, the terrible pressure was gone, but more importantly my mother saw that I had accepted being in charge instead of her and was grateful.

By the time the kids came home from their trip, I had the second, the third, and many other opinions. Most of the doctors were reluctant to talk until they had done their own tests and personally examined my mother, but a few of Anya's close friends agreed to look at the existing results. All of them said the same thing. There was no sense in starting with the surgery, because the tumor was too large for a safe removal. The best option was to start with chemo and see if it worked. They were especially reluctant to discuss the prognosis, but one of them said that in the best-case scenario, my mother would have up to a year.

I didn't know whether I should tell this to my mother. I knew that Americans always chose honesty with terminal patients. But Russians did not. As a Russian I was required to lie; as an American I was required to tell the truth. In the end I did both. I told my mother that her prognosis was grave, but it wasn't like there was no hope. There is always hope, right? Even if a tiny one? Nobody can tell you that there isn't hope.

My mother smiled for the first time in days and said how strange it was that she'd been scared of cancer her whole life, but now that she had it, she wasn't scared at all.

"What do you want to do?" I asked. "Do you want to go for a walk? I can drive you to the beach. It's not too cold. Or maybe we could order some food?"

My mother said that she wanted to watch a video. She had a boxed set of *Sex and the City*, which she'd never opened.

In the middle of the pilot episode she pressed pause and asked if I was going to tell people. "So I don't have to?" she said. I said that I would.

I called Uncle Grisha later that day. There was such a long silence on the other end that I thought that the call was disconnected. I said: "Grisha? Grisha! Are you there?" Then I heard him sobbing; it was like the barking of a deranged dog.

The kids arrived the next day around five. They were messy, loud, gushing about their trip, happy to see me, and eager to go and greet their grandmother. Len was hovering behind, impatient to leave.

I told the kids that their grandmother was asleep and sent them upstairs. I said I'd be there shortly. Then I asked Len to come to the kitchen with me, where I told him everything, about myself and about my mother.

"Is there any hope?" he said.

I shook my head.

Len covered his face with his hands, and when he took them away, I saw that he was crying.

There had been so much ugliness in our marriage, but his tears at that moment canceled all that. At least for me.

He offered to help us in any way, or even to move back into the house. I thanked him, but said getting back together would be a very wrong thing for both of us. He agreed and left.

As I saw him to his car, I thought how bizarre it was that a few weeks ago, I had three men in my life. Now I had zero. It was as if my whole life were screaming "ERROR" at me.

I found both kids in Dan's room, leaning over his desk, arguing about the best way to upload Mexico photos. I sat down on Dan's bed and asked them to come to me.

The conversation that I was going to have was probably among the most daunting tasks a parent could face, and as with many daunting parental tasks before that, I didn't handle it very well.

My speech was vague, convoluted, and broken by sobs.

"But she's not going to die, is she?" Nathalie asked in the end.

"Of course she is going to die, you stupid idiot!" Dan screamed.

TWENTY-THREE

Six months before my mother died, one of her doctors offered her good math.

"With this brand-new experimental chemotherapy there is a 15 percent chance of up to five-year survival," the doctor said.

The doctor had a perfectly immobile face and round, glassy eyes that she was shifting from my mother to me, as if she were a remotely controlled doll.

"This is good math," the doctor added.

Was this good math? I thought. At first glance, it seemed as if my mother was promised an additional five years, but if you looked at it carefully the math started to crumble. Not five but "up to five," which meant what exactly? Two years? A year? And then there was a 15 percent chance of chemotherapy working at all. Fifteen seemed like a lot, like a pretty good chance, unless you thought of the other 85 percent for which the grueling treatment didn't work.

I looked at my mother, expecting her to be crushed by the numbers. She wasn't. There was a hopeful smile on her face. The numbers that seemed tragically meager to me sounded infinitely better to her, as she had no other option but an imminent death. She leaned toward me and whispered as if she were embarrassed to appear greedy: "I think I want to live for a little while longer." In the end, however, the math turned out to be bad.

TWENTY-FOUR

Four months before my mother died, we happened to see a chemo party. We were sitting in the patient lodge of the World's Greatest Cancer Center, waiting for her chemotherapy appointment.

All of a sudden a loud group of middle-aged women rushed in, all festively dressed, carrying balloons, a pastry box, and a bottle of champagne. One of them was bald and wan and visibly in pain, but the others looked chipper as hell, laughing, chatting loudly.

"Are they insane?" I asked my mother.

"No," she said. "They are doing a chemo party from *Sex and the City*."

My mother explained that in season six of *Sex and the City*, Samantha discovers that she has breast cancer. The news is upsetting, but everybody is so set on Samantha's beating the cancer that she has no choice but to beat it. Beating, beat, upbeat. You need to stay upbeat in order to beat cancer. That's what they all do, Samantha, and Carrie, and Miranda, and Charlotte. They throw an upbeat chemo party right in the treatment room. They are trying to defy death by denying that death is even a possibility.

By that time, my mother's MRIs started to show that the chemo wasn't working, but we didn't have the heart to stop the treatment. We continued to defy the death that had already won.

TWENTY-FIVE

Three months before my mother died, she asked me if my publisher dealt with nonfiction. I didn't understand where she was going with this. I said that they did.

She asked, "Will you show my book to your editor?"

It took me a moment to react. My initial thought was, "What book?" At that time, all that my mother had were random notes scribbled on her yellow flash cards, some of them barely legible.

But I managed to get my bearings fast enough and said: "Of course I will! Of course!"

I thought I was lying to her. But it turned out that I wasn't.

Note to my editor. My mother's book is contained in these pages.

TWENTY-SIX

Two months before my mother died, I walked into Dan's room. He sat hunched over his computer playing *Minecraft*, his hands hovering over the keyboard, his arms moving slowly and methodically, his back shifting left and right ever so slightly.

He was sitting in a wooden chair we had brought with us from Brooklyn.

I don't remember how that chair ended up in Dan's room, but I do remember how Dan loved rocking in it when he was younger. "Stop rocking!" we would say, since this wasn't a rocking chair. "You'll flip backward!" And he would say, "No, I won't!" He didn't flip backward; what happened was that his butt got stuck. He kept pushing it against the back of the chair, and it ended up wedged into the small rounded space between the back and the seat. He was only seven. He yelled: "Mom!"

I rushed into the room and there he was, his little butt jammed in so firmly that he couldn't wiggle it out, and when he tried to stand up the chair would stay attached to his body and pull him back. I wanted to help, but I couldn't. I slid down to the floor and laughed for five minutes or so, unable to stop. Then I managed to stand up and approach him, but I was still laughing. I tried to free him by pulling on his legs, but when that didn't work I had to come up to the chair from behind and push Dan's butt out with my foot. I was laughing even after Dan was finally free. I couldn't stop for an hour or so.

Even nine years after that incident, I still couldn't look at Dan in that chair without snickering.

"Are you laughing at my butt?" he asked me without turning.

I said that I was. But then I stepped closer and saw the computer screen. A true disciple of my mother, Dan was building a *Minecraft* version of an Escher house, a pixelated structure inspired by Lobachevsky's twisted geometry and the concept of impossible architecture.

I wanted to hug him, but I was afraid that I'd start to cry and left the room.

TWENTY-SEVEN

Six weeks before my mother died, it was Nathalie's middle school graduation. She got four tickets for the ceremony, for me, Dan, Len, and my mother.

My mother hadn't lost all her hair yet. She had a few long wisps. Ghoulishly white, light as pillow feathers, barely touching her scalp.

I ordered a special chemo hat for the graduation. Made of the softest cotton. In the softest blue color—my mother's favorite. Boasting incredible Amazon ratings. One woman said that the hat gave her comfort and joy. Another said that her dad loved his hat so much that he was almost grateful for the chemo. My only worry was that the hat wouldn't arrive in time for the graduation, but it did, it arrived the day before.

My mother put it on and took it right off. "Is it uncomfortable?" I asked.

"No," she said, "it's fine. I just don't feel like wearing it."

"But you can't go to the graduation like this," I said.

I said that everybody would stare. My mother said that she didn't care. I asked if she understood how much she would embarrass Nathalie on the day of her graduation. My mother said that Nathalie wouldn't care. I insisted that she would. Until Nathalie herself said that she wouldn't.

Note to a reader. I still don't understand what compelled me to insist. And it looks like I will never be able to forgive myself for that.

The ceremony was in the huge gym of a local college. The AC wasn't working, so they had to put huge fans all over the room. We sat in the first row. One of the fans was blowing right at us. It made my mother's hair fly up and flutter over her head. Like a halo of death.

She has a defiant smile in all the photos.

TWENTY-EIGHT

Six weeks before my mother died, I threw out my back. It happened because of my grief and greed. I picked up a flyer advertising free trial membership at a new gym and decided to go there. I was out of shape, both physically and mentally, and I thought that this free gym would be the most accessible option to get me into shape. I had only thirty minutes to use the gym that day, so I decided that the most efficient way of getting into shape would be skipping warm-ups and going straight for the machines with weighted plates. I felt a tug while using the leg press. It felt as if somebody had pulled on my spine and tied it to a tree or something. It was only two hours later that the pain truly got me.

My back pain lasted for two weeks. During that time the only way I could walk was by bending almost ninety degrees, so that my upper half was perpendicular to my lower. The kids couldn't deal with it.

"Sorry!" they would say while sliding off the couch to the floor in convulsions of laughter.

I wasn't mad at them, because they clearly got the sick laughter from me. Just like I got it from my mother.

TWENTY-NINE

Five weeks before my mother died, she wrote her last note.

The card read: "6 + 3 =." The sum was left blank. Then I figured that "6 + 3" was the date. She meant June 3. She must've forgotten how to write down dates.

I wondered what would be the sum of the month and the date. The life you'd lived from the beginning of the month up to this date added to the life you'd lived from the beginning of the year up to this month? Life lived up to that point?

The next day I couldn't wake her up for her chemotherapy appointment. She would open her eyes and then close them right away and shake her head. At one point she started to cry. I let her be. She fell asleep.

I called her doctor. The receptionist said that she'd call me back right away. When she finally called, in four hours, my mother was still asleep.

I told the doctor about it. She said that we didn't have to come to the appointment. I asked if we should reschedule. She said no. I was too scared to ask her why.

Ten minutes later her nurse faxed me a referral for a hospice service.

THIRTY

Four weeks before my mother died, the hospice people came to my house to arrange things. It took them less than an hour to furnish my mother's room for death. A hospital bed, an oxygen tank, a little box with three vials inside.

Ativan for the fear of death.

Atropine for the death rattle.

Morphine for the death agony.

The vials were signed by a doctor I would never see in person. I was worried that all these people—moving furniture, checking the bathroom, signing papers—would frighten my mother, but she chose to ignore them. I expected her to ask me about them, and I was scared to say the word "hospice" to her, but she didn't ask anything.

The nurse told me I was fortunate to be able to keep my mother at home. This was a rare situation. My mother had both Medicaid and Medicare. She had her own space in the house. And she had a responsible adult by her side willing to provide continuous care. I had a fleeting proud feeling that somebody took me for a responsible adult.

"But what about when my classes start?" I asked.

"When do they start?" the nurse asked.

"September," I said.

"September? Don't worry about that, hon."

I didn't understand her. Then I did. I started to sob. She patted me on the arm. I found her touch unbearable.

THIRTY-ONE

Three weeks before my mother died, I walked into a church in Brooklyn. I was passing by and some impulse made me enter it. There was something important I needed to ask God, and I felt like this time I needed to do it in an actual place of worship. This was a Russian Orthodox church. I recognized it by the paintings and the smell of lamp oil.

B. once told me how much he loved that smell. He kept sending me email after email; I kept methodically deleting them without reading. I was proud of my resolve, but if I had to be honest with myself, denying B. didn't take much willpower. I learned that the process of watching a loved one die was somewhat similar to falling in love. I was focused on my grief with obsessive intensity; the entire outside world had become muted and blurry.

I didn't know how to pray in church. There were a few people around. They looked like they knew what they were doing. One woman bought a candle. I went and bought a candle too. But then I didn't know what to do with it. I was afraid to do something wrong and be exposed as an impostor. I hid behind a column, squeezing the unlit candle in my fingers, and started to pray. Or rather, not to pray, but to beg God to take mercy on my mother. I wasn't asking God to cure my mother, or to prolong her life. I knew to be humble. I was asking God to spare her suffering. I wondered if I should be more specific about suffering. The hospice literature listed three things that horrified me: unbearable pain, intestinal blockage, and inability to breathe. I pondered if I should list all three, but then decided against it, because what if there were some unknown forms of suffering lurking in the dark? Ultimately I begged: "Please, don't let her suffer!"

Then I went and lit the candle from the other lit candles and tried to put it in the candleholder, but it wouldn't stay up, so I left it there. Lying sideways on the tray among all those erect candles.

THIRTY-TWO

Two weeks before my mother died, the confusion set in. She mistook her six-foot-tall Jamaican nurse for her tiny friend Rita. She thought Uncle Grisha was their father. She kept wondering why we weren't living in our Moscow apartment. "Because of the war?" she would ask. "Because of the Nazis?"

She couldn't remember how to use a fork. Or rather she invented her own way of using the fork. She would pick up a piece of food off her plate with her hand and push it onto the fork's tines; then she would carry the fork toward her mouth, remove the food from the fork with her fingers, and put it into her mouth.

She remembered about her book though. She kept insisting that I prop her up and give her her yellow flash cards. Once I noticed that she was holding her pen upside down, so I took it from her and turned it back up.

"Are you my editor?" she asked.

I shook my head, thinking that she took me for her editor. But it turned out that she was being sarcastic.

"If you're not my editor, don't tell me how to hold my pen!" She was putting me in my place; she was being mean just as she used to be.

One time, when Dan and Nathalie walked into her room, my mother smiled and said how lucky she was to have three beautiful kids. Then she said that Katya had always been the most difficult of the three, but that she knew that deep down Katya was a good girl.

"But Grandma," Nathalie said. Dan shook his head at her, and she fell silent.

THIRTY-THREE

Ten days before my mother died, the kids and I were sitting by her bed, trying and failing to have some sort of conversation. All of a sudden my mother reached for Dan's hand and looked at him with a troubled expression.

"Grandma, what?" he asked.

"Mama, what is it?" I asked, rushing to her.

"I—" she said. "I—" But the rest of it wouldn't come to her. Then she raised two fingers up.

"Mama, what do you want?"

She was turning panicky, but she kept thrusting two fingers at us, as if begging us to understand.

Then Nathalie yelled: "Toilet! She needs to do number two!"

Dan and I took her to the toilet. She went. We took her back. She lay down and closed her eyes.

My mother couldn't remember how to ask us to take her to the toilet, but she found a way to communicate what she wanted. She had always been resourceful, ingenious like that. Her math textbooks had been famous for urging kids to come up with un-orthodox solutions.

What impressed me the most was her ability to keep her presence of mind in the face of losing her mind.

THIRTY-FOUR

One week before my mother died, it was her birthday.

I woke up and remembered that it was her birthday and that I had forgotten to buy her flowers. The kids and I had this routine. I would usually buy the flowers the day before—daisies, she loved daisies—and hide them upstairs, and in the morning I would gather the kids and we would bring the daisies to her along with the presents. It was important to do this first thing in the morning, so that the first thing she saw that day was the flowers.

This was going to be her last birthday and I had forgotten to buy her flowers, as if she were already gone. I went to check on her. She was still asleep. I left Dan in charge, got in the car, and drove to the florist. As I drove, I thought about the especially important birthdays in a person's life, milestone birthdays. The first, the eighteenth, the thirtieth, the fiftieth. I wondered why the Last Birthday wasn't considered important. Of course, you couldn't always know which one was going to be your last. But sometimes you did know.

When people asked my mother how old she was, she never said she was fifty-five or sixty-one; she would always say, "I'm turning fifty-six this summer," or "I'm turning sixty-two in two months." I guess that was her ingrained pessimism talking. About two months earlier, one of her nurses asked my mother how old she was. She was about to say, "Turning sixty-seven soon," when she stopped and appeared to be embarrassed. She didn't know if she'd live to sixty-seven. Nobody knew. But she did live to sixty-seven. Today was her birthday and it would definitely be the last one.

The florist didn't have common daisies. She offered me marguerite daisies in a large pot.

I was holding the pot with both hands so I had to knock on the door with my foot. Dan answered the door. He was beaming.

"Grandma's up!" he said. "She's better!"

I carried the pot into her room. She was sitting in bed propped against the pillows, eating a crumbled hard-boiled egg off a saucer. Her expression was almost normal, if a little agitated.

Nathalie was sitting by the bed, holding the saucer.

"She asked for a soft-boiled egg, but we messed up," she said. She was beaming too. Both kids thought that their grandmother was on the way to recovery.

I had read about this in the hospice literature. They called it "a striking temporary improvement that usually lasts up to a few hours and comes no more than a few days before death."

No more than a few days before death.

My hands started to shake.

Dan took the flowerpot from me and brought it closer to the bed.

"Look, Grandma, daisies!"

"Pretty," she said, "but I'd rather have a bouquet. I'm not sure if they allow potted plants There."

The kids exchanged puzzled looks, but I knew what "There" was.

She took another bite and closed her eyes. The kids looked alarmed.

"Grandma, are you going to finish your egg?" Dan asked.

She shook her head, without opening her eyes. She wouldn't open them again.

THIRTY-FIVE

Four days before my mother died, I gave her morphine for the first time. I didn't know if she needed it or not, because by that time she couldn't communicate at all. She was moaning and moving her arms in a strange twisty way. She looked as if she was in pain, but I couldn't be sure. I called the nurse.

She said: "Honey, don't ever hesitate to give her morphine!"

"But what if I give her too much?"

"Think about it: What's the worst thing that could happen?"

"She will die!" I said.

"Yes! And if you don't give her morphine?"

"She will still die."

"Exactly!"

I hung up and thought that I had given the wrong answer to the nurse. My mother dying from too much morphine wasn't the worst thing. She was bound to die very soon anyway. The worst thing was that it would be me who killed her if she died from too much morphine. But this would be the worst thing for me, not for my mother.

Administering morphine was easy—a few drops into her mouth from a tiny syringe. She stopped moaning and moving her arms. Her features relaxed. Yet there was something about her expression and the position of her body that frightened me. It looked as if she was farther away now. It looked as if by giving her morphine I had pushed my mother farther into that other world.

THIRTY-SIX

Two days before my mother died, she opened her eyes, but they were barely focusing, as if she were looking at me from a great, great distance.

I leaned over and called her. I whispered, "Mama, Mamochka!" not into her ear, but over her face. My words were foggy with need. I could almost see them land on her face as a damp cloud. She stirred a little, but otherwise didn't react to me. I wanted to call her again, but then I thought that I probably shouldn't. This was her journey. It wasn't my place to impose on it, or distract her with my neediness, or disturb her in any way. My duty was to follow her needs, to help her along as much as I could.

THIRTY-SEVEN

On the day my mother died, she was shaking and spewing up thick rusty-brown liquid that looked like volcanic lava. By then she was deep in a coma, or rather her body was in a coma; I wasn't sure if my mother was there in that bed. The lavalike liquid didn't look painful, or human. Didn't look like something that could come out of a human being. Didn't look like something that could come out of my mother.

The hospice nurse had warned me about feeling this way. "Remember that the dying person is still there up until the very end." She had also told me that hearing is the last sense to go and that I should continue talking to my mother. I didn't know what to say. I whispered: "I love you." That wasn't true. I loved my mother. This wasn't my mother. This was an unresponsive shaking body spewing lava. I refused to believe that this was my mother. But whoever this being was, she didn't have anybody but me to protect her, to take care of her, to shield her from the horror. I made an effort and leaned closer. The sparse downy hair on her head flew up, disturbed by my breath. I kissed her on the forehead and said: "Don't be afraid. It's not scary over there." I didn't know where "over there" was, but I suddenly became certain that it was somewhere, that my mother wasn't turning into nothing as my Soviet teachers wanted me to believe; she was traveling, to another realm. I knew that her essence had already left her body, but I also knew that it hadn't disappeared.

THIRTY-EIGHT

A student once asked me why Tolstoy would drag out the scene of Prince Andrei's death in *War and Peace*. This was such a perfect scene, he said, arguably the best scene in the entire Western canon.

The student insisted that Tolstoy should've stopped after the words "Where has he gone? Where is he now?" But instead, he wrote three more seemingly unnecessary paragraphs before he ended the chapter. The other students were annoyed.

"What are you doing, Kevin? Are you trying to workshop Tolstoy?" one girl asked him.

I looked at the paragraphs and I too found them pointless and even bland compared to the rest of the chapter. But they were necessary. Very necessary, because without them the reader would've been plunged into the raw horror of awareness of death.

"Tolstoy is trying to hold your hand there," I said to the students. "He wants to be there for you for a little bit longer, until you get your bearings and are ready to continue reading."

Note to a good reader. This is what I am doing right now. I'm holding your hand.

THIRTY-NINE

Some time after my mother died, I saw that the body lying in the bed in front of me was a corpse.

I will never know the exact time she died. I missed the moment she took her last breath. I will never know how much time passed with me staring at my mother's body trying to figure out if she was still alive after she had already died. You would think that you'd know right away, but you don't. I didn't.

She had been perfectly still for some time, and I reached and touched her hand with my fingertips. It felt cold and stiff, but it didn't feel all that different from the skin of a person who had walked in from the cold.

I called the hospice nurse and described what I saw and felt.

"She's gone, honey," the nurse said.

I asked, "Are you sure?" and she said: "Oh, yeah." She promised to send the service for the body right away.

I took one look at what was on the bed and saw that this wasn't my mother anymore. This was the body.

FORTY

I exited my mother's apartment and went upstairs, where Dan sat at the TV console playing *Skyrim*. He saw me and dropped the control to the floor.

I said: "It happened. It's over."

Nathalie was at Len's. I had asked him to take her, even though she had begged me to let her stay. She was coming home tomorrow. I would have to tell her then.

Dan asked me if he should go there. I said no. I thought it was important that he not remember what was in that room as his grandmother.

His grandmother was gone. She wasn't there anymore.

We sat together on the sofa for some time, the *Skyrim* universe frozen on the TV screen.

Then the service came to retrieve the body. They asked me not to enter the room while they were performing their task.

I wouldn't enter it after they left either. I was scared to see nothing there. An actual tangible nothing.

FORTY-ONE

An hour after they retrieved the body, I found myself going up and down the stairs. Dan was in his room. Asleep, or at least I hoped that he was asleep. The house had only three floors, and only two flights of stairs. But it seemed to me that it had turned into a bizarre labyrinth, like in Escher's drawings. You could go up and down and then up and down again, until you couldn't understand whether you were going up or down.

FORTY-TWO

Several hours after my mother died, I woke up on the floor of my room. I heard the clatter of dishes in the kitchen, and thought that my mother was up and cooking breakfast for us. Then I remembered that this wasn't possible, because she had been bedridden for weeks. Then I remembered that she had died.

I went down to the kitchen. My son was there, fixing himself a bowl of cereal. He looked embarrassed that I'd caught him doing something so ordinary on a day like this. I fixed myself a bowl of cereal too. We sat side by side in silence and ate our cereal.

After breakfast, I went outside to check the mail. I was dressed in the clothes that I had put on the previous morning, when my mother was still alive. There was a thick, damp envelope stuffed in the mailbox. My first thought was that it was from my mother. From There. But it was from our divorce mediator. The final papers. Signed and executed. How strange, I thought, that my marriage officially ended on the same day that my mother died.

But I didn't have time to ponder that. I saw the car bringing Nathalie home pulling up the driveway. I put the envelope back into the mailbox and went to tell Nathalie that her grandmother had died.

We spent most of the day holed up in my stuffy bedroom, sitting cross-legged on top of my bed, avoiding the rest of the house, because it seemed frighteningly large for the three of us, until I decided to drive us to the beach.

The time was about an hour before sunset, when most of the beachgoers had already gone and the fishermen were starting to arrange themselves along the water's edge, with their plastic buckets and their long and short rods, and their fishing lines bobbing over the sand.

We walked in perfect silence for a long time, until Nathalie said: "Look at the shadows!" The bright light made our shadows especially pronounced. Every detail was visible, even separate wisps of our hair messed up by the wind. Dan's shadow was longer than mine. Nathalie's was the same length. We didn't look like a mother and children, but like three orphaned siblings.

Now that my mother was gone, I needed to become their mother. I wondered if I'd ever be able to master that.

FORTY-THREE

Two days after my mother died, there was a funeral. We had a
very small service followed by a very small reception at our house.
No speeches. My mother wouldn't have wanted that.

Grisha and Bella brought lots of food from NetCost. Anya
brought the flowers. Dan and Nathalie brought a friend each.
Len brought back my copy of *War and Peace*. Yulia brought a
crate with twelve Sancerre bottles left over after yet another Résistance party. Sasha flew in from Germany and brought some
duty-free schnapps. He wanted to bring his mother, Rita, but she
was too sick to travel.

I hardly understood what was going on, because I was simultaneously drunk on Yulia's Sancerre and high on my mother's
leftover OxyContin. At some point I brought all of my mother's
notes for her new book upstairs and spread them over the table. I
kept telling everybody how this was a great idea. A self-help math
book, imagine that!

I didn't see B. right away. I was at the kitchen table with a glass of Sancerre in one hand and one of my mother's flash cards in the other, forcing Anya to read it out loud. "I can't read her handwriting," Anya said. "But it's so good," I insisted, splashing my wine.

Then I saw B. across the room, standing timidly in the corner, staring at me with a pained expression. In my confused state, I thought he was a hallucination. I thought that while my mother was dying I had been protected from thinking about B. But now that she was gone and I was exposed, was this a return of my longing, my obsession? And was it so powerful that it made me hallucinate?

Then B. started to speak. He was talking about respect. Respect? Did I hear him right? How he respected my silence. How he had heard what happened from Sasha. How he felt like he had to come today. He needed to see me. He needed to know that I was okay. He cared about me. He loved me.

Don't they say that OxyContin is supposed to make you kinder, happier, mellow, at peace with yourself and with others? It didn't work that way for me.

I picked up a kitchen chair and raised it above my head. It was so heavy that I almost toppled over. Then I made a swing and threw it at B.

I missed, Sasha told me. I don't remember it myself. I don't even remember throwing the chair. I don't remember anything that happened after I heard B. talking to me.

Apparently, Anya and Sasha dragged me upstairs, gave me two Ativans, and sat with me until I fell asleep. Len took the kids to his place for the night. And all the guests cleared out.

FORTY-FOUR

The next morning, I woke up dizzy and nauseous and confused. I walked into the kitchen and saw that somebody must have cleaned up. Everything was in perfect order, paper plates in the garbage bins, wineglasses drying in the dishwasher. There was a chair-sized dent in the wall, but I didn't notice it until later. What I did notice was the notes for my mother's book still strewn across the table.

I poured myself a glass of water and sat down at the table. This was when it hit me for the first time. I didn't have *a mother* anymore. Before that I had been mourning the loss of *the specific person, my mother*. Now I realized that I had also lost *a mother*, a person who would love me and forgive me no matter what, even when I was being stupid, cruel, awful.

Which meant what? That I'd have to grow up? But how? How did one do that?

There was nobody and nothing to guide me. Except for those twenty yellow sheets of paper. Twenty disjointed, barely legible notes for my mother's book. Which she had left for me.